Praise for the works

If I Don't Ask

If I Don't Ask adds a profound depth to Sabine and Rebecca's story, and slots in perfectly with what we already knew about the characters and their motivations.

-Kaylee K., *NetGalley*

Overall, another winner by E. J. Noyes. An absolute pleasure to read. 5 stars.

-*Lez Review Books*

If I Don't Ask was just the right mix of old familiarity and exciting newness. It was a lot of fun reading about Rebecca's feelings during the early years of their relationship. This book is one of the many reasons that I will read anything that E. J. Noyes writes in the future, it is a guaranteed hit. Her work is consistently good, characters always entertaining and full of heart. I'm definitely a reader for life.

-Ashlee G., *NetGalley*

Go Around

Noyes excels at writing both romance and intrigue and it shows in this book. Her characters might as well be real they are so well-written. I'm a pretty big fan of second-chance love stories, and I love the way this one is done. You get the angst you expect from the two women trying to get past the pain of their separation and work their way back to being a couple in love. The outside forces that had a role in their breakup are still around and have to be dealt with. Add in a nasty bad guy (or guys) who are physically and psychologically stalking Elise and you get a tale full of danger, excitement, intrigue, and romance. I also love the Easter egg the author included for her book *Alone*.

I actually laughed out loud at that little scene. E.J. Noyes' works always get my highest praise and recommendation, and this novel is no different. You really need to read this book.

-Betty H., NetGalley

In *Go Around*, E. J. Noyes has dipped her toes in the second chance romance pool and was masterful in blending angst, enduring love and suspense in it. The chemistry and dynamics between the pair were thick and palpable but what stood out for me throughout the book was the type of love everyone wished they had; fierce and protective, grounded in loyalty, passionate yet to be able to just be when you are with the other. Noyes also made Bennet, Avery's dog another highlight for me. He was the tension breaker and a giant darling.

-Nutmeg, NetGalley

Pas de deux

Pas de deux doesn't disappoint: the writing is excellent, the pace is ideal, the characters are layered and, yes, relatable, including the secondary characters, from Caitlyn's groom Wren, to Addie's friend Teresa and, of course, Dewey the horse. One of the many things I loved in this book is the way the MCs deal with problems. They do this very adult and very rare-in-lesfic thing: they talk to each other. This book is proof that miscommunication isn't required for drama. Neither is a breakup. Well-fleshed characters with very human hang-ups bring all the angst and drama necessary. It's all the more interesting here as *Pas de deux* is part enemies-to-lovers romance, part second chance, depending on whose point of view is playing.

-Les Rêveur

This story is not the traditional enemies-to-lovers romance, and I love that. Noyes really puts emphasis on how skewed memories can become as you get older, and how an experience may appear different to another person who had the exact same one. Even if you are unfamiliar with dressage, Noyes' writing is still spot on and delivers the same compelling, fun, and intriguing story with loveable characters of both the two-legged and four-legged kind. This love letter to a sport she obviously has a passion for is so evident and I felt honored to have her share her passion with me and every reader who picks it up. If you love horses, enemies-to-lovers, or even just Noyes' stories in general, this one will definitely be a favorite on your list.

-The Lesbian Review

This romance hit two main tropes. For one main character this is a second chance romance, for the other character, this is an enemies to lovers romance. I loved the two different sides of how the character saw things and I think it gave the book a little zip that caught my attention from the beginning. I was very happy that while this was first person, the POV is actually from both main characters. It was perfect for this book especially since both mains can't even agree on their past. Seeing how each character thought and why, was the right choice for this romantic story. As long as you are a fan of horses, or at least are okay with them, then I would absolutely recommend this one. Noyes writes really well and makes smart choices so that is why she is one of the best.

-Lex Kent's Reviews, *goodreads*

Reaping the Benefits

The story is quite eccentric with its paranormal context but in fact is a pure romance at heart with a nice dose of humor. The book is written in third person, from the point of view of both protagonists, which is not common for Noyes, but it is executed perfectly. With all main elements done well, this makes an awesome read which I could easily recommend to all romance fans.

-Pin's Reviews, *goodreads*

I've read many love stories that entertain the idea of soul mates, but this one does something even more interesting. This one explores the depth of love and its ability to transcend death. This story plays with the idea that love has no limits or boundaries. Its exploration provides a unique setting for this heartfelt romantic tale. At its core it remains a romance. The love story between Jane and Morgan is tender and sweet. It's so cleverly and delightfully done; I've never read anything quite like it before. Noyes possesses the ability to see a story where others don't and turn that into something unique and captivating. She uses rich storytelling and engaging characters to enthrall and delight us.

It's fresh and original. It's everything you crave when you want to dig into a great romance. I highly recommend it.

-Deb M., *NetGalley*

I'm spectacularly smitten with Death, to be specific with E. J. Noyes' personification of death as Cici La Morte in this new and most wondrous book. Cici is not one of the main characters but she is the fulcrum about which the whole plot rotates. She simultaneously operates as a beautiful symbol of our fascination with the theme of death and loss, and as a comedic but wise Greek chorus guiding Morgan through the internal conflict threatening to tear her very soul apart. All of E. J. Noyes' previous books have had emotionally charged first-person narrative, so I was curious how her switch to writing in the third person would play out here, but it really works. Despite many lighthearted and genuinely funny moments I found that this book not only had E. J. Noyes' signature ability to make me cry, but also fascinating ideas and philosophies about grief, loss, and hope.

-Orlando J., *NetGalley*

If you're looking for a lesbian romance, but with a twist of something different, I recommend *Reaping the Benefits*. It's sweet, sexy, and fun.

-*The Lesbian Review*

If the Shoe Fits

When we pick up an E. J. Noyes book we expect intensity, characters with issues (circumstantial and/or internal), and a romance that builds believably. Considering this is *Ask, Tell* #3 we expected all of the above layered with epic seriousness. We were pleasantly surprised and totally floored by the humor in addition to what was already expected!

-Best Lesfic Reviews

Alone

E. J. Noyes is easily one of the most gifted writers pulling us into whatever world she creates making us live and feel every emotion with her characters. Definitely, loudly, vehemently recommended.

-Reviewer@Large, *NetGalley*

Alone is an absolutely stunning book. This book is not a 5-star, it is well above that. You don't see books like this one very often. Truly a treasure and one that will stay with you long after the final page.

-Tiff's Reviews, *goodreads*

There are only a handful of authors that I will drop everything to read as soon as a new book comes out, and Noyes is at the top of that list. It seems no matter what Noyes writes she doesn't disappoint. I will eagerly be waiting for whatever she writes next.

-Lex Kent's Reviews, *goodreads*

There are only a few books out there so compelling they seem to take control of you and force you to read them as quickly as possible. You can't put them down. You just want the world to go away and leave you alone until you can finish this story. *Alone* by E. J. Noyes is that book for me. This novel is absolutely wonderful.

-Betty H., NetGalley

Not only is this easily one of the best books of 2019, but it has worked its way onto my personal all-time top 10 list. There is not one formulaic thing going on, and it's "unputdownable."

-Karen C., NetGalley

I cannot give this anything more than five stars, but damn I wish I could. I would give it 15.

-Carolyn M., NetGalley

Ask Me Again

Not every story needs a sequel. *Ask, Tell* demanded it, and Noyes delivers in spectacular fashion. Sabine and Rebecca show us their fortitude and their strength in their love for each other...Thank you, Noyes, for giving us a great story, a great series, and amazing women that teach us the best things in life are worth fighting for.

There really is only one way to tell this story, and Noyes executes it perfectly. She gives us events from the first person perspective. However, she alternates each chapter between Sabine's point of view and Rebecca's point of view. You're able to get the full perspective of their inner feelings and turmoil they hide from one another. In addition, you're able to get the complete picture of the unconditional love Sabine and Rebecca have for each other. It's this little light of love that propels the reader to keep going and hope these women will finally reach the end of the darkness.

-The Lesbian Review

Gold

This is Noyes' third book, and her writing just keeps getting better and better with each release. She gives us such amazing characters that are easy for anyone to relate to. And she makes them so endearing that you can't help but want them to overcome the past and move forward toward their happily ever after.

-The Lesbian Review

This book is exactly the way I wish romance authors would get back to writing romance. This is what I want to read. If you are a Noyes fan, get this book. If you are a romance fan, get this book. I didn't even talk about the skiing... if you are a skiing fan, get this book.

-Lex Kent's Reviews, *goodreads*

Turbulence

Wow... and when I say 'wow' I mean... WOW. After the author's debut novel *Ask, Tell* got to my list of best books of 2017, I was wondering if that was just a fluke. Fortunately for us lesfic readers, now it's confirmed: E. J. Noyes CAN write. Not only that, she can write different genres... Written in first person from Isabelle's point of view, the reader gets into her headspace with all her insecurities, struggles, and character traits. Alongside Isabelle, we discover Audrey's personality, her life story and, most importantly, her feelings. Throughout the book, Ms. Noyes pushes us down a roller coaster of emotions as we accompany Isabelle in her journey of self-discovery. In the process, we laugh, suffer, and enjoy the ride.

-Gaby, *goodreads*

The entire story just flowed from the first page! E. J. Noyes did a superb job of bringing out Isabelle's and Audrey's personalities, faults, erratic emotions, and the burning passion they shared. The chemistry between both women was so palpable! I felt as though the writer drizzled every word she wrote with love, combustible desire, and intense longing.

-The Lesbian Review

Ask, Tell

This is a book with everything I love about top quality lesbian fiction: a fantastic romance between two wonderful women I can relate to, a location that really made me think again about something I thought I knew well, and brilliant pacing and scene-setting. I cannot recommend this novel highly enough.

-Rainbow Book Reviews

Noyes totally blew my mind from the first sentence. I went in timidly, and I came away awaiting her next release with bated breath. I really love how Noyes is able to get below the surface of the DADT legislation. She really captures the longing, the heartbreak, and especially the isolation that LGBTQ soldiers had to endure because the alternative was being deemed unfit to serve by their own government. I applaud Noyes for getting to the heart of the matter and giving a very important representation of what living and serving under this legislation truly meant for LGBTQ men and women of service.

-The Lesbian Review

E. J. Noyes was able to deliver on so many levels... This book is going to take you on a roller-coaster ride of ups and downs that you won't expect but it's so unbelievably worth it.

-Les Rêveur

Noyes clearly undertook a mammoth amount of research. I was totally engrossed. I'm not usually a reader of romance novels, but this one gripped me. The personal growth of the main character, the rich development of her fabulous best friend, Mitch, and the well-handled tension between Sabine and her love interest were all fantastic. This one definitely deserves five stars.

-*CELEStial books Reviews*

SCHUSS

Other Bella Books by E. J. Noyes

Ask, Tell
Turbulence
Gold
Ask Me Again
Alone
If the Shoe Fits
Reaping the Benefits
Pas de deux
Go Around
If I Don't Ask

About the Author

E. J. Noyes is an Australian transplanted to New Zealand, which may be the awesomest thing to happen to her. She lives with her wife, a needy cat and too many plants (and is planning on getting more plants). When not indulging in her love of reading and writing, E. J. argues with her hair and pretends to be good at things.

SCHUSS

E. J. Noyes

BELLA
BOOKS

2022

Bella Books, Inc.
P.O. Box 10543
Tallahassee, FL 32302

Printed in the United States of America on acid-free paper.

First Edition - 2022

Editor: Cath Walker
Cover Designer: Heather Honeywell

ISBN: 978-1-64247-430-5

Acknowledgments

Writing characters I already know is always such a joy, and when those characters are spending so much time skiing, it's doubly so. When I wrote *Gold*, I never anticipated that two of the peripheral characters in that novel would demand their own book, but I'm so glad they did. Gemma and Stacey have been two of the easiest characters to shape into actual people (does that say something about my mental age?), and creating this novel never felt like work—except for figuring out the title, but I hope it makes sense as you move through the book.

Of course, there's also a double handful of people who helped me shape this work and assisted with the scary research…

My gratitude to Kat, who is not only a fabulous pool partner, but who patiently explained the US college system to this Australian who never went to college.

Thanks to Laura, who helped an old person understand some of what young people are doing in American high schools nowadays.

Claire, rah-boom-bah! That's you cheerleading, in case it wasn't clear.

Kate—I never know how to express my gratitude to you, so I won't even try. You know what I mean.

Linda, Jessica, and the Bella crew—it's always a pleasure. And an easy one at that when I have all of you backing me.

Cath, we make a great team. Or should that be you and I make a great team? Me and you…I and you…Cath and me… me and Cath…? I'll get it right soon, I promise.

And, Pheebs? Ta, babe.

CHAPTER ONE

Stacey

"That is *so* unfair!" I sounded like a bratty kid, and was surprised I hadn't crossed my arms over my chest and stomped my foot.

Aspen's expression was sympathetic. "I know you're upset about it, Stacey, but that's the way it is." My coach's calmness was infuriating. In the face of that calm matter-of-factness, my annoyance always vaporized.

"But—" I protested weakly.

"But *nothing*. In the last five months, as well as the Winter Olympics and the U.S. Team spring speed camp, you've had *nine* competitions, and podiums at every event." As she spoke, she ticked off the locations on her fingers, as if it might strengthen her point. "Lake Louise, St. Moritz, Val d'Isere, Aspen/ Highlands, Cortina, Garmisch-Partenkirchen, Crans Montana, Lenzerheide, Courchevel/Meribel. Add in Beijing in February, and speed camp at Mammoth Mountain last week, and it's no wonder you literally fell asleep leaning on your car after training today. I had to grab you before you faceplanted."

"That's just Nap-o-matic taking care of things. No big deal." Some friends on the alpine ski racing circuit had dubbed me Nap-o-matic because I could, and did, sleep anywhere and at any time and in any position.

Aspen's face was the epitome of *Mhmm, exactly*. "You're exhausted and Nap-o-matic has been working overtime. So, we're skipping the Downhill at Mammoth next week, and you're having from tomorrow through Tuesday off training too. You can come back refreshed and ready to go hardcore with spring race training and the push into our off-season training."

"But…" It was even weaker this time.

"*But* you don't need more World Cup points this year, especially not from the one remaining race we had planned. This season's globes have already been decided. You need to rest and reset both your body and your mind. You need to take a break from traveling. You need to look forward to future seasons, to the next two Olympics, if not the next three, look at protecting your career and not over-racing yourself. When you get tired, you lose focus and mistakes creep in. When mistakes creep in…" Her eyebrows rose as if she was just thinking about finishing that sentence.

We crash.

My coach knew this better than anyone. I couldn't really argue with her logic, and tried a different tack. "Did my parents make you do this?" It was tradition to go to Mammoth for my last race of the season. The fact I'd won the Downhill there the last three years in a row didn't hurt.

"Of course not. You're twenty, Stace. An adult. Legally at least." Aspen grinned, and I returned it. She gripped my shoulders, jiggling me side to side. "You know your parents want you to succeed and have fun and stay safe, but you also know they don't tell us how we train and compete. You're not being punished, so calm down. It's four days off training. You know, a vacation? Not *even* a vacation, just a tiny break."

Most people on the circuit took a vacation mid-to-late April, heading somewhere tropical to defrost once the globes— the crystal-ball trophies handed out not only to the season's highest points earners in each alpine racing discipline, but also the highest overall point scorer on both the men's and women's circuits—were handed out and all the "important" races were done. Not me. I was a winter person through and through, and lying inactive on a beach was close to my definition of torture.

So I'd take some chill time skiing wherever I could, as well as hiking and mountain biking with my best friend, Gemma. That was enough relaxation for me. Why go somewhere else when there was still snow on the ground? Nearly all the mountains would close to the public on May 1st, just over two weeks away, and there were no guarantees that the snow would hold, or that we'd get a top-up dump so we could make good on the "If there's enough snow, select U.S. Alpine Ski Team members can train at Copper Mountain past official closing" clause thing. I huffed out a sound that I hoped conveyed that I wasn't happy. It sounded more like I had asthma.

"A break will give you time to enjoy some normality." Aspen glanced around. "Maybe you could finally unpack these moving boxes and buy some more furniture? Make things a little more homey? Settle in for real?"

Settle in… Late last year, I'd bitten the bullet and officially moved out of home and into a rental. Kind of. The four-bedroom house my parents owned in Edwards, Colorado, close to the mountains where I trained most often—Copper Mountain, Beaver Creek, and Golden Peak—was used to generate Airbnb income. Was. Now it generated a much smaller rental income from me. And to twist the knife, Mom and Dad had put all the furniture into storage, saying they wanted to give me plenty of space to store all my skiing gear and set up my home gym. Like a couch and coffee table and dining table were going to get in the way of gear storage.

Knowing my parents, emptying out the house was less about "giving me space," and more about teaching me to be an adult by…making me buy a bunch of furniture. But I *was* adulting, in a very baby-steps kind of way. I'd moved in and promptly forgotten about shit like furniture and unpacking, more focused on training, and traveling around the world chasing points and a spot on the US Winter Olympic Team for Beijing 2022. My house had the necessities of course, but ninety percent of my belongings were still in boxes.

"Boring," I muttered, still stuck in petulant-kid mode.

"Boring but necessary. I don't want you living like a hobo. It makes me look bad," she joked.

"I set up my gear room, and the gym with the simulator," I pointed out. "I even put up my posters. That's making it homey." Because who wouldn't want alpine race legends Mikaela Shiffrin and Lindsey Vonn and Ted Ligety and Bode Miller watching them train?

Aspen looked over to Brick like she was passing him the baton. Aspen, Steven "Brick" Mabrick—my agent and also Aspen's former agent from when she was a pro—and I were standing around my breakfast bar. I'd thought it weird he was waiting for me when I'd arrived home, and also weird that Aspen had insisted on coming around after my afternoon gym session when I'd already seen her that morning. Now I knew. This was an ambush.

Brick pushed away from the breakfast bar. "Yeah, but you need to buy some furniture, kid. Or did you forget you've got that interview with Amanda Debnam next Friday? It's too late for me to move it to a studio location, so you need to at least get some chairs or something for you two to sit on. Aspen's right, you living like a hobo makes us look bad."

Shit. I totally *had* forgotten about the interview. I raised my hands. "Okay, okay, fine. I'll go buy some furniture and finish unpacking. But I'm still registering my strong disagreement to you pulling the plug on the season."

Aspen sighed a sigh I knew well—the sigh of *I know how you feel, but I'm still the boss.* "Come on, Stace. Stop and think for a minute and you'll see this is the best thing right now. You've given it everything this season and then more from the reserve tank. It's time to rest."

I looked between the two of them, unsurprised by their complete lack of contrition. "You guys are so mean."

"We know," they said in unison, both of them smiling.

This was a familiar routine, one we'd been through before. I never wanted to back down. I would race every day if I could, and was constantly being pulled back by my team and reminded of the importance of balance, and in particular—resting body and mind.

Aspen tugged me close for a side-on hug. "You've kicked ass this season and we're all so proud of you." She pulled out her ace card. "Now it's time to practice what you preach and look after your physical and mental health ready for next season."

She was right. Umph. I knew how important body-brain balance was for racing, and a few years ago, I'd partnered with the organization Smooth Tracks to promote the importance of mental health in athletes.

Aspen Archer also knew all about the importance of caring for your mental health. She was at the top of her game, gold-medal favorite, multi-Olympic medal winner already, when she crashed out of the Vancouver Olympics and shattered her leg, yet again. Only this time, it was serious enough for her to decide she couldn't go through another year of recovery and rehabilitation. So, she'd retired. Not long after she became my coach, Aspen told me she'd been trying to out-ski her fear for years but it'd finally caught her. I knew her personal experience was why she was so insistent that I take care of myself both on and off the mountain. She was the best coach I'd ever had and not just in the "make me a better ski racer" way. I knew I could talk to her about anything, and I trusted her with my life. Literally.

I reached up to pat between Aspen's shoulder blades. "I know, I know. But it's still unfair."

"Your objection is noted. Take these four days to rest. Just cardio and light strength training if you must, okay?"

"Okay." Oh, I must.

"Light," she warned, with a teasing finger wag.

"Light," I agreed as I saluted. I'd be a good Stacey and do as she said, and probably spend some zen time skiing off-piste or in the backcountry. She hadn't said I wasn't allowed to ski, just no training, and cruising around the mountain wasn't strenuous on body or mind. It was the opposite, setting me firmly in the chill zone.

"But I'm gonna kick your butt at Copper on Wednesday, so rest up good."

I grinned at the thought of all that work. "Can't wait."

"Masochist."

After Aspen and Brick left, I spent an hour unpacking a few boxes of clothes. There, I was practically moved in. So what if I still didn't have a coffee or kitchen table or entertainment unit or anything in my bedroom aside from the bed and bedside table I'd brought with me. I was just about to call Naomi, my friend and fellow U.S. Alpine Ski Team member, to tell her I wouldn't be seeing her in California next week, when I heard the unmistakable sound of tires on gravel on the turnaround out front.

I peeked through the blinds, my bad mood falling away instantly when I saw the green Subaru Forester. Gemma. My best friend, and one of the few people I felt truly comfortable being myself around. Gem was Aspen's stepdaughter, so we'd met right after Aspen became my head coach at the end of 2017, and had fallen into the easiest, most comfortable friendship.

I didn't have many friends, because the friends I'd had as a teenager had fallen away after high school. Sure, I had people on the race circuit that I could have unforced, friendly conversations with during races, people I cheered for and enjoyed spending time with when I was away, but I wouldn't call any of them if I had a problem. I could probably classify Naomi as a good friend, but our friendship wasn't what I'd call deep.

But Gemma? She'd help me bury a body, and vice versa.

Gem slammed her car door—which would have given her away as my visitor even if I hadn't peeked to see who it was—and walked carefully up the path to my front door. I pulled the door open before she could press the doorbell, and without a word opened my arms to her.

Gemma fell into the hug, pressing her face against the front of my shoulder as she squeezed me. "Hey," she mumbled against my hoodie. I felt her deep inhalation a second before her body softened with relaxation.

Wrapping my arms around her waist, I picked her up, holding her tightly against me as I spun her around. "Hey yourself," I said before setting her down again. Hugging Gemma always made me feel safe. Having her there made everything okay.

Gem pulled back, and I just caught the expression in her huge, light-blue eyes before she managed to hide it. She looked at me that exact same way every single time I saw her, but it hadn't taken her long to figure out a way to mask it after that millisecond of giving herself away. She looked at me like I was the best thing she'd seen all day. She looked at me like she wanted to say something, but was too frightened to let it out. She looked at me like she wanted to kiss me.

And if I wasn't so freaking scared of ruining the best friendship I'd ever had, and one of my most important non-family relationships, then I'd probably have just grabbed her already and kissed her. Also, not to mention the fact she was my coach's daughter, which could make things weird for all of us. I hadn't always felt this desperation to kiss her…and more than just kiss her. Early in our friendship, when we were both in high school, I'd been aware that she seemed to have a crush on me, and had just ignored it—without being mean about it, of course. But somewhere in the last two years, it'd dawned on me that I not only loved her as a friend, but that I kinda loved her as more than that. Tricky tricky.

"You're on spring break now, right?" I asked. When she nodded, I added, "So you can come weekday skiing with me a few times?"

That brightened her like nothing else, even though we skied together as much as my training and racing schedule allowed. "Absolutely." Gem pulled off her wool hat, and her curly blond hair made a break for it. "Will Bree come too?" She tried to sound casual, but the forced neutrality of her expression told me she felt anything but.

"Doubtful." My girlfriend tolerated skiing but was more invested in her acting stuff and circle of friends at CU Boulder, two hours-ish drive away.

"So it'll just be you and me. The dream team."

"Yup." I carefully tucked a piece of hair that was trying to get into her mouth back behind her ear. "I didn't think I'd see you today."

"Aspen said you might need someone to talk to. I thought something bad had happened, but…" Gem's eyebrows creased together, highlighting the little concentration line between them. "You just look…murderous, not sad."

"I *am* sad, but annoyed is winning out. I got totally blindsided. Aspen says we're done competing for the season, and I have to take four days off training. I mean, it was only Mammoth next week left on my race calendar. Just one more race. But nooo, I need to rest." I huffed, and tried to stuff down my annoyance. I didn't want to waste my time with Gem by being a grumpy ass.

"Shit," Gem commiserated. "Sorry, Stace, that really sucks." Ever loyal to Aspen, even as she remained loyal to me, she added, "I'm sure she's just thinking of what's best for you." After pulling off her boots and leaving them lined up neatly on the rack, she shucked out of her coat and carefully hung it and her camera bag on one of the coat hooks. Gem rarely went anywhere without her digital SLR, and I couldn't count how many times I'd stood around while she'd photographed or filmed something on a hike.

"I know. But it's still shitty."

"It really is," she agreed. Then Gem grinned, squeezing my arms. "But, at least you'll be around to keep me company for the first days of my spring break. Aaaaand, I know it's selfish, but I really wanted to get some more footage of you training and if you raced at Mammoth then we might have run out of time, and good snow for me to film you on. So…win?" Gem fluttered her eyelashes at me. She did that a lot whenever she was trying to get me to agree to something—which I always did, without needing any persuasion.

I'd agreed to "star" in a short film to add to Gem's portfolio and was a little nervous about the final product. Not because I thought she wouldn't do a fantastic job, but because I was worried I might do something stupid and ruin her footage.

She'd already applied to her colleges, so it wouldn't mess that up. But it'd be there when she was ready to apply to her dream institution after college—the American Film Institute in LA. The thought of her living in California, or New York or Boston or Chicago or wherever she'd go for college and beyond made me feel kinda sick. We spent time apart when I was out of state or overseas racing, but she was always right here when I came home, and college would change that. Of course I was *super* proud of my best friend, and wanted her to chase her dreams to the end of the earth. But selfishly, I also wanted her nearby.

Smiling, I agreed, "Yeah, you're right. It's a win." Determined to mope no more, I changed the subject to one of my favorites. Food. "You hungry?" When she nodded, I pulled open the fridge. Without asking or being asked, Gem grabbed a cutting board, extracted bread from my pantry, and slathered slices with mayo. I handled ham and turkey while she dealt with salad and cheese. Double meat for me, ham only for Gem.

"How much more stuff do you need?" I asked. "Raw footage stuff I mean." She'd already filmed me training on snow— start drills, ski drills, GoPro footage from my PoV (or, more accurately, my helmet's PoV), drone footage, more drills.

"Can you give me a session at the gym? Maybe another on-snow training session, or even just some non-training skiing? And I still need you to record some voiceover too."

"Yup, no worries, can do. Tell Aspen I'm cool with whenever you want to film my on-snow training."

"Thanks, Stace. The more I have, the more I can work with. I'm trying something different with this one, making it kinda unscripted, just seeing how I'm feeling the footage and stuff, and how it wants to come together." She passed me the mayo knife to lick clean.

"You know," I said around licks, "you could just give up your dream of making documentaries for Nat Geo and make ski movies instead. Come with me on the racing circuit and I'll give you my best side every day. Promise."

Gem's laugh was short, but she packed a whole lot of mirthful disbelief into it. "Surrrre. I'll just follow you around forever and film everything you're doing, like a 24/7 Stacey Evans reality show."

"Sounds awesome." I stole a slice of tomato from her, blowing her a kiss when she mock-scowled. "Are we doing a formal interview, or…?"

"Nah. Unless you want to?"

I shrugged. "It's your thing, Gemmy Gem. I'll do whatever you want."

She paused for a moment, her mouth twisted into its thinking expression. "Okay. Let's just do question-answer to lead you into giving me some soundbites. You've done enough media stuff since Beijing."

Enough media stuff since Beijing was an understatement. Winning a bronze medal was amazing, but it came with a whole lot of media commitments. I loved talking to people, but answering the same questions over and over was super draining.

Gemma continued, "And if I don't get what I need from just us talking then we can record you doing some cool lines like 'I have no fear' or 'I am Stacey Evans, Olympic bronze medalist and winner of World Cup races, and I am the greatest speed skier in the world!' or 'I love skiing!' or…something." She'd adopted a deeper voice to put forth her ideas about what I could say for her video project. "And then we'll have Aspen saying 'Stacey Evans is the best skier I've ever coached, except for my daughter, Gemma, who will never be a ski racer so she doesn't really count.'"

I snort-laughed. "Yeah, you really need to work on those lines. And I'm definitely not the greatest speed skier in the world."

"Ye-etttt," she singsonged.

"*Ever* if Aspen and Brick have their way." It was a really unfair thing to say about the people who had my back at every turn, and I regretted it instantly. "You know what I mean," I mumbled.

She bumped me with her shoulder. "They're just looking out for you. That's what coaches and trainers and managers are supposed to do, right?"

"Right." I sliced my sandwiches into rectangles, and Gem's into triangles.

She grabbed her plate and sat opposite me at the breakfast bar. "And I know you're mad, but I kinda agree with them. You've kicked ass this season and I don't want you getting hurt because you're exhausted."

"You're too sweet," I said.

"No, I mean it. If you get hurt, then this film project will go to shit." She smiled around her mouthful of sandwich to show me she was kidding. Mostly. "You went to the freakin' Olympics, Stace, and you won a medal there. At your *first* Olympics. You've stood on the podium for all of your World Cup races this season. You've got nothing more to prove to anyone right now. Not ever."

"Yeah, I know, it's just…I want people to be proud of me. I just wanted a little more this season, and I *know* I could have gotten more from myself."

Her smile started slowly, but quickly turned bright, brilliant. "Of course you could have. And we *are* proud of you. I'm proud of you and I love you just as you are."

I forced myself to smile goofily when all I wanted to do was climb over the breakfast bar and hug her. "Do you love me enough to brave furniture shopping with me? I've got a journalist coming round Friday to do an interview."

"It's *because* I love you that I'll go, because if I don't, you'll end up buying the ugliest stuff and it'll be all over television for the whole country to see."

CHAPTER TWO

Gemma

I wandered through the house to find Aspen. Again. When I'd come home from school, after a quick hug and "How was your day?" she'd suggested that maybe my best friend needed someone to talk to. So I'd done an about-face and gone straight out again. Now Aspen was in the laundry, shooing away our ridgeback, Taylor, who had her nose in the laundry basket. Taylor abandoned her sniffing to come say hi, and Aspen glanced up from where she was bent over stuffing clothes into the washer, her swampy not-green-not-hazel eyes lighting up. "Just in time to help out with the dirty laundry."

"Gee, thanks." I leaned against her, relaxing immediately when she straightened up and pulled me into a hug.

Aspen was *tall*, over six feet, and her hugs were amazing—almost as good as Stacey's. Maybe good hugs were a tall-person thing? Stace was a few inches shorter, but *way* more muscular than Aspen, in that hot "I'm an elite athlete who treats my body well" sort of way. My best friend was also an enthusiastic hugger, which suited me just fine.

With a final squeeze, Aspen kissed the top of my head and released me. She shoved her short, wavy brown hair back, trying unsuccessfully to tame it. Her hair declined the invitation to behave and immediately flopped back across her forehead. "Everything okay?"

"Yeah."

Aspen frowned, which always looked weird because she was usually super calm and cheerful. "I guess she told you?"

"She did. You know, *you* could have just told me," I said.

"I thought she'd want to tell you herself." Aspen leaned against the washer. "I know she's pissed off, but it's for the best. Did she talk to you about it at all? Had the steam stopped coming out of her ears by the time you got there?"

I laughed at her description. I'd never really seen Stacey get mad. Fired up, passionate, maybe a little belligerent when she was told to chill, but never mad. "Yeah. I think she's okay. I'm kinda glad. I hate it when you guys are away." Since Aspen had started coaching Stacey four and a half-ish years ago, Mom and I had taken a few trips to join them at ski races. We'd watch Stacey ski and stand on a podium to get her prize, see the scenery, and do some skiing of our own. But it wasn't the same as having Aspen at home and Stacey just a few blocks away. "Plus," I added. "You're right. She needs to rest."

Aspen laughed dryly. "I hope you told her that."

"I tried. I think I was maybe…eighty percent successful in getting my message across?"

"Better than zero percent."

"Yeah. We're going furniture shopping tomorrow, and skiing Sunday and probably Monday and Tuesday as well, so whatever you said to her seems to have sunk in. I think she's accepted that she's home for a while now so she'd better sort her house out and finish unpacking."

Aspen's shoulders dropped. "Oh good. Thanks, Gem. She's lucky to have such a good friend in you."

"Think I'm the lucky one too."

She grinned. "I think you're right."

It was a weird twisty thing that someone as confident and extroverted as Stacey, and someone as shy and borderline-introverted as me clicked so well. But we just...worked, and had from the beginning. Of course, there was the teensy-tiny problem of my raging crush on her, which thankfully she didn't seem to notice. I was pretty sure anyone who was attracted to women would have a crush on her, because personality aside, Stacey was Hot with a capital H—tall and athletic and ripped, a sexy-as-hell full-sleeve tattoo, the cutest batch of freckles over her nose and cheeks, and the most incredible light brown eyes framed by thick, dark lashes, which I'd always found a little weird given she was a natural blonde. She had an interesting face, for real. She was gorgeous, not movie-star gorgeous, but her face was bold, yet soft at the same time. Yeah, I spent a lot of time thinking about her face. And her other body parts.

Being in love with your best friend was both great and shitty, and I'd been managing my crush since pretty much the moment I'd first seen Stace. Maybe when I went away for college in the fall it'd be easier. Sure, it was going to suck, but not being close to her all the time might help me cool my feelings.

I picked up the empty laundry basket and put it up out of reach of Taylor's teeth. "Oh, hey. I need to get some more footage of Stacey training. She told me to tell you, but she's okayed it. I'll stay out of your way again."

"Sure," Aspen said easily.

"When would be the best time?"

"Just pick a nice sunny day and we'll go with that. Everyone else will be fine with having professional media around us again." She winked. "Do you want us to go easy on her while you're filming?"

"Nah, Stace would hate people not seeing her putting everything into training." I bit my lower lip. "Do you think someone would be able to follow her down the course with the GoPro again? Just so I know I've got every possible shot I can get. I just...can't ski that." There was no way I'd ever be able to match Stacey's speed on a racecourse, even during training and even on a run that I wasn't petrified of doing, like the *Birds of Prey* Downhill course at Beaver Creek.

Aspen's face softened. "Of course." She pulled me against her. "It's okay to be anxious about doing some runs, Gem."

She'd know. Aspen had retired from her lucrative pro ski racer career partly because of snowballing injuries and partly because of crippling anxiety she said came from the procurement of those injuries. I'd seen enough race crashes—including some of Stacey's, which made me sick to my stomach—to totally get Aspen's anxiety. I had no idea how they just rehabilitated themselves and went back at it just as hard, if not harder. Brave weirdos.

"I know." I leaned against her shoulder. "I don't mind going slow down those runs with you or Stace where I can stop and get my confidence back, or sideslip some bits. I just don't want to go zoomies."

She kissed the top of my head. "And that's totally okay. Ski your own run, remember?" Aspen set the washer, then slung her arm over my shoulders, guiding me out of the laundry room and to the living room. "Okie dokie, Kathryn Bigelow. Now you're officially on spring break, what are your plans for the week? Think you could find a day so you, me, and your mom can ski?"

"Of course. I'll just be hanging out with Stace while she's having her break, prepping for finals next month, editing Stacey's film, sleeping in…Oh, and I wanna go out and take some photos of the start of the spring thaw."

"Sounds great."

It'd been Aspen who'd bought me my digital SLR for our first Christmas together. At the time, I'd thought it weird because while I enjoyed taking photos, I wasn't obsessed with it then. I used to think I wanted to be a veterinarian but after a few months playing around with the camera, taking stills and videos, I was hooked. I still loved science, but weirdly and totally unexpectedly considering how focused I'd been on academic stuff my whole school life, I'd discovered I loved film stuff more. And talking to a veterinarian at a job fair thing had also kinda made me realize it wasn't for me. I just wanted the science and animal part, not anything to do with the people-who-owned-the-animals part. Then I'd talked to a filmmaker at the same fair, who was nerdy and introverted and so passionate about making films that I'd tumbled head over heels and hadn't looked back.

So I'd decided I wanted to blend my two loves and make science and nature documentaries. (I'm available, Nat Geo!) Of course, Mom and Aspen had diligently asked me if I was sure I wanted to move away from veterinary science to something more arts centric, then they'd had A Discussion, then I'd pointed out that I was only fifteen and still figuring my life out and didn't people change their minds all the time? When I was four I wanted to be a spoon. Definitely changed my mind about that one.

I'd changed my mind about a lot in the last few years, some things not so important, some things sorta important, like about finding out who my donor was. When I was younger I was sure I'd use the identity release he'd signed, which meant when I was eighteen I could find him. But now I had Aspen and my family felt so perfect that I didn't want to know the guy who'd contributed half my genes anymore.

We'd met Aspen back when Mom's and my last name was Tierney, and Mom was lonely and miserable. Who knew that when we'd taken a family-and-friends ski trip to Australia in 2017, I'd end up with a stepmom? I hadn't really wanted to go, but Mom's best friends wanted to confirm it really did snow in Australia, and Mom thought a dual family vacation with her good friends and their kids was a great idea.

I didn't really love skiing, mostly because it scared me. So, I'd agreed to take some lessons in Australia. Turned out my coach was Aspen, a former professional ski racer, who also lived in Colorado when she wasn't traveling around teaching noobs like me how to ski, which was super cool. Also super cool was the swoony look Mom gave Aspen when she first met her. I'm pretty sure it was love at first sight, but then we went home to Idaho Springs, Colorado and Aspen stayed in Australia to finish their ski season. If you've ever wondered what it feels like to watch your lonely, sad, scared-to-trust-women Mom fall in love with someone awesome and then break up with that person because of a dumb reason, I can tell you it freaking *sucks*.

Thankfully they sorted out their stuff, because no exaggeration—Aspen was the best stepmom in the world. Not that I had much of a gauge, but I knew the woman who'd been with Mom when I was conceived, right up until I was about eleven, wasn't a nice person or a nice mother. But Aspen was both a great person and a great mom. She'd never treated me like I was a silly kid, was always there if I needed to talk to her about anything from personal stuff to school stuff to weird stuff, and would probably jump into a burning building to save all of us, Taylor included. But she was also the biggest kid at heart and was the first person to suggest we should build a combustion engine, or that we should take an afternoon off school as a mental health break to go for a hike or to the museum or a movie.

Aspen ran a hand over my head and down the back of my neck to gently massage. "You okay? You look totally zoned out."

"Mhmm, totally. Just thinking." Everything felt so perfect right now, and I was scared of it all changing at the end of next month when I'd graduate.

"Don't think too hard. Why don't we go surprise your mom and meet her after work? I'm craving Italian. We could go to Figaro's for dinner?"

I gave her arm a few rapid-fire pokes. "You mean you don't feel like cooking?"

She snuck in with threats of tickling. She'd tickled me once, learned how much I hated it and had never done it again. But she always pretended she was going to. "Do *you* feel like cooking?"

"Hell no." I never felt like cooking, but it was part of my allowance chores so I diligently did my part in our rotation and even produced completely edible meals.

"Exactly. Let's use me being tired from wrangling Stacey as an excuse. And your mom's been at work all week so it's not fair for her to cook. Plus, you're technically on vacation so why would you want to cook?" She glanced at her watch. "We'll leave in…thirty minutes? Then we can be back early for a movie or whatever."

A movie sounded amazing. But… "I have some English reading to do." Though senior finals were a month away, and my college applications were done, it felt weird to not keep up with schoolwork.

"What are you reading?"

"*The Things We Cannot Say.*"

"Ah." Aspen's face went blank. "Never read it. But I bet it's better than *1984*, *A Tale of Two Cities*, and *The Grapes of Wrath* which is what I remember reading in the twelfth grade. Boring."

I wrinkled my nose as I reminded her, "I read those last year." Just because I was interested. They weren't as interesting as I'd hoped.

Smiling, Aspen wrinkled her nose right back at me. "I know. Why do they always assign really profound and hard-to-wade-through books in school?"

I leaned against the doorframe. "Yeah. Just once it'd be nice to read a girl-meets-girl romance."

"Well we know why that's not being assigned..." she grumbled. Then she perked up. "Y'know, I always thought someone should write a story about how your mom and I met. It's got everything you need—romance and drama and a dramatic romantic gesture, action and suspense and an amazing kid. And! It's got lots of skiing!"

"It'd be a bestseller," I deadpanned.

"Brat," Aspen laughed.

I flashed her an angelic smile, and turned to leave.

"Hey, Gem?"

I spun around, catching myself on the doorframe to swing myself back into the room. "Yeah?"

"Thanks for talking with Stacey. She's really lucky to have such a good friend as you."

"Makes your job easier, right?"

She grinned widely. "Right. But I know you didn't do it for me. You did it for Stacey."

Yep. I'd do *anything* for Stacey.

We took Aspen's Land Rover into town to meet Mom, and when Aspen spotted her locking up the front door of her PT practice, she jumped out of the car and rushed over to help. I stayed where I was because standing around while your parents got reacquainted was boring and a little embarrassing. As soon as Mom realized Aspen was there, she reached up to pull Aspen's face down, kissing her before hugging her tightly. They talked quietly. Mom laughed.

The change in both of them was immediate, like they'd both been holding their breaths for a week and had finally inhaled. Love was great. But they also seemed to actually like and respect each other. I'd never seen them fight. I mean, they had little arguments but always resolved them quickly. I really was that person who never complained about their parents because there was absolutely nothing to complain about—we were basically a television-commercial family. Mom and Aspen had the kind of marriage I wanted one day, with someone great. But I had nobody in mind, of course. Ahem.

Once they'd finished with their PDA, I got out of the car and waited for them to come back. Mom greeted me with a hug, kissing my temple. "And here I was going to surprise you guys with Chinese for dinner. This idea is so much better." She smoothed my hair back. It was a futile exercise—I'd inherited her blond curls, and I'd apparently also inherited the unruly hair gene from the donor. She looked between Aspen and me. "So. Where are we going?"

"We were thinking Figaro's," I said.

"Sure," she agreed. "Let's leave my car here and we can pick it up on the way home." Mom pulled both of us to her for another hug. "I missed you guys today. Love you both so much."

I wrapped my arms around them. "Love you both too." I really did have the most amazing family. Yeah, I know…it's gooey. But it's also really great.

CHAPTER THREE

Stacey

Bree was spending the weekend with friends, doing group practice for acting auditions, and who knew what else for school. Despite my best efforts to share some time with my still-kinda-new girlfriend, we just couldn't seem to find the time to meet up regularly. So I spent Saturday morning furniture shopping, and buying new Lego sets and Warhammer figurines (Gem had turned me on to both hobbies—no judging, I was still super cool), then the afternoon arranging all my newly delivered furniture with Gemma, chilling with her on my new couch, and planning a day's skiing together for the next day.

Gem left around five p.m. to squeeze in some study for her senior finals, and the emptiness of my house was so smothering I decided to slink back to my parents' house to sneak a place at their table for dinner. It was the right thing to do, to go in person to let them know they were off the hook early this season. The fact it was dinnertime was just a happy bonus. Honestly.

Every season, once my racing schedule was completed, it was time for Mom and Dad to do things they wanted—like visiting my brother, Max, at college in Chicago and spending some time in Florida with my grandpa—instead of getting up at 4:45 a.m. to make sure I went off safely to training, or tag-teaming to make sure one of them was always at my races to support me, regardless of what country I was in. Mom and Dad were appropriately supportive of how bummed I felt about missing Mammoth but I could tell they were fully in agreement with Aspen that I should rest. It was also clear they were relieved they wouldn't have to trek to California with me for the final race of the season, which led to them talking about moving their flights to Florida forward a week now that they were "free." I knew they needed and deserved a break, but geez, don't act so eager to get away from me, guys.

Mom sent me home with a mountain of leftovers, and the moment I'd stashed the food in the fridge I collapsed on my couch and called Naomi to tell her I was done for the season. She was the appropriate mixture of angry, upset, and pleased that she'd have one competition where she wasn't trying to beat me, though she was usually unsuccessful in that goal. "Surprised you found time to call me," she said around a laugh. "Thought you'd be spending your enforced break in bed with that hot girlfriend of yours."

I made myself laugh back. Because the truth of it was Bree and I hadn't slept together, though it wasn't for her lack of trying, or my lack of hormones. But it was for my lack of desire to sleep with *her*. Sure, Bree was hot and she was an okay kisser, and I could easily have gone to bed with her. Except for the fact she was also not a person I wanted to share that special thing with. Nobody I'd dated so far was a person I wanted to share that special thing with. When I was fourteen and fifteen, I'd thought I'd probably have sex with the first girl I was serious about. But then I was sixteen, seventeen, eighteen, nineteen, and now twenty and I'd never really been in love with, or fully trusted, any of my girlfriends and so it had just...never happened.

I probably wouldn't have agreed to date Bree if she hadn't been so persistent. We'd met in January at the Aspen/Highlands race and she'd asked for my autograph, then given me her number, then DM'd me on Instagram. The timing was spectacularly bad, given I was in the lead-up to the Winter Olympics, but she was so hot that I'd called her. For the first month, Bree had seemed so undemanding, swearing she totally understood how much of my life I had to dedicate to my racing career, especially in an Olympic year. Seemed so undemanding…until after Beijing. Now it seemed like my training and racing schedule was just pissing her off, and a little snark had crept into her responses whenever I talked about skiing.

We'd never really had a chance to get close, so I couldn't say we were drifting apart, but we definitely weren't drifting together. And I wasn't sure if it was that we were just so busy with our stuff, or if there was something more. But…people liked the social media posts of us that I occasionally put up, so even though we hardly saw each other I was sort of just rolling along with our relationship, because it was fine and wasn't interfering with my training or racing.

"She's busy," I said, and hoped that was enough of an explanation.

"Mmm. So, you're doing what? Sitting alone, trying to pretend you don't want to run back to your parents' place, stewing about your early season's end and forced days off?"

I already had run back to my parents' house today, but I left that part out. "Nah, I spent the day with Gemma. And I had my stewing-mad time and now I'm…resigned, I guess. Time to forget about what I can't change and look forward."

"That's very mature of you."

Laughing, I said, "Don't get me wrong—I hate it, but it's not going to kill me to skip Mammoth. And Gemma said taking a few days to rest and recharge wasn't such a bad thing."

"Gemma said, huh? Gemma says a lot of things." Her tone was singsongy, like she was leading me to a confession.

I didn't need to be led. "Yeah, she does." I'd confided in Naomi about my feelings for my best friend when she'd commented that Gemma had seemed to feature more in my social media stuff than anyone, even current girlfriends. I'd also confided that when Gem and I had first met, by accident when Aspen and her family had caught me out skiing when I'd been told to rest an injury, I'd picked up on some definite crushing vibes from her. My revelation had sent Naomi down a spiral of practically planning the wedding.

"You still don't want to go there?"

My laugh caught in my throat. "Oh I absolutely want to go there, but I can't."

"Why the hell not? God, I *dream* of finding a guy who I can actually talk to, who loves the same shit as me, who I can just hang around with without feeling like I have to be switched-on all the time, a guy who I can pick my nose and fart around. You've got all of that right there, my friend. You do not know how lucky you are."

That was true. But just because Gemma and I were completely comfortable with each other didn't mean we'd be able to magically make romance work. *If* we got to romance, which I doubted we ever would. I wasn't scared of much, but I was scared of losing Gem's friendship. "You ever been in love with your best friend?"

"Can't say I have," Naomi mused.

"Imagine it, then imagine if you started dating and it was amazing and then for whatever reason, it all went to shit. You might lose your best friend as well as your partner. *That's* what I'm afraid of." The thought of losing my anchor was so awful it made me feel trembly inside. "Yeah, it'd be awesome to have friend plus girlfriend in one package, but is it worth the risk?"

"Yeah, that would suck," Naomi said breezily. "But maybe you need to think about what sucks more—*maybe* break up and lose the tight friendship, or not dating her and experiencing all that awesomeness. If your friendship is as solid as it seems to be, why couldn't it weather a dip into the dating pond?"

I took a little while to think about that. Gem and I had never really had an argument—little disagreements, yeah, but nothing major—so I had no idea how we might bounce back if we dated then broke up. But neither of us were antagonistic people, and we got along so well and loved each other so much as friends, so maybe… Maybe nothing. "It might. But I can't be sure and she's too important to me to risk it."

"I get it. So you're just going to stick it out with whats-her-face?"

"Bree," I said absently. "Not forever, but yeah." Or more accurately? Not for long, based on our three-month relationship which was still as shallow as a puddle. We were girlfriends, sure, but it felt more like we were a bit more than acquaintances, who sometimes kissed. I rarely found myself thinking about Bree when we were apart; she was just there sometimes and then she wasn't. "I dunno," I groaned. "It's nice to have someone, even if sometimes she feels more like a cousin I just met and we're still awkwardly getting to know each other."

"That, my friend, sounds like the biggest waste of your time ever. All I can say is I hope the Instagram likes are worth it and that she's a great lay."

I chuckled—yes, chuckled—and hoped it sounded appropriately casual, instead of me panicking inside. "A gentlewoman never tells."

"Okay, okay. I read you loud and clear. Now, speaking of great lays, I was in the middle of a conversation with this cute snowboarder I met on Bumble so I'm going to get back to that. Unless you have any other gossip?"

"Nope, nothing more to tell. And a snowboarder? Eww," I joked.

"I know, I know. But he's so sweet and funny and hot that I'm forgiving him this transgression."

"You're a better person than me."

"I know. Take care of yourself, okay? Use this time to rest."

"I'll try."

As I wandered around checking the locks before bed, I sent a quick text to Gem with the time I'd pick her up in the morning. I hadn't bothered asking Bree if she wanted to join us, even after Gem's reminder, because I was sure she'd say no. And even if she agreed, I knew we'd just get frustrated with each other.

Bree skied, and was more than capable, but she preferred to use her on-snow time to pout on Insta with the mountain behind her. We'd spent a few days at Vail together and by the end of each day were bickering because I wanted to do what people usually did at a ski resort, while she wanted to sit around and take selfies. Bickering was not the vibe I wanted when I was on skis, and we'd come to a silent understanding that we should keep this activity separate.

It was clear Bree was more interested in the perks of dating a ski racer rather than the shitty, gritty behind-the-scenes stuff. The stuff where I was training all the time, didn't drink even at parties (or more accurately—didn't really attend parties), stuck to reasonably strict dietary needs, was injured and upset about it, or was away at races or training camps for half the year.

Gem, on the other hand, was intimately familiar with all aspects of my racing—partly thanks to Aspen, but mostly because she wanted to be. My best friend and my girlfriend were such complete opposites, right down to their career aspirations. Bree wanted to be on-camera, where Gemma was most comfortable—and also awesome—behind it. And I knew when it came down to it, who I would choose to hang out with. And it wasn't the girl I was kissing…

I'd just finished brushing my teeth when my app alerted me that someone had driven up. I checked the video and cursed under my breath. Bree. What was she doing here? If only I'd been a minute earlier in my routine and had already turned out the house lights for the night, then I could have pretended I was asleep and ignored her. I stuffed my feet into Uggs and went to meet her, not wanting to prolong things any longer than necessary. It was bedtime, and my brain had already begun switching off.

I flung open the front door, wrapping my arms around myself. The blast of cold air was super unpleasant while I was just wearing pajama bottoms and a tee, but Bree didn't seem to realize I was freezing my ass off while she dawdled her way to the door. When she reached the stairs, I smiled. "Hi. Didn't expect to see you, especially not so late. I was just about to go to bed."

She ignored me, jumped up the last two stairs and after pushing me inside and closing the door, looped her arms around my neck and kissed me hard. "Hey, baby. I missed you so much.

How was, uh…your training camp thingy?" We hadn't seen each other since I'd come back from spring speed camp almost a week ago.

"It was great," I enthused. As she should know, given she'd pounced on the Instagram posts of me ripping down the Downhill training course, and had spent an afternoon bleating on social media about how that was her girlfriend. Nothing about her being proud of me, nothing about love—thankfully—and no congratulations on my great season. Just Bree, Bree, Bree.

"Did you miss me?" she asked through a pout.

I realized then that I hadn't responded to her telling me she missed me with an obvious and obligatory "So did I." I grinned. "Sure I did." It was a lie. I'd thought of her in abstract ways, the way you think about what you're having for dinner, but I'd allocated no great brain or emotional power to her. Maybe it was that we didn't have that sort of relationship. Or, I admitted to myself, maybe it was that I just didn't care about her as much as I probably should, given I was her girlfriend.

"Good." She kissed me again, hard, and her tongue intrusively pushed into my mouth.

I tried to engage with her but honestly, all I could think about was how tired I was. "Come sit down with me." Once she'd hung her coat and stepped out of her boots, I took her hand and led her into the living room. The moment we'd settled on the couch, she pressed herself into my personal space.

Bree ran her hand up my arm then back down, her fingertips playing over my tattoos like she'd never seen them before, though she'd seen them plenty. The sleeve on my left arm was ski-themed—all grayscale of snowy mountains, trees, the silhouette of two people on a chairlift, a pair of skis (Atomics of course—you're welcome, sponsors) etcetera. But embedded in the tattooed snow at the base of the mountains was a small, sparkling red gemstone. And Bree wouldn't leave it alone.

I thought I knew why she was so intensely focused on the ink, and regretted telling her why something that seemed so out of place was there. Gemma's favorite color was red, and I'd put it in there as a tribute to my best friend who was always there for me, even when she wasn't physically with me. My Gem.

Bree's hands moved from my arms to my stomach, and I squirmed away as they slipped under my tee. "Wait, wait. Can we talk a minute?"

"What is there to talk about?" Bree kissed my neck, which made it very hard to concentrate on the fact I didn't really want her kissing my neck.

"A whole bunch of stuff. I haven't seen you in over a week. I want to know what you've been up to."

Bree shrugged. "Just the usual stuff. Going to classes, a few parties. I'm staying in town with some friends tonight. Or… staying here?" She moved so she was lying on top of me, and I shuffled to shift her weight off me. She wasn't heavy, but she still felt smothering. Bree's hands wandered again and when I tensed, she sighed. "Stacey, seriously, why don't you want to have sex with me? Are you…like…weird or something?"

I carefully disengaged, sliding backward on the couch so I was away from her hands which had been an inch from my boobs. Her statement and accusation that I was weird made me feel so icky it was hard not to jump off the couch altogether. "There's nothing weird about people who don't want to have sex, and I say this as someone who *does* want to. And you saying that is cruel and honestly, kinda bitchy."

Her eyes narrowed slightly, even as she seemed to accept she'd been nasty. "So what is it then? You want to fuck, but you don't think I'm hot enough?"

"I'm just…I'm not ready. I don't think we know each other well enough and I'm not really a sex for sex's sake sort of person. I need to feel a connection that's more than just my hormones." Though I didn't want to apologize for not wanting to sleep with someone for whom I suspected it would mean nothing more than just feeling good, I thought it might soften things. I was so not in the mood for an argument. I just wanted to go to bed and sleep. "I'm sorry, Bree. It's not that I'm not attracted to you, but I guess I'm just wired differently. It takes me time to get comfortable enough with someone before that happens." And as yet, I was nowhere near that stage with her. Or with anyone I'd dated.

She tried another pout. "Haven't I made you feel comfortable?"

Not really, no… And it wasn't anything she'd done or not done, I just honestly didn't think there was anything that would convince my brain that it wanted to have sex with her. But again, being totally honest would hurt her feelings and cause more issues than I wanted to deal with right then. "It's not about that sort of comfort. Look, it's hard to explain. And I know it's such a shitty cliché but it really *is* me, not you. I'm totally attracted to you, but I'm just not ready for sex yet. Sorry," I added again.

"I see…" She pursed her lips. "Do you have any idea when your brain might be ready for sex with me?"

"I really don't, no. It's not like I'm consciously choosing this." I apologized to the universe for my little lie.

Her mouth fell open as she stared at me. "Wait. Are you a… *virgin*?" She could have won an acting award for her portrayal of "incredulous girlfriend."

I felt suddenly exposed and completely vulnerable. Sure, she was my girlfriend, but admitting to her that I was waiting, like some eighteenth-century maiden, for the right person to have sex with for the first time was embarrassing. Embarrassed! Me! I knew my being embarrassed was more about her reaction if I admitted that yep, I hadn't had sex with anyone yet—probably more incredulity and derision, and even teasing that wasn't really teasing. I didn't want to lie outright, but I had no idea how to be evasive. So I said nothing. Bad idea.

Bree gaped. "Oh my god! You are!" She bit her lower lip, and again, her hands slid under my tee, though this time she cupped my boobs. "I can help with that."

I extracted her hands, though it took a lot of willpower when her thumbs were doing interesting things to my nipples. "No. Thank you. But no." I leaned forward and kissed her, careful to keep it light. "Look, it's late and I'm tired, and I have an early start in the morning. You can stay here if you don't want to drive home. I'd feel better if you weren't driving all the way back to Boulder in the dark."

Her eyebrows slowly arched. "I'm staying in town with friends, remember? I swear you don't listen to me."

"Right. Sorry. Just tired. I'd still feel better if you weren't out driving this late."

She sighed, then pushed away from me and stood, a hand on her hip. "It's not late for the rest of the world, Stacey. You know, the normal people."

Ouch.

With another exaggerated sigh, she turned and walked toward the front door.

I caught up with her as she was putting her ankle boots back on, and touched her arm to grab her attention. "I'm skiing with Gemma tomorrow at Beaver Creek, if you wanted to join us? I mean, you're already here, right? We're leaving early." I had no idea why I'd just said that, because I knew I didn't really want her there. But I hated this feeling of her thinking I was an idiot. Even worse? I sounded stupidly hopeful, which again, was not like me, especially when it came to asking Bree to do anything, *especially* skiing.

"No thanks. I've already got plans." She kissed me, lingering just enough for it to be uncomfortable given our recent interaction, and I wasn't sure if it was intentional or she was just cluelessly horny. "Call me when you've got some time for me."

Double ouch.

CHAPTER FOUR

Gemma

Mom followed me into the dedicated ski-equipment room on the bottom floor of our house, talking at me the whole time. The main theme of her conversation was, "Do you need me to make you something for lunch?"

I sorted through ski-boot liners on wooden pegs along one wall until I found mine. With Aspen's coaching and skiing-for-fun gear, and Mom and I skiing at least a few times a week during the season, the room was stuffed with everything you could ever need for ski adventures. "I'm good, thanks. I've got some energy bars and trail mix." And if I wanted something more, I was capable of creating it.

"That's snacks for the day, not a lunch." She handed me my boots.

"Then I'll buy lunch on the mountain."

"What if you get hungry while you're somewhere away from food?"

"Then I have the energy bars and trail mix."

Mom kept quiet while I reinserted my liners and stuck a boot in each of the pockets on the side of my gear backpack. I really didn't care what I ate during a ski day, and Stacey generally brought enough food to feed a ski team anyway. But…Mom was helicoptering. My mom didn't helicopter. Neither did Aspen. They were always there if I needed, mothered the shit out of me, but they weren't hovery, let-me-do-everything-for-you parents. So something was up.

"Why don't I just make you a couple of sandwiches anyway?" she asked cheerfully. Too cheerfully for her at this time of morning.

Yep, helicoptering. My best guess was her mood something to do with my imminent graduation and move away to college, even though the college part wasn't really all that imminent. But, if Mom wanted to make sandwiches, then I'd take sandwiches. If nothing else, Stacey would always eat them. "Sure. That'd be great. Thanks, Mom." After checking I had helmet, goggles, mittens, and buff, I zipped up my backpack.

"Don't forget to grab your skis."

"Thanks," I said dryly. "I think I would have totally forgotten them if not for you."

She swatted me. "Smartass."

I grabbed my all-mountain Atomics and put them and the backpack down in the entryway. I'd just finished filling my CamelBak bladder when Taylor scooted past the kitchen to the front door. A few seconds later, the doorbell rang, prompting a round of barking. "I'll get it," Mom said, passing me two sandwiches.

I heard Stacey's cheerful and super polite, "Hi, Mrs. Archer. How are you?"

Stacey's voice was naturally kinda deep, not as deep as a guy's, but not super-high, and for some reason, whenever she talked to Mom, her voice suddenly turned angelic. And despite Mom assuring her it was fine to call her Cate, Stacey had always called her either Ms. Tierney, or now, Mrs. Archer. It was hilarious, and adorable, and when I'd teased her about it she'd been aghast, and spluttered, "She's your mom and the partner of my coach, Gem. I can't call her by her first name!"

Yeah, but Mrs. still sounded *so* weird to me for Mom. I'd thought she'd just keep her name when she married Aspen but before the wedding, there'd been A Discussion where she'd told me she was taking Aspen's last name. Something about Aspen's old-fashioned family ideals and family units and stuff, and Mom knowing how important it was to Aspen. I had no great attachment to my last name, and Gemma Archer sounded as good as Gemma Tierney, so I'd legally changed mine too and now we were a family of Archers.

Mom's response was muted, but I heard her laughing, then Stacey's exuberant, "T-Swift! Sorry, I wasn't ignoring you. How you been, gal? I missed you."

I arrived to find Stacey kneeling on the floor hugging the dog and kissing the top of her head, while avoiding reciprocal dog kisses which involved a lot more tongue than anything else. If I kissed Stacey, there'd be tongue, but not like that. The thought made my cheeks warm.

Stacey abandoned her love of my dog and stood. "Hey, Gemmy Gem. You all set?" In the warm light of our entryway, her brown eyes seemed darker than usual, but they still creased at the edges the way they always did when she saw me. She opened her arms for a hug.

I hugged her back, and indulged in a sneaky whiff of Stacey's distinct scent. Even when she was sweaty from a workout or skiing, or a hike or bike ride, she always had an undertone of cologne, slightly masculine but also with something feminine, like a bottle of perfume and aftershave were mixed to create a delicious-smelling scent-baby. "Yep. And we have sandwiches, thanks to Mom."

"Oh cool. Thanks, Mrs. Archer. That's really nice of you." Stacey finally seemed to register that she still had her arm around my shoulders from our hug, and casually let it drop.

Mom's smile was both benevolent and sly. She seemed to have taken great delight in Stacey taking her side with the damned sandwiches. "You're most welcome."

Aspen wandered in and fist-bumped Stacey, before she hugged me. She wrapped an arm around Mom's shoulders. "Okay, we'll see you when you get back this afternoon. Text us when you're leaving Beaver Creek."

"Yep," I agreed.

"Have fun, be careful. Both of you."

Stacey flashed my parents a winning smile. "We will. Promise." She grabbed my heavy backpack and slipped it over both shoulders while I slung on the CamelBak and nabbed my skis. Mom and Aspen stood in the doorway, arms around each other's waists, watching us pack everything up in Stacey's U.S.-Team-sponsored Toyota 4Runner. They waved until Stacey started the car, then went inside more quickly than I'd ever seen them disappear from saying bye.

As she backed out of the driveway, Stacey said, "I love your parents." After a pause, she added slyly, "Was it just me or did they seem desperate to get you out of the house?"

I shrugged. "I guess they just want to have some quiet time without me."

Stacey almost choked laughing as she said what I'd been trying not to think about. "Oh yeah. They're going to be having sex allll over the house while you're gone. Loud sex. All day. That's why Aspen wanted you to text before we leave the mountain. It'll give them time to finish up and put everything back where it was after they've trashed the house with all that sex."

"Oh, gross. Shut up." I shoved her shoulder, which just made her laugh more. Of course I knew they had sex, and they weren't shy with affection for each other—a good affection role model for me, Mom had said when I'd eww'd at catching them making out on the couch—but I didn't need to have that stuff anywhere near my brain. "Aspen wants me to text so they know when to expect us home, you juvenile. You know, in case you skid off the road and put us in a ditch somewhere. The same way I always text when we've arrived?" Maybe it was overcautious, but all it cost me was five seconds of my time and it gave my parents relief to know I'd gotten safely to my destination.

Stacey inhaled a shocked gasp. "I would *never* skid off the road!"

"I know," I conceded, patting her thigh. "You drive like you're eighty years old." It was the most hilarious contradiction, considering she spent the rest of her life at top speed.

She glanced at me, flashing a bright smile. "Gotta keep my pal safe." Her attention went back to the road. "Also, how annoying would it be to ruin my body in a car crash so I couldn't ski anymore? If I'm gonna end my career, I want to do it racing. Full tilt, giving it everything and going out in a blaze of bone-snapping glory."

I cringed. Stacey spoke about race crashes the same way she talked about what she'd watched last night on Netflix. Acknowledging the dangers of her sport instead of pretending they didn't exist was a coping mechanism, because locking those fears away was sometimes worse than facing them. I reached over to rub her shoulder. "I'd prefer it if you retired from alpine ski racing because you've won everything there is to win, multiple times, and have decided it's time to move into a life of commentary or coaching. With all your bones and tendons and ligaments happy and intact."

She laughed. "I guess that's an option. I'm not sure Bree would enjoy that unglamorous lifestyle though."

"Well…" I said carefully, trying to ignore the uncomfortable sensation I always had when Bree was mentioned. "Your retirement is still a long while off yet."

"True," Stacey agreed. "She won't hang around me that long." There was no sadness or malice in the statement. Just pure matter-of-factness. The fact Stacey didn't think vapid, kinda standoffish Bree was marriage material softened some of the weird feeling I had about them as a couple. Their relationship always seemed so odd to me, and I still wasn't sure what Stacey was getting out of it. Except sex, of course.

"Speaking of Bree…Is she still AWOL?"

Stacey's knuckles went white around the steering wheel, then relaxed. "Nah. She came around last night as I was about to go to bed."

"Oh." My skin felt clammy. I had no idea what to say and knew that how I felt about my best friend sleeping with her girlfriend was a jealousy problem I really needed to get over. But also, everyone important to Stacey knew her routines, and none of us would dare just come around near her bedtime, or during her middle-of-the-day naptimes, or bother her during training unless it was a true emergency. So Bree was thoughtless as well.

As if sensing my discomfort, or maybe just because she didn't want to talk about Bree either, Stacey said, "Can you change this music? I have no idea what playlist this is but it's not great."

I grabbed her phone and when FaceID inevitably failed, input Stacey's passcode. "It's Road Tripping Volume Two."

She huffed out a *hungh*. "No idea how it got on to that. Can you please put on Ski Tunes…uh, Volume Four?"

I scrolled through playlists. Long Flight Volumes 1–5, Race Day Hype, Race Day Chill, Road Tripping Volumes 1–6, and finally found Ski Tunes Volumes 1–16. Stace really loved music. Once it restarted, she quietly echoed what I'd been thinking. "I just wish Bree wasn't so oblivious to my job. She obviously knows my schedule and my boundaries for training and downtime because she reaps the benefits of dating a ski racer. But it's like she just forgets them. Or she doesn't care."

Personally, I thought she didn't respect Stacey enough to care. "You wanna talk about it?"

"I don't want to talk or think about Bree today." She glanced quickly at me to grin. "I want to enjoy a day on the mountain with my best friend."

Best friend. There it was. That was all she'd ever think of me as. I returned the grin, though it felt like my face was about to crack. "Me too."

Once we'd parked at Beaver Creek, we dragged all our gear out to wait for the shuttle. Stacey got more than a few second glances, but nobody said anything about being in the presence of a recent Olympic medalist. Once we'd filed off the shuttle, we found a quiet-ish place to gear up. She passed me the sunscreen and as I smeared it over my face, she double-checked the contents of her backpack.

"Am I rubbed in?" I asked.

Laughing, she answered, "Not at all." Stacey moved until we were toe-to-toe and carefully rubbed in what I'd apparently missed over my cheek, chin, and eyebrow. "Now you are," she said quietly.

"Thanks."

A girl, probably around ten, and her mom, walked up behind Stacey. From the nervous twisting of the girl's hands and the way the pair were lingering, everything screamed "nervous fan." I nodded at Stacey, then indicated with a tilt of my head that she should turn around. This wasn't our first Stacey-fan rodeo, and I knew she'd get what I meant.

Stace plastered a genuinely excited smile onto her face and turned to greet the newcomers. "Hey!"

The girl, still twisting her hands, said shyly, "You're Stacey Evans, aren't you?"

Stacey nodded. "I sure am! Now, you know my name… what's yours?"

Stacey's kind acknowledgment seemed to relax the girl, and her response was a little more confident. "Maya. Your helmet is really cool. Orange is my favorite color."

"What a coincidence," Stacey exclaimed, dialing up her enthusiasm. "It's mine too." Whenever she wasn't training or racing, Stacey always skied in a bright orange helmet, which made it easy to find her if she'd zipped off in front.

The woman gently shook the girl's shoulders. "Was there something you wanted to say to Ms. Evans, Maya?"

Maya's voice wobbled when she asked, "Could I please have an autograph? Maybe a picture with you?"

Stacey held out her hand. "Of course! Come on over here."

I shifted out of the way so Maya's mom could snap a bunch of photos without me lingering weirdly in the background, and when they were done, Stacey unzipped her jacket and extracted a Sharpie from an inner pocket. "What do you want me to sign?"

Maya pulled off her helmet and swept her fingers along the side. "Here please. I just started ski-race school last year," she added as she passed the helmet over.

"Yeah? That's awesome! I bet you're really good."

"I am," Maya said confidently.

That made us all laugh. Once Stacey had carefully written "Ski fast, Maya!" and added her signature on the side of the helmet, she handed it back. Maya looked like she'd just been given a bar of pure gold.

"Not the first time you've been asked to sign skis or a helmet, huh?" the mom asked, laughing.

"Definitely not," Stacey said cheerfully, stuffing the pen back into her pocket.

Maya's mom made appropriately wowed noises as her daughter showed off the autograph. "Thank you so much—she really looks up to you."

Stace flashed a luminous smile. "My pleasure. Keep up that race training, Maya!" She waved bye to the pair, then turned back to me. "Right. Sorry about that."

"Don't be sorry. You know I love watching you with fans. They love seeing their ski hero."

"Am I *your* ski hero?" she asked me, teasingly, but I caught a hint of vulnerability under the question.

I patted her shoulder. "You know if I had a ski hero, you'd be it." I shrugged into my CamelBak and clipped all the straps up tightly. "Now, let's go make some turns."

She gave me a double thumbs-up. "Speaking my language."

We spent the morning moving back and forth across the mountain from Larkspur Bowl to Bachelor Gulch Mountain and Arrowhead Mountain, just taking chilled-out runs. When we skied for fun at Beaver Creek, we rarely went to Beaver Creek Mountain or Grouse Mountain, where the Downhill training and racecourses were. I'd skied down *Birds of Prey*, the world-famous Downhill course, a couple of times. Very slowly, and sideslipping some of it. Most of it. Stacey and Aspen usually sideslipped with me even though I knew they could whip down it at eighty miles an hour if they wanted to.

I loved watching Stacey ski, whether it was training, racing, or like now when we were having fun. She was fluid and easy, carving turns with an intuitiveness of where I was in relation to her, never cutting me off or ruining my carefully thought-out rhythm by getting in my way. Unlike me, she skied like skiing was breathing, like she never had to think about a single aspect of it. Aspen was the same with the instinct and natural talent, but Stacey seemed to have something Aspen didn't, a certain grace. Though like Aspen, every time Stacey skied—even when we were messing about—it was with the mindset of perfect turns, of what would make her a better racer.

And despite the chasm between our skill levels, Stace had never once made me feel like an idiot or a burden or that I might be holding her back somehow as I slowly made my way down some of the steeper, harder stuff. She just loved to ski, and I knew she loved skiing with me. If you'd told me five years ago that I'd be spending so much time on skis, I'd have died laughing. But, here I was—definitely not an expert but still having fun.

We paused, as always, at the start of the green run *Aspen Alley* on Bachelor Gulch, and I sent a pic, as always, to Aspen. There was no response. She was probably engrossed in a TV show or something. I'd once asked her if they'd named the run after her, given she'd been based at Beaver Creek during her pro career, but she'd offered only vague answers. Aspen rarely bragged, so I knew they totally had named it after her. Should have given her a double-black diamond run…

We skied off *Pow Wow*, onto the tree-lined trail that would take us to the Arrowhead Alpine Club Yurt—a private ski club restaurant at the top of Arrowhead Mountain—and stopped just above the lower tree line. After we stowed our skis tail-down in the snow, Stacey took a photo of the pair of side-by-side Atomics and sure enough, less than a minute later I had a notification that @*staceyskeez* had posted on Instagram.

Hey @atomicski! Helps when your BFF has excellent taste in gear too! #weareskiing

I raised my eyebrows at her and received a nose wrinkle in response. We plonked down to the side of the trail, almost in the trees, so people could easily pass. Stacey shucked out of her backpack and lowered herself to sit beside me, her long legs stretched out. She flexed her ankles, moving her feet up and down, then fell onto her back to gaze up at the sky. "You ever just feel like everything's suddenly right where it's meant to be?"

I set my provisions between us on the snow. "Sometimes, yeah. What's with the philosophy?"

Stace dug her heels in and sat up. She pulled out a container of cold pasta salad and with a wink, nabbed one of Mom's sandwiches too. "I was so bummed about my season ending early, but now I'm starting to see the wisdom and benefit in it." After a huge mouthful of pasta, she elaborated, "I hate admitting it, but I really was tired after Beijing. It's been nice to take a break, and now I'll get a head start on my training for next season." She bumped me with her shoulder. "And I get to spend more time with you."

I unwrapped my sandwich. "That's the part I like best. Plus also, you not getting burnt out early."

She hmmed her agreement and we sat quietly for a while, eating our lunch. As soon as she was done with her pasta, she said, "Gimme some of that trail mix?" Stacey opened her mouth for me to trickle in a handful, and as she chewed, she unwrapped Mom's second sandwich, studying it as if it contained the meaning of life. "I don't know what it is, but your mom's sandwiches are always amazing."

"It's just a PB and J, Stace. Not caviar and gold leaf on a home-cultured artisan sourdough."

"Gross. Who'd eat that?"

"Bree?" I said teasingly. But I didn't get an eye-rolly smile or a reciprocal joke the way she usually would. Instead, I got a tight smile which prompted me to ask, "You okay?"

"Mhmm, of course."

She didn't seem okay. Not *not* okay either, but just not... Stacey. I hastened to say, "Sorry, that was out of line."

Stacey huffed out a dry laugh. "No it wasn't. It was spot-on."

Ah. Bree problems? A part of me did a tiny dance of "Thank goodness" and the rest of me just wanted to hug my best friend. Even though to me, Bree didn't seem like the right person for Stacey, she was still Stace's girlfriend and it was my job to be supportive.

She dug her heels into the snow, pushing them deeper while she worked on the PB&J. And I sat quietly, waiting until she found what she wanted to say. After a minute, she did. "I don't know, Gemmy. I mean, I'm not going to marry her, obviously. And I know what we have isn't going anywhere. But it's a 'fine for now' situation, you know? I just can't be bothered changing it, because breaking up with her is probably going to cause drama I don't need."

I tried as hard as I could to be both supportive and neutral. "Yeah, I know." Gosh, I wanted to tell her that us together would be so much better than a "fine for now." We'd be amazing. Our friendship was so perfect, that why couldn't us as girlfriends be even more perfect? But that big worry always butted in with, "What if it isn't perfect, what if it ruins everything?"

Stacey exhaled a loud sigh. "I don't know, maybe it's already moving into drama I don't need. I'm not an emotions expert, but…it kinda feels like she's shitty with me all the time, because I can't rush off to Boulder just to spend an hour with her, or find full days to do stuff together whenever she comes here."

"Maybe she just doesn't really get what it's like to be close with a ski racer, and how important racing is to you." Important was an understatement. Ski racing was basically Stacey's whole reason for existing.

"Maybe. But you'd think she'd know that by now. I told her straight-up, and she swore she understood and that it was cool." Stace glanced over at me. "I mean, you got it right away."

Well yeah, but I knew from Aspen how important it was. And I loved Stacey and wanted her to have everything she needed to succeed. "I think," I said carefully, "if your relationship with her isn't causing you massive grief, then why not just see how it pans out? You've only been dating her for what, three months?" And she'd been away at races and the Olympics for most of that time. So realistically, how well did she and Bree know each other?

"I guess. And about that, yeah."

Three months. It was kind of Stacey's MO, to date women for less than six months and then break up with them, usually because her girlfriends didn't like taking a back seat to Stacey's true passion—skiing. Even when she'd dated a fellow ski racer, it'd fizzled, and they saw each other way more than anyone else Stace had dated.

"Can we sit in the truth bubble?" I asked.

Stacey's focus snapped to me. "Sure."

We were so close that I wasn't worried about what I had to say, or that she'd get pissed off at me for being honest. "You've got this thing…like you only date women for three, four, maybe five months and then that's it. I know you're honest with them from the start about what you've got to give them, time-wise, so either you just keep dating women with poor listening comprehension skills, or maybe there's something else going on."

She frowned. "Something else like what? Care to elaborate, Therapist Gemma?"

I inhaled slowly before I told her what I'd observed being her best friend for years. "Or maybe, in the time you do share with them, you're not *really* sharing all of yourself, and they're feeling doubly excluded from your life. That'd make me feel kind of snarky, if it were me." *If.*

It took her a little while to answer, but I could tell she was really thinking about it. Still, all I got in answer was, "Maybe. I dunno."

I tapped the side of her calf with the toe of my ski boot. "Something to think about?"

"Yeah." Stace grinned at me. "But another day and place though. Come on, we're wasting good snow." She stuffed the last bit of sandwich into her mouth, sucked down some water from her CamelBak, then stood, offering a hand to help me up. As usual, she pulled too hard and laughed when I almost collided with her. She offered her usual semi-swaggery, "Don't know my own strength."

"Nope," I agreed. I loved her strength; all that lean, useful muscle was super sexy. I shuffled backward, forcing myself out of sexy muscle-touching range. "Ready for round two?" As soon as I spoke, I realized how innuendo-y that had sounded. But I could definitely go a few rounds with her, and not on the mountain.

Stacey unstuck my skis from the snow and put them down so I could easily clip in. "Let's do it."

We backtracked slightly and paused at the intersection near the top of the Arrow Bahn Express chairlift to wait for a gap in the stream of skiers and boarders so we could continue down the mountain. Stacey held up a hand to stop me from leaving, then fished her phone from her outer chest pocket. She frowned at the screen. "Bree's here?" Stace peered at me, and though her eyes were hidden behind goggles I could still discern her emotion from the twist of her mouth. A little pissed and a little frustrated and a little confused.

"Where?" I glanced around, half expecting to see her skiing toward us.

"Down at Broken Arrow." The restaurant at the bottom of Arrow Bahn Express. "I guess I should go meet her." Stacey stuffed her phone back into her pocket and adjusted her pole straps with uncharacteristically jerky movements.

"Do you want me to come down with you?"

"Of course I do, if you want to. But I shouldn't be too long, so if you'd rather hang out up here and take a few runs while I do this, that's cool too." Her smile was forced, and I wasn't quite sure what she was thinking.

I made my smile extra cheery, hoping to pull her out of her mood. "I'll come along. Boring skiing by myself."

Stacey's shoulders slumped. "I'm really sorry, Gemmy Gem. I've got no idea why she's here. I'll be quick so we can get back to our fun day."

I reached up and patted the top of her helmet. "It's fine. Come on, let's head down before your girlfriend gets shitty."

Instead of turning off *Cresta* onto *Tomahawk*—a black run— the way we normally would, I suggested we just rip all the way down *Cresta*—a blue run—because I was slower on blacks. Stacey skied down with short snappy turns like she was racing Slalom. Her usual fluidly graceful style had gained some tension, and I wanted to do or say something to help, but had no idea what that might be. I knew, and had known before our earlier conversations in the car and on the mountain, that Stacey didn't seem to love Bree and that this wasn't going to be a long-term relationship for her. But seeing her so obviously annoyed by something her girlfriend had done was both upsetting, yet also made me grossly hopeful.

I wasn't hopeful that she'd break up with Bree and then ask me out, but that it might ease some of her tension when she talked about her girlfriend. Not that it was my place to judge, but if being with someone made you feel that way, was it worth it? Stacey was my best friend and I just wanted her to be happy.

Bree was easy to spot, because she wasn't dressed for a day on skis. We slipped our skis into the racks, draped our pole handles over the top and headed toward her. Stacey led the way, and I let myself think she was protecting me from what was about to come. In the few times we'd interacted, Bree had never been nasty to me, but she always made me feel small, like she didn't think I was worth her time.

Bree stepped out from a small crowd of similarly aged, similarly dressed women and walked right up to Stacey. "Hey, babe." She kissed a startled Stacey full on the mouth.

"Hey," Stacey spluttered. She lowered her voice, but I still heard her say, "What are you doing here? I thought you said you weren't interested in coming to the mountain today."

"Changed my mind, thought I'd bring some friends to meet my girlfriend." The *girlfriend* was accompanied by a double cheek pinch which Stacey ignored, even though I knew she hated her cheeks being pinched.

"Hi, friends," Stacey said, grinning. It was a forced grin. Bree's friends, a crowd of four, all waved and said hi. A few of them looked me over, their appraising glances thankfully not nearly as burning as Bree's. None of them were wearing ski or snowboard boots, or carrying any gear, so apparently "meet my girlfriend" was exactly that. There would have been heaps of other opportunities for Bree to show Stacey off to her friends, but for some reason, she'd decided to drag them here while Stacey was with me.

I instantly realized why. She was shitty that Stacey was hanging out with her best friend instead of her girlfriend. My suspicions were confirmed when, before Stacey could introduce me to Bree's crew, Bree gestured vaguely in my direction and asked, "Who's your little friend?" The question was quiet, but not quiet enough, and the emphasis on the *little* was unmistakable. It was an obvious dig at my age, because while I was nowhere near Stacey or Aspen's height, I'd never considered myself short. Half the crowd around Bree snickered, the other half looked embarrassed.

Stacey pounced immediately. "That's Gemma. You've met her before, a few times. And yeah, you know she's my best friend. And she's not little, or young." She said something under her breath that I couldn't hear, but that made Bree slap a fake smile on her face as she turned toward me.

"Gemma! Didn't recognize you with the helmet and goggles and stuff. How are you?" I'd give her one thing, she was good at hiding her dislike of me when she wanted to.

I knew I was blushing fiercely, and had to force myself to not drag my buff up to my nose to hide it. Instead, I set my goggles on top of my helmet so I could make eye contact, though Bree's were partially hidden behind designer sunglasses. Calmly, I said, "I'm great, thanks." Before Mom and I had moved to Edwards to live with Aspen, I'd had some bitchy bitches at school who reminded me of Bree. My parents' advice about dealing with bullies—aside from tell adults when it crosses a line—rang in my head. Kill them with kindness, but obviously not literally. I cleared my throat as quietly as I could. "I love that jacket. It's gorgeous and you look great in it. Is it new season?"

Bree ran her hands over the front of her Spyder jacket, smoothing out imaginary imperfections. "Next season prototype, actually."

"Ah, well that explains why I've never seen it on anyone before. You must be pretty special to have gotten an early release." If she didn't fall over dead from my kindness, I was going to be super disappointed.

One of her friends, a short woman with a mass of black hair artfully escaping her beanie, said, "Spyder asked Bree to model their gear, get it out in the public eye before it's on sale. They saw her pictures on Insta and thought she'd be perfect."

"Wow, that's really cool," I said.

Bree agreed, "Mm, yes, it is."

Stacey was between Bree and me, standing more still than I'd ever seen her. Stacey was never still; it was like she had a motor inside her that ran even while she slept. She seemed to finally recognize that this conversation was about to become circular with me throwing crumbs of praise at Bree and Bree lapping them up, and spoke up. "Are you guys skiing, or...?" She peered around slowly, as if making the point that they were dressed for fashion, not ski runs.

"No, I just wanted to see you. We'll have lunch then go home. You coming in for lunch, Stacey?" Stacey. Not Stacey and Gemma.

Stace shifted uncomfortably. "Gem and I just had lunch up top."

Bree's expression was masterfully neutral. "Ah. Well then, I suppose you want to get back to your skiing."

I wondered if Bree's friends felt as awkward and uncomfortable as I did. Stacey's smile was full-charm. "Yep, guessed it in one. Sorry."

She didn't sound all that sorry, more matter-of-fact. Bree turned to her friends with both hands raised in a "Well, whaddaya gonna do when your girlfriend is an Olympic-medal winning alpine ski racer" gesture. They all laughed. Bree turned back to us. "Then we'll leave you to it. Call me, babe."

Stacey nodded. Bree kissed her with as much possessive demonstrativeness as she had when we'd arrived. Then, with a flurry of double-hand waves, the group disappeared into the restaurant. When the door had closed and we were safe from ears, Stace turned back to me, huffing out a visible puff of air. "Well. That was pointless." She cackled out a laugh. "And god, I love you. Completely deflated her. Oh it was so hilariously awkward. You're so clever."

It certainly was awkward, and not just for Bree. "Thank Aspen for that. She taught me the old 'kill 'em with kindness' trick."

She grinned, leaning close. "Is there anything she can't do?"

I pretended to think about it. "You know, I actually don't think there is."

Stace hmmed, glancing back at the building. "I'm sorry about her. I don't know why she did that."

I appreciated the apology, but it wasn't Stace who should be apologizing for her girlfriend's behavior. I almost told her I thought Bree hated that Stacey found time for me, but not her, but I'd already said enough about my best friend's dating life today. "She's definitely one of the more, um, interesting women you've dated."

"Yeah," she said noncommittally. "You know, Spyder didn't actually find her on Insta and ask her to model that jacket? Her cousin works for them and she gets all the next-season stuff from him." Stacey held a finger to her lips. "But don't tell her adoring fans. Oops, I mean, *friends*." She winked.

"Oh my gosh. That's…" I thought of a bunch of words like *ridiculous*, *sad*, *deceitful*, but kept them to myself. Eventually, I just shrugged.

As if she knew what I was thinking, Stacey murmured, "Yeah. It is." She pulled me in for a quick hug. "You ready to head back up?"

I reluctantly released my grip. "Lead the way…"

CHAPTER FIVE

Stacey

My enforced days off hadn't been as annoying as I'd expected. Gem and I had hung out, skiing Monday and Tuesday as well as watching movies, taking Taylor for walks, and playing with my new Lego sets. And as I'd promised Aspen, I'd kept away from structured cardio and strength training, and in addition to activities with Gemma, I'd just done some gentle stretching. Look at me, so relaxed.

After my first few training runs on Wednesday, I had to admit to Aspen that I did feel rested. She couldn't have looked smugger if she tried. And because Gem was off school for the week, she was ready to hang out in the afternoons when I was done with training, so it was actually a pretty good week. Aside from a few texts, Bree had been conspicuously absent after her performance at Beaver Creek. Unsurprisingly, I didn't miss her at all. And neither did my new zen vibe.

But Friday, interview day, came way too fast. We trained on a four-on-one-off schedule, but we'd reset everything to make Friday my day off. The lack of activity had me so antsy and hyped up that I'd snuck out for a ten-mile run at dawn. I'd done dozens of media things—podcasts, interviews at races and in studios, but I'd never invited (or more accurately, had Brick invite) a film crew into my home.

Brick had told me the idea for the interview was "staged informality." I'd show Amanda Debnam—the gorgeous, effervescent host of the local YouTube streaming channel *Hello, Vail*—around, she'd probably try the simulator (I'd told her to bring her ski boots if she had any) and then we'd talk in my living room, set up so it looked fancier than my living room.

After my shower, I chose the burgundy button-up that Gemma loved, paired with tan chinos instead of jeans, because we'd planned to play around on the simulator, and the last thing I wanted was for people to make jokes that Stacey Evans skis in jeans. The ultimate insult.

Amanda Debnam arrived at eleven a.m. with a small crew laden with equipment hardcases. Someone who I assumed to be a producer type—Gem would have known—introduced herself as Julia, then got right into surveying the space and rapidly giving orders about how she wanted things arranged. Then, with my permission, she was off with a camera guy to tour my house, presumably to get an idea of how they'd do the "walk and talk" part of the interview. That left me with Amanda, and Brick, who was in the corner of the room doing something on his iPad.

Amanda was television-personality pretty with shiny dark-brown hair, clear skin, and an engaging personality that immediately put me at ease. She started by complimenting my house and the furniture, laughing when I told her most of it was literally just purchased last weekend, then went through the questions—which Brick had already okayed—with me, and explaining the general vibe of the interview. *Hello, Vail* aired one one-hour episode per week, usually focusing on local news stories or personalities. The show was overwhelming skewed toward Vail's main drawing card—skiing and snowboarding— and I'd been on it once before, just after my first World Cup race in 2018.

Amanda's smile was practiced, but kind. "I just want you to feel comfortable, so think of it as a conversation rather than an interrogation."

I smiled back. "I am comfortable."

Julia came back from her reconnaissance, apparently satisfied with what she'd seen. We had a short rehearsal for the part where I'd show Amanda through my house, then I had my hair—including re-buzzing the sides and tidying the top before they styled it—and makeup done, my clothes lint-rolled, and a microphone taped up under my shirt. Despite the supposed informality, the whole setup was still formal, and a little stilted. But as Brick had said, I'd need to either stop winning so much or get used to this kind of journalism.

As we walked through my hall, I tried not to look at the camera guy and mic-holding guy both walking backward in front of us. We talked about the skiing photos on the walls, and the trophies and medals I'd unpacked and set up especially for this interview. And as promised, I booted up for a simulator session.

The simulator was amazing. It was basically a platform with parallel sliding tracks that had bindings attached, facing a huge screen. I could clip in, choose which real course I wanted to run virtually, and simulate a race complete with accurate g-force replication. Aspen loved it too. While I was cooling off and stretching after a sim session, she'd jump on it. She was like me—hated being off skis, and together, we grew steadily more antsy as we waited for the Southern Hemisphere to produce enough snow for us to train on during the racing off-season.

I ripped down a cyber-version of *Birds of Prey* a couple of times for the camera, then adjusted the bindings so Amanda could have a virtual run. She was a good sport about it and I could tell she was a capable skier, but she still skied out of half the gates, even though she was taking it slowly.

Julia directed us all back to the living room, where the camera crew set up two cameras. There was some kerfuffle about sightlines and backgrounds or something, and while that was being dealt with, I texted Gemma. *Wish you were here. So much filmy stuff you'd love.*

Wish I was there too. Heart emoji.

My hair and makeup were refreshed, my microphone rechecked, and I was directed to sit in the chair across from Amanda. She started off by introducing me and listing a condensed version of my achievements to date, before she moved into the meat of the interview—the part where vultures usually circled. "What about people saying you should have won gold or silver in your best disciplines, the Downhill and Super-G, from Beijing earlier this year?"

After inhaling slowly through my nose, I answered, "I think the women who won gold and silver in the Downhill absolutely deserved it. I think the women who won gold, silver, and bronze in the Super-G absolutely deserved it. I would have liked to get more from myself but…" I held my hands out, palms up. "I skied the best races I could have on those days, and that's all I can ask of myself."

"You have an extraordinary amount of self-confidence. Does having people making negative comments about your performance dent that confidence at all?"

"Not at all, no. I mean, having people bombard me with negative things isn't nice, but at the same time I take the view that what these people say doesn't matter to me. They're not my team, or my friends and family, not fans who've supported me for so long." I smiled, grateful we'd had some time to prep before this interview, and continued, "So, I don't listen to the 'haters.' I stay away from social media as much as I can, aside from putting up numerous Insta posts of snow stuff or my gym sessions. Everyone's entitled to their opinion but…the pressure on athletes is immense and unfair. Those people aren't skiing in my boots, they don't get to see everything that happens behind the scenes. They're not on a steep, icy course, in sometimes poor conditions, making split-second decisions at eighty miles an hour or more. I'm twenty years old and I'm human, and every time I go on course, I ski the best I can in those few minutes. Some days I win, others I don't. I wish it was a win every time I stepped up to that timing arm, but that's impossible."

Leaning forward, I made sure to keep eye contact. "I came top five in both of my best events at my *first* Winter Olympics. I won a medal in the Downhill. And for a little while, I stood on the podium next to my heroes for my Super-G." Laughing, I amended, "Until a few of the competitors after me put down some amazing times and pushed me out of the medals, that is. Despite the enormous amount of pressure put on me, I feel like I won." I exhaled, pleased that I'd gotten all of that out clearly.

"But a lot of people think elite athletes should be able to deal with the pressure. What do you say about that?"

"I think people forget that we're humans with emotions. I'd challenge anyone to switch their emotions off at a moment's notice, to not only ignore their personal expectations but to shut out every external thing, every external pressure from media, fans, sponsors and brand partners, event organizers, then put their bodies on the line to ski a racecourse. Yes, we're incredibly fortunate to be able to travel and do what we love, and yes, we work hard at focus and managing our emotions for race day, but we're not robots. We have fears and anxieties and dreams, the same as everyone else and we don't *owe* it to anyone to go out there and win.

"Think of a runner. Do they run a better time every single run? Of course not. We're limited by our body and how we've trained it, by our equipment, by the conditions, limited by our brain. We can't improve infinitely on a constantly upward-moving line—at some point we hit the limit of what we can do and that limit is variable based on a number of factors. Do you see what I'm saying?" When she nodded, I said, "What I'm saying in a very roundabout way of course, is that we're human and we can't be at our peak one hundred percent of the time. And that's what I wish people would understand, and be empathetic about, when they come at us about not winning every race." I made myself smile. "Sorry. Athlete mental health is something me and my team are very passionate about."

Amanda flapped her hand. "It's okay, we can edit it out."

I gaped. "I don't want you to edit that out." I glanced at Brick, who gave me a thumbs-up to indicate he was fine with it, then turned back to Amanda.

She paused a moment, looking to someone off-screen. Apparently, off-screen person had given her the go-ahead to go ahead. "Your coach is four-time Olympic alpine-ski-racing medalist, Aspen Archer, who certainly knows something about external fears. Has her influence changed your perspective on how you manage your mental health?"

I smiled at the understatement of Aspen knowing fear. She was adamant that I have the tools to control mine so I didn't have an early career end the way she did. "Yes she does, and yes she has. Aspen's very aware of the consequences of pressure, and that's why I refuse to let other people's expectations dictate how and when I race. Amanda, as I said, I'm only twenty, I had my first World Cup start just four years ago. I have plenty of years left in my racing career, plenty of time and opportunity to win medals and globes. I'm just getting started."

We talked about my goals, my background, and a bunch of other things I'd discussed with other journalists a million times before. Amanda checked her notes. "Now, from what I've seen, ski racing is a full-time career. Do you have any hobbies outside of racing?"

"Sleeping. Eating." I laughed. "I love being outside, so hiking and mountain biking in the off-season to break up the gym training. Relaxing on the couch with some movies or TV. And my best friend got me into huge Lego constructions and, uh, I don't know if you've heard of the game, but, Warhammer?"

She nodded. "My son loves it."

"Yeah...I don't play with them but I love the intricacy of painting the figurines. It's super soothing and gives me some time to turn my brain off."

Amanda smiled. "One of the things I hear people say most often about you is how much they love watching you race because of...your 'self-commentary' on-course. The camera mics often pick up the sound of you talking to yourself during races. Tell me about it. Have you considered a career in racing commentary?"

"Well I'm not sure I'd know what to say about other racers. Just myself. Uh, it's something I've always done. It's my way of focusing, of keeping my energy high." Laughing, I added, "And talking while I'm racing keeps my face warm."

"How did it start? Was it a coaching tool or…?"

"I used to do it as a really young kid when skiing, even before racing, reminding myself to shift my weight, use my left foot and now right foot, and it stuck. Everyone has different focus zones—some are totally quiet and zen, but I'm like a puppy who's eaten a bag of gummy bears—I need to keep my energy up, keep myself hyped the whole way through a race, and processing aloud is how I do that."

She stared into the camera over my shoulder. "We have some footage of Stacey skiing as a child, and a warning to our viewers, this video contains scenes of absolute adorableness."

Julia yelled, "Cut."

I'd been told they'd add in all these videos and photos later. This video would be one that Dad had taken of me as a five-year-old. As I wobble-skied through makeshift slalom gates, I was shouting, "Heavy left foot! Heavy right foot! Heavy lefttt…whooooaaa!" Little me turned to get back on course. "Heavy left foot. Don't fall over, Stacey. Now heavy right foot. Gogogogogo zoom-zoom-zoom to the end!" The video had a soundtrack of young-me laughing hysterically as I crossed through the finishing gates.

The hair and makeup person touched up both Amanda and me, lint-rolled me again—who knew my house had so much hidden lint?—then stepped back. I drank some water, and took a few deep breaths. Be charming, be witty, be real, be honest.

Julia raised her voice, as if she thought we couldn't hear her over the almost-silence of my house, and called, "Three…two… one, action."

Amanda stared intently at me, smiling softly. "Oh that was *adorable*. I can see you had skills from an early age." We laughed together. "Did you always want to be a ski racer?"

"Actually, no. I wanted to be a caterpillar." Laughs all around. "Then a racecar driver. Then a helicopter pilot. Ski racing was always something I did for fun, even when I started realizing that I was winning a lot, and people were telling me that I should take it more seriously. It wasn't until I was about twelve that I decided this was it, that I was going to make it my career instead of just my hobby, and in order to do that I really needed to focus my entire life on it, which is an interesting thing for a middle-schooler to take on. But it was always fun, even through all the work and the things I didn't get to do with my peers at school, the things I might have missed. And I think fun is the key to my success, alongside all the work my team and I put in. The moment I stop having fun with it will be the moment I know it's time to retire."

Amanda's smile was dazzling. "I'm sure every fan of alpine ski racing hopes you don't retire any time soon, myself included. Now, let's see you fifteen years later."

This was apparently going to be network footage of me in Beijing during my medal-winning run. There was no hair-and-makeup break this time. Instead, the cameras kept rolling as Amanda checked her notes before turning a soft, sweet smile on me. "I can't even imagine walking down that, let alone skiing down it at eighty miles an hour, and you were doing it as a child."

"Well, I wasn't going quite that fast as a kid. Maybe only sixty miles an hour." I winked, then paused to check my joke had landed—yes. "I think kids have no fear until they learn something is scary. And I was lucky that by the time I had my first big wipeout, I was so in love with ski racing that it didn't matter."

"You must be utterly fearless. You look fearless. Are you ever afraid?"

I'd always been truthful when asked this question, and now was no different. "Of course. I'm afraid all the time. Ski racing isn't about having no fear, though I know there are racers who really are fearless. Racing is about managing that fear and knowing I have the skills and the strength, and I've done all the homework and groundwork to make it down to the bottom of the course and onto the top of the podium. I can't control variables, I can only control myself, so I do my best to do that." I paused for a breath. "My strategy has always been full risk for full reward. Most of the time that pays off, sometimes it doesn't. I race with the mindset of either being on the podium, or not finishing the race because I've pushed beyond my limit and crashed or skied out. I always ski like I either want to win, or leave the hill on a stretcher. I mean, I never go in with the mindset that I'm going to crash, but it's an all-or-nothing kind of thing."

"You have had some big crashes, and some big injuries."

I nodded. "Yes, I have."

"How long does it take to rehabilitate from a major injury?"

"Depends what you define as major. Things like serious fractures or ligament ruptures can take up to a year. Small things like sprains, strains, or dislocations I can ignore if they aren't my ankles or knees."

"You've had some knee issues in the past, right?"

"In the past, yes. I had a few minor knee injuries, then I ruptured my ACL a few years back and had surgery."

Amanda paused and reset her expression again, a cue that they'd be adding something in later. This edit would be a picture of me in a hospital bed after my ACL repair in 2020, surrounded by balloons and flowers, and pointing behind myself to the banner Gem had made. Instead of reading "Get Well, Stacey" or something else as mundane, she'd played with the ACL theme—Another Crash Lol.

Amanda made eye contact. "You look like you have some very good friends who support you."

"I do." I laughed. "And I know that get-well sign seems like gallows humor. But it's one way I deal with the disappointment of being injured and I'm so fortunate to have friends who understand how best to support me."

"Have you given any thought as to what comes after your racing career?"

"Not yet, but I have a lot of options. Coaching, or commentary, working with the U.S. Team or even the International Ski Federation." I smiled as widely as I could. "But whatever it is, it's not going to be for many years."

"Whatever you choose to do, I hope you have as much success as you have in your ski racing career."

Amanda faced the camera again and wrapped things up with a recap of who I was and what I'd done so far, and then Julia called, "And cut. Nicely done, everyone."

My living room suddenly came to life, and Amanda shook herself as if she was shaking off something unpleasant. Hopefully that unpleasant thing wasn't me. She flashed me a warm—and thankfully genuine—smile. "Stacey. That was fun. Thank you for being such a good sport."

"I'm all about good sports," I quipped.

Amanda grinned. "You certainly challenged me beyond what I thought. Your comments about mental health have made me think about how, as a journalist, I frame my interview perspectives. So rarely do my interviewees do that. So, thanks."

"No problem. And you were great on the simulator by the way. Maybe it's time to try the real thing when it's set up for racing?"

She almost doubled over laughing. "Not in this lifetime. Take care of yourself, now. I want to see you in the gold-medal positions in Milan in 2026." She walked off, pulling the microphone pack from her waist and fiddling with the corded mic. The crew were pulling down lights and cameras, rolling cables, and moving the furniture back into place. It only took them twenty minutes to pack up, and then they were slipping out the front door and saying goodbye.

I exhaled. Formal interviews took so damned long. My body was tight from so much time sitting still, and I rotated my torso side to side to loosen up. Brick had also gathered his things and was checking around to make sure he hadn't left anything, which he usually did. He gripped my shoulder and shook me gently—his version of a hug. "You did good, kid."

"Thanks." I peered at his face, trying to gauge his mood. He seemed his usual chilled self. It took a lot to rattle him, a benefit of his having represented a bunch of snow-sports athletes who were a lot wilder than me. "Didn't cross the line with the mental health stuff?"

"We'll see. But that's for me to worry about. You gave her something to think about next time she speculates about an athlete's performance. And you told the truth, a truth people should hear. Now, you forget about the interview and concentrate on training." He let me go and fumbled in his pocket for his keys. "I'll call the producer and make sure we get a copy before it airs."

"Cool, thanks."

"Now, take some time and relax for the rest of your day off. I'm sorry we couldn't fit this in another time."

"It's okay." And it really was. It wasn't physically taxing, just mentally. And now it was done and I could switch off. "I'm gonna go see Gemma while I'm looking so fine." I checked my reflection in the hall mirror. "She'll die laughing at the height they got in my hair."

"Good for you. You kids have fun now." With a shoulder pat, he slipped out the front door.

I texted Gem to ask if I could come around, and once I'd received a thumbs-up, I grabbed my peacoat, checked my hair again, and jumped in the car to see my best friend.

Aspen answered the door, her face easing into a smile. "Hey, Stace. How'd the interview go?" She pulled the door wider and ushered me inside.

"It was…long. But harmless. Amanda Debnam is nicer to look at in person than she is in photos, and she can ski." I hung my coat. "On the simulator at least."

Aspen nodded slowly. "Good to know. I assume you're here to see Gemma, not me?"

"Aw, don't sell yourself short, coach."

"Yeah, yeah," she drawled. She leaned on the banister leading up to the second floor and called out, "Gemma? Stacey's here."

Gem barreled down the stairs a few seconds later. "Ohmygosh," she rushed out on a cackle. "Look at you, Fancypants." She laughed again, reaching out to mess up my hair.

I leaned backward. "Nuh-uh. No touching." I used both my forefingers to point at my hair. "I can't waste this. You wanna come grab something to eat with me? I feel like this needs to be out in public."

Gemma glanced at Aspen, who shrugged and said, "Doesn't bother me. If you're happy with your study schedule, then I'm happy. And it's your mom's night to cook so I'm sure she won't care either."

Gem turned and started back up the stairs, gesturing for me to follow her into her bedroom. "Come on up. I'll just get changed. Where are we going? Should I dress up or are we just going to get pizza or something?"

"How about we head into Vail?" Way more options for food. "We can get something medium-fancy."

She sighed like I'd just told her the best news. "Perfect." Gemma turned down her music and went straight into her en suite. From behind the partially closed door, she asked, "How was the interview? Aside from long."

I kept my eyes averted in case she accidentally passed by the gap in her underwear. Or less than her underwear. My neck heated and I was sure I sounded squeaky when I answered, "It was okay. Kinda stressful trying to make sure I didn't sound like an idiot."

Gem poked her head through the gap in the door and rolled her eyes. "You never sound like an idiot." She popped back before I could respond.

"You would have found it super interesting though, there was so much TV shit going on in the background all the time."

"I'm bummed that I couldn't be there. But I really needed to study. Next time someone wants to interview you, can you ask them to do it when I'm not approaching finals?"

I laughingly agreed. "Sure. But you won't have high school finals ever again, so you can just ditch a college class or something, can't you?" I asked slyly.

Even with the door partially closed and the music, I could hear her snort. Gem called, "Can you turn off the music and disconnect the speaker please? I'm almost ready."

I noticed Gem had changed her phone screen and it was now a picture of us. It took me about two seconds to realize it'd been taken right after I'd skied the winning Downhill race at Aspen/Highlands in January. After I'd clipped out of my skis,

I'd rushed over to hug my parents, then Gemma and then Mrs. Archer. As usual, they were waiting at the finish line because Aspen was always up at the start with me.

I'd been dimly aware of the sound of cameras going off all around me, but this wasn't a professional photo. Mrs. Archer must have taken it. Taken from side on, it was Gemma and I just about to hug. We'd already gripped each other's arms, and even with my helmet and goggles I could see how damned delighted I had been as I looked down at her. I smiled, thinking the photo had captured my emotion perfectly.

Gemma's smile was utterly ecstatic, and from this angle the picture captured the little dimple that was low down on her left cheek, almost level with her mouth. She was gripping my forearms hard, leaning into me. The little rumble of excitement in my stomach wasn't unexpected. Nor was the weird feeling of realization that I'd met Bree that same day.

Gem came out of the bathroom wearing jeans with just a bra on top, and went straight to her closet. I snapped my eyes back to her phone. "I didn't know you had this picture."

"Hmm? Oh…yeah. Mom took it. Remember?"

I didn't. "Can I have it?"

"Sure. There's a bunch more, she did the burst thing she always does. Just send them to yourself."

"Thanks." I know it sounds weird that she was so casual about me looking through her photos, but we'd always used each other's phones for music, sharing pictures and stuff like that. I trusted her completely, as she did me, to respect those unspoken boundaries. I scrolled through her album—mostly selfies of us, pictures of Taylor, a couple of Aspen and Mrs. Archer, and nature shots until I found the group from the race. I sent them, and a couple of selfies of us, to myself.

Gem came out of her closet with a gray coat slung over her arm. "Okay, I'm ready to go. How do I look? Suitable for an outing to celebrate…your hair?"

I finally felt brave enough to give her more than a passing glance. She'd put on a little eye makeup, let her hair down and done something so it fell in thick curls around her shoulders. I tried not to stare, but the moment I saw her long brown boots, I was a goner. Skinny jeans hugged her thighs in ways that made my throat feel tight, and she'd put on the clingy pale green dippy-neck top I loved—the one that somehow made her eyes seem even bluer.

There was only one response, and it came out hoarsely around the overwhelming sensation of wanting her. "Yep. You look…incredible."

CHAPTER SIX

Gemma

It was the first day back after spring break and I'd had a hellishly hectic morning. For some reason, some of my most brain-intense subjects were packed into the block of classes on Monday before lunch, and by midmorning I felt so fried I could barely form a sentence. But I had advanced video production directly after lunch, which balanced out the combination punch of a morning of math and honors biology.

Erin Lawson, my closest school friend, pushed her way through the cafeteria, a lunch bag tucked under her elbow and an iced coffee in each hand. Every day she gave up fifteen minutes of her lunch period to go out and collect our iced coffee. I also had permission to leave during lunch period, for the occasions I just couldn't be bothered making lunch or had woken up craving a burrito, and could have gone with her. But she'd said she enjoyed the tiny amount of quiet alone time away from the cacophony of school, and was more than happy to pick up my coffee too. Erin sat across from me and slid one of the clear cups over. "Your afternoon wake-me-up, ma'am."

I sagged with gratitude, unable to say anything until I'd gulped my drink. I'd been slowly inching closer to the wall of tiredness, and coffee should halt the progress 'til school was done. "You're a lifesaver, thank you."

"I know." Erin unzipped her cooler bag and dragged out a sandwich along with her usual miscellaneous snack foods. "How was your spring break?"

"Same as any weekend, but longer. Photography, study, skiing, hanging out with Stacey. Usual stuff. How 'bout you?"

"Study. Sneaky dates." Her nose wrinkled in distaste. "Then I had to go to Denver for my cousin's birthday thing on Saturday. Whole bunch of drama of course, Mom and Dad yelled at each other most of the way, but of course they were angelic during lunch while there were people around. I wish they'd just get divorced already and give up on this charade." She raised both eyebrows at me. "You have no idea how lucky you are to have such amazing parents."

"Oh, no, I know how lucky I am." I gave her what I hoped was a sympathetic smile. "I'm sorry home is so shitty for you." She adopted me as her friend not long after I changed schools, and for as long as I'd known her she'd had parent-fighting troubles.

"Mmm, thanks." Erin smiled bravely. "Whatever, it's not like them fighting is anything new, right? But at least now I have a bright spot, and I am counting the days until I skip off to college and I hardly have to see them ever again."

I turned the cup in circles. "Does it feel weird to you? That we're almost done here?" It was still so odd that everything was just continuing as normal, as if we weren't a month out from graduating high school.

"Oh hell yes. I still feel like I'm in seventh grade or something, not like I've just agreed to the plan for the rest of my life. Scary thought."

"Same," I sighed. Aspen had caught me fretting about this exact problem a few weeks back, and I'd confessed that I was feeling strange about being expected to be an adult and a kid at the same time. I still wasn't sure I'd made the right choices for college, and technically for the rest of my life. I mean, I'd been convinced for years I was going to be a veterinarian and now I wanted to make films?

And when I was wondering what the hell I was doing and just wanted to cry about it all, she'd said, "You know...I don't remember much about college. Barely remember the people. I don't remember who was mean or nice. What I do remember are the things I did during those times that made me feel good and that made me happy."

I'd nudged her and asked dryly, "Like ski racing?" Aspen and Stacey were peas in a pod—skiing was life.

Aspen had laughed, and enfolded me in a hug. "Right, like ski racing. I just want you to know that college is really important, but it's not the end of your world, and you have options after you're done. So you need to find the things, or people, that make you happy so your time at college is easier. Because those are the important things, the things that'll be there long after you're done learning to be whatever it is you decide you want to be."

The things that made me happy... Learning. My family. Stacey. Photography. Making films. Being outdoors. Skiing. So all I had to do was figure out a way to keep those things close when I went away. Piece of cake apparently.

"You figured out where you're going yet?" I asked Erin. College and graduation were the main topics of conversation at school right now, and I was getting tired of the constant refrain of "You had any acceptances yet? Which one are you going to choose?" I knew intellectually that I was eighteen, an adult, and about to begin the next stage of my life which would theoretically set me up into "old" adulthood. But I still felt like a fourteen-year-old, and trying to reconcile my actual age and the age I felt was tricky. I think I was in denial that high school was almost done. I couldn't wait to get out of this place and start my college life, but I still had this weird sense of being both ready and unready at the same time.

Erin shrugged nonchalantly. "Probably Harvard. Hard to pass that one up, right? I mean...Harvard Law just sounds so good, doesn't it?"

I'd always considered myself super studious, and had always worked hard, and gotten really good grades, but Erin made me (and everyone else at the school, including some of the teachers) look like dunces. But she wasn't uptight, or arrogant about her brains, just honest.

"It really does," I agreed.

She inhaled a bite of her chicken salad sandwich. "And Anthony is probably guaranteed an acceptance to MIT, so we'll be close to each other."

I nudged her shin teasingly under the table. "Riiight. The important point to consider when choosing the place that's going to shape the rest of your life is where the guy you're secretly dating is going to go to college."

She grinned. "It is. Why wouldn't I want someone I'm close to nearby? And come on, Gemma, tell me you're not sweating at the thought of leaving your family and Stacey behind? I mean, I know you're not going to miss me," she joked.

"Liar," I rebutted instantly. "Of course I'll miss you." We weren't best friends, but we were friendly enough that we ate lunch together every school day, and hung around outside of school for both study and non-study related activities when we could find time, and her parents allowed it.

Erin's expression softened. "Yeah I know. I'll miss you too."

"Well, no matter where I end up, we'll stay in touch, and when you're appointed to the Supreme Court, I'm going to tell everyone I know you and how you made me sit with you at lunch my first day here."

"Made you?" She coughed out a laugh around swallowing her mouthful. "I think you mean I saw you standing by yourself looking totally lost and wondering where to go, and I ever-so-kindly indicated you could come sit with my table of cool people." We'd bonded over academia and our shared love of year-round iced coffees, even when it was bucketing snow outside and most people were reaching for hot drinks. The other "cool" people had melted away into new friend groups, but Erin and I had stuck it out.

"Yeah okay," I agreed, "you saved me." Changing schools, and in the middle of the year, was an introvert's nightmare. I added musingly, "Maybe I'll make a documentary about you, start with how you enfolded a poor lost soul, move through your rise to academic stardom and your acceptance into every top law school in the country, and then to how you've single-handedly reversed injustice throughout the nation."

"Oh, that's a terrifying thought." She shuddered. "The documentary, not me fixing injustice. I'd love to figure out a way to get my law degree and change the world, but all in secret." Surprisingly enough for her career aspirations, Erin was a bigger introvert than me. "And you do know when yet another one of your documentaries sweeps the awards, I'll be shouting from the rooftops that you were my high school friend."

"And likewise when you're nominated to the Supreme Court."

We ate quietly for a few minutes until Erin asked, "How's that project about Stacey coming along?"

"It's coming along. I've been playing around with editing, seeing what sort of film it wants to be. But I like what I'm seeing."

"I bet you do," Erin said, her tone laced with faux innocence. "I can't wait to see it when it's done. You should have a premiere or something. Even just a small one at home, or here in the gym. May as well start practicing for all the red carpets you'll be walking."

I almost choked on a mouthful of iced coffee. "Yeah," I wheezed. "You know, I've kinda been hoping to just avoid all of that? I was thinking it'd be a great image if I'm the mysterious and rarely seen documentary maker." I wasn't so introverted that I couldn't talk to people, but a spotlight shining on me was a terrifying thought. Unlike Stacey, who seemed to relish the spotlight without actively seeking it out. "I'm hoping college includes a class about how to not be anxious about showing your work."

"Yeah, I'm hoping law school has a 'how to not be anxious in front of judges' class. I'm pretty sure I'm going to pee at my first court appearance." She finished the other half of her sandwich. "You got any strong feelings about where you'll go?"

"Not sure. Still waiting on a couple of acceptances. Or rejections. So it's just speculating until I know for sure what my options are." I shrugged. "It's just…so much pressure, trying to decide this one thing. And I'm going to get the necessary education wherever I go, right? So do I *need* to go to the University of Southern California when CU Boulder will give me the same skills and experience? And what about after? *Should* I apply to the American Film Institute? Is more schooling better than real-world experience? This is all way harder than when I wanted to be a veterinarian, which was just go to vet school, the end."

"Right," she agreed. "I don't know, maybe filmmaking is more a mix of school for technique and all that and then just going out and making movies and stuff and getting experience and a feel for what style you want to apply to your work. So maybe it doesn't really matter where you go." She grinned around her straw. "Or maybe I don't know shit about it."

"Mmm. I'm pretty sure I don't know shit about it either, but I think deep down I'm crossing my fingers for CU."

"CU is close to your family," she pointed out unnecessarily.

"It is," I said neutrally. Just two hours away in Boulder.

Erin flashed me a knowing look. "Funny, isn't it? I can't wait to get away from my home situation, and you just want to stay in yours."

I groaned, trying to smother my embarrassment. "I know, I'm so lame. College is supposed to be about going out and getting away and magically turning into a real adult, and I just want to be near Mom and Aspen. And Stacey," I added, hoping like heck that I sounded more chilled than I felt.

"I probably would too. Your parents are amazing." Erin leaned closer and murmured, "And Stacey Evans is seriously cool. If she was my BFF, I'm not sure I'd want to move away to go to college either." Erin was a skier, and she'd nearly fallen over herself when she'd learned who my stepmom and best friend were.

"You should tell her you think she's seriously cool," I teased. "I'm sure she'd love to hear it."

"Maybe I will," she drawled. "Speaking of telling her…" She pointed at me with a carrot stick. "You ever going to tell her?"

My heart thumped hard, and I stalled with a bland, "Tell who what?"

"Stacey. That you've had a crush on her for what? Four years?"

I knew I was blushing, and hid my face in my sandwich. "No way. She's got a girlfriend and I'm just her best friend. I don't want to ruin that."

"Isn't her girlfriend an Insta airhead?" I'd honestly only whined about Bree to Erin once, but she never forgot anything you told her. Probably one of the reasons why all the schools in the country were dueling each other to have her.

My face heated when I thought of the look Bree had given me at Beaver Creek, the way she'd ignored me, like I was less than dirt on her designer snow boot. "Yeah, and…she's also kind of bitchy to me, but it feels so sneaky that I'm not sure Stacey's picking up on it." Stacey hated bitchy bullies and I couldn't believe she'd knowingly let her girlfriend talk to me like I was a piece of pond scum.

"Seriously? That sucks. Even if you weren't totally in love with Stacey, it must be shitty to see someone you care about with someone totally unsuitable."

"It really is," I admitted quietly. I had no idea what Stacey saw in Bree aside from her face and body. They were complete opposites in every way—except the hotness part—and I couldn't see what on earth they'd ever talk about. I stalled with a long gulp of chilled caffeine. "I know it sounds stupid and clichéd, but I really just want Stace to be happy in her life outside of skiing. And I don't think Bree makes her happy."

"You'd make her happy," Erin said.

"I like to think I would." Shrugging, I added, "It doesn't matter anyway. It's never going to happen between us."

"Well, I'll just keep crossing my fingers for you." And then thankfully, Erin didn't push any more.

We'd been over this subject before, my feelings about Stacey and how I'd give almost anything to be her girlfriend…except give up our amazing friendship, which was the risk. And it was a huge risk that I was too scared to take.

Erin nudged me under the table. "Speaking of relationship shit, Noah's coming over, making a total beeline for you." She rolled her eyes. "Just to one-eighty our conversation."

I stifled my groan and took a few moments to compose myself. This was going to be painful. I'd been trying to ignore the looks he'd been sending my way since he'd sat down a few tables over. No small feat given their consistency and velocity. Noah stopped beside me, and before I'd even turned to face him, he'd mumbled, "Hey, Gemma."

Solid opener...

I smiled up at him. "Hey. What's up?" I didn't want to be rude, but I wasn't going to hand him a conversation on a platter.

"I, um, was just wondering if you got notes for math class this morning? I had an orthodontist appointment and missed it."

"Yeah, I did." As if I wouldn't have class notes. As far as desperate attempts to interact with me went, this one was right up there.

"Cool. Uh. Would you mind sharing with me? Maybe you could come around after school today and run through the class with me?" His desperate awkwardness would have been amusing if I wasn't so uncomfortable about being burdened with his lingering crush. "You're really great at explaining stuff."

"I can't, sorry. I'm really busy with study and my film project and stuff. But I can photocopy the notes for you. Or you can meet me at my locker after last period and you can take a photo or something?"

His shoulders fell so much his knuckles nearly scraped the floor. "Uh, sure. That'd be great. Thanks." He seemed to force himself to stand upright again. "So, um, how's your film project going?"

"Really great," I enthused.

My enthusiasm seemed to give him confidence and he perked up before asking, "It's about...snowboarding, right?"

I bit down on my laughter. I could just imagine Stacey growling at the insinuation that she was a boarder. "Skiing. Alpine ski racing. A short feature on Stacey Evans."

"Oh right, yeah, of course. Your friend. Didn't you do a physics assignment on her too?"

"Yeah, I did." The physics of skiing as the basis for an assignment was way more interesting than some boring thing about jellybeans sliding around a table or making energy beams to stop criminals. It'd been a solid A assignment too.

"Cool," he mumbled, shuffling backward. "I'd love to see your movie sometime."

"You can," I said cheerfully, feeling bad when he brightened like a lightbulb. "With everyone else when it's done," I pointed out.

The light dimmed. "Oh, right. Yeah, that's really cool."

I was almost out of small talk, and the bell wasn't going to save me. I was about to give Erin the signal that it was time to bolt, but thankfully one of Noah's friends came over and gave him shit about standing around looking like a "Fuckin' weirdo, dude" and he left with a doubly dejected, "See ya."

The second I was free, I muttered, "I wish he'd get the hint." It wasn't even a hint, because I'd told him I didn't want to date him again, but he kept asking me to come by his place after school, but just as friends—promise! We had sort of dated last year, but only for a few months. Early in his quest to rekindle what was never a flame in the first place, I'd caved, and within minutes he was talking about how great it'd been when we'd dated. Then he'd tried to kiss me. Then I'd left. The "just friends" was bogus, and I wasn't interested in being friends with someone who tried to pressure me like that. I'd tried being nice, I'd tried being firm, I'd tried flat-out ignoring his innuendo and pleas, but nothing seemed to work. The only way he'd back off was if I started dating someone new, but there was not a single person at the school who I wanted to date. Outside the school, on the other hand? There was just one person.

As if she'd read my mind, Erin said, "You know what would give him the hint? You dating someone else." She leaned closer, her face utterly angelic, and stage-whispered, "Like Stacey. Didn't you once tell me you were thinking about her while you were making out with him?"

"Mhmm."

"And thinking about Stacey when you were making out with Ashley?"

"Mhmmmm." Then Ashley had decided she wanted to get back with her ex-girlfriend, and had dumped me. Given we'd only dated for three weeks and all we'd been doing was making out, I wasn't heartbroken.

"Your Honor, the Defense rests."

I slumped back in my chair. "If Stace felt the same, then she'd have made a move. She isn't shy. But she hasn't, so she's obviously not interested, and I'm not gonna shove my feelings onto her."

"Or maybe she *is* interested but doesn't want to risk ruining what seems to be a great life. Amazing supportive BFF, hot piece of arm and bed candy, successful racing career. She's got it all."

My heart sank. Erin was right. Stacey had everything she needed, right now, as it was. Why would she want to change any of that? I wadded up my empty sandwich wrapper and threw it at Erin. "I hate it when you're logical."

CHAPTER SEVEN

Stacey

I was on snow all Monday morning for a session of drills—no speed training—and after lunch, a nap, and some keep-sponsors-happy social media it was time for a gym session. My trainer, Charlie, was as ruthless as always, and I spent the first of our breaks walking slowly around the rubber gym mat, trying to drag some oxygen into my lungs while my quads and glutes and shoulders and biceps screamed, "What the hell are you doing to us?"

I was fit. Really fit. And proud of how hard I worked to keep myself in peak performance condition. But Charlie somehow found a way to make me feel like I'd never stepped foot into a gym in my life. He interrupted my breather with a pumped-up, "All right! Break time is over! Let's go! Next set of sled pushes! You psyched? I'm psyched!" He held out his fist for a bump and I obliged.

I pretended to snarl. "Let me at it." My quads and glutes called me mean names.

Sled pushes and pulls, weighted pistol squats, core killers, and more. Midway through a ninety-second block of ball slams, the Garmin watch on my wrist buzzed. I ignored it. It buzzed again. Then again. From the corner of my eye I could see my phone, resting on a nearby weight bench, now lighting up with a call, instead of the series of three texts. Everyone important in my life knew not to contact me during training unless it was an emergency, so I never bothered to put my devices on Do Not Disturb. Charlie knew this "rule" too, and told me to stop the set so I could check what was going on.

Bree.

I stared at the texts to make sure there was no threat to life or property—no—then quickly turned off my watch notifications and flipped my phone facedown. Charlie bent to retrieve the abandoned thirty-pound slam ball. "Everyone okay?" he asked.

I tried to talk around gulping down air. "All fine. Sorry. Can we redo that set, please? Make up for that half-assed attempt."

"You got it!" After resetting his timer and making a quick note on his ever-present iPad, Charlie gave me the signal to restart my set. From the bench, my phone buzzed again.

I slammed the ball down extra hard.

An hour and twenty minutes later when I was done with my workout, my frustration at Bree's interruption had been overtaken by familiar exhaustion. As I rehydrated and ate a banana, I read the messages in full. Not an arduous task.

I'm bored.

I miss you.

What are you doing?

I can come around tonight.

The voice mail she'd left me was basically her texts in verbal form, with an added, "Call me ay-sap! Byeeee."

Then another text. *Why aren't you answering? Can we go out tonight?*

I never wanted to go out at night, especially not when I was in full training with both snow and gym work. Going out at night was so rarely on my radar, I didn't even know what going out at night looked like. And Bree was twenty-one, so her idea of a night out usually involved a bar or club which counted me out until August when I'd turn twenty-one as well. Even if I'd been old enough to get in, I wasn't really a partier or a drinker—except for the occasional celebratory champagne if I'd had a particularly good race.

My annoyance was so strong that I knew I'd need to take a while to calm down before I could talk to her, even in a text. I'd just pulled on sweatpants and a hoodie after my cooldown and stretches, and said bye to Charlie, when my phone chimed another text. Gemma. *Puke or pass out?*

We ranked our gym training sessions from one to ten, with one being me sitting on a bench the entire time, to ten which was me puking or passing out. Most of our gym sessions were a solid eight or nine where I just *felt* like puking or passing out.

As with all Gem's texts during the day, this one was perfectly timed to avoid interfering with on-snow or gym training. Well, yeah, that's because Gem knew my schedule because of Aspen. And yeah, well…so did Bree because I'd always made sure to keep her in the loop so she'd know what I was up to and where, and as a hint that I'd be focusing on training during those hours and not able to be with her. My days were regulated to the half hour, and Bree knew this. But it seemed lately that she'd been stricken with amnesia regarding my training schedule, and a tiny niggle told me it was because she just didn't care. I'd always known she was a little self-centered and I now realized she viewed my racing career as less of a career and more a thing that got her Instagram likes. I'd known when we started dating that we were never going to be a long-term thing. But I was starting to realize we might be more short-term than I'd first thought.

I sat in my car to drink my post-workout nutrition shake, then opened the message thread with Gem and tapped out a reply. *Neither. Obvs I'm too lazy.*

Her response landed quickly. *Do better next time.* She'd added a tongue-poking emoji.

More puke. Got it.

The "I'm typing" indicator lingered and disappeared before Gem's message appeared. *Rest up, relax, take care of yourself.* Heart emoji.

I sent a flex emoji.

Why was the woman who was supposed to be my partner so completely disconnected from my life, and my best friend so connected? I knew the answer to that but was too afraid to dive deeply into it just now. Since that day at Beaver Creek, when Gem had suggested that I didn't really share myself emotionally with my girlfriends, the thought had kept popping up at inconvenient times. I squashed it again, and decided to address my elephant and text Bree. *Got your messages. Was at the gym. I'm exhausted, so just going to eat then go to bed.* I almost added *sorry* but decided I had nothing to apologize for.

I waited for her to respond that she'd just come around to share dinner and hang out for a few hours, but all I got was: *Kay.* Well…'kay then. I put Bree out of my mind, and turned my attention to social media. I'd had a heap of responses to my cross-platform post from today—two photos, one of me leaning on my poles and studying the tops of my skis, and one snapped from the start of the training course looking down.

I'm thrilled to be training on my home turf @CopperMtn to be stronger and faster next season with @atomicski and @oakley keeping me on track #weareskiing #BeWhoYouAre #AlpineSkiing

Bree had shared it and added some drivel about "My superfast girlfriend" and was probably absorbing the reflected attention like it was oxygen. There were a few hundred likes and shares, comments—mostly positive—and then the expected negatives, like *Practicing failing again?*

People could be such dicks. "Come say that to my face," I muttered as I put my phone, and negative thoughts of haters, away.

Gem had liked or loved it on all three platforms—Twitter, Instagram, and Facebook—and added a heart emoji comment as well. She shared my things occasionally, mostly just results and stuff where she'd gush over how proud she was of me, or if I put up pictures of us skiing or at the movies or something on my days off. But she was definitely shy and social media adverse. And I never forgot that. That thought always rushed to the front every time I had a particularly intense bout of wanting to ask her if maybe she wanted to go on a date sometime and see if friendship could turn to relationship.

Because if I let my feelings run away, if I told her how I felt about her and something happened between us, then she'd be exposed to all that social media stuff through me. And that wasn't fair. So we'd remain firmly in each other's friendzones. And honestly? Being in Gem's friendzone wasn't a horrible place to be, even as I wanted to be in the girlfriendzone.

As I pulled out of the gym's lot, I asked my phone to call Gemma. She answered almost immediately. "Hey. What's up? Can you talk or are you still catching your breath?" she teased.

I pretended to wheeze, which made her laugh. "I've recovered. Almost. You wanna come round tonight for dinner and a movie?" Unlike Bree, who unfailingly stayed past the time I wanted to be in bed, or tried to come to bed with me, Gem had never stayed past 9:15 p.m. on a training night. "Or we can do some of your voice recording stuff if you want?"

"Sounds great. What's for dinner?" she asked.

"A lot of chicken. A lot of tasty carbs. And dirt foods." As a kid, I called vegetables "dirt foods," and Gemma had been so gleeful upon learning that fact that I dragged it out again whenever I wanted to make her laugh.

"You had me at dirt foods. When do you want me?"

"I'm on my way home now, so…whenever. I'll be showered and ready in half an hour."

"Cool. Do you mind if I film you preparing dinner?"

Laughing, I clarified, "You mean, do I mind if you don't help me cook dinner?"

"Well I can't do *both*," she said with fake indignation.

"Mhmm, sure. I guess I'll put on something nicer than a hoodie."

"Whatever you want to wear is perfect."

"Makeup?"

"Up to you. What about filming something like us doing Lego or Warhammer after dinner?"

"Hell no! It's enough to mention that stuff in an interview, but I draw the line at people seeing my nerd tuft." I had a thing about hair in my face, especially when I was trying to concentrate on important tasks like creating a Lego model of the Mandalorian's ship—the Razor Crest—and pulled the longer hair on top of my head into a little silly-looking topknot.

"But you look so cute," she pleaded. "I love the nerd tuft."

"I'll see you soon," I said, and hung up before she could persuade me to let the nerd tuft loose for public consumption.

After my shower I decided just some eyeliner would do, but paid careful attention to my hair. It was still in good shape from being doctored for my recent interview, and stayed in its quiff without too much argument or too much product. I dressed in a navy button-up and faded blue jeans, and after much consideration, decided Uggs were as good a footwear choice as any. I was in my own home and this was supposed to be not staged, so warm and comfortable feet it was.

When I heard a car door slam I rushed outside to help Gem with her hardcases of gear. The moment we'd set it all inside, she told me to, "Stand still." Gemma carefully moved a stray piece of my hair back into place, patting the standy-uppy bit into place. "There. Perfect."

I stuffed my hands into my jeans pockets. "Thanks."

She didn't need any help setting up, so I stood around and just enjoyed watching her. When Gem was concentrating on something, like her photography or videography or skiing down a hill steeper or bumpier than was comfortable for her, she got this intense look on her face—scrunchy eyebrows and tongue poking out, which showed her little cheek-chin dimple. She was adorable.

Gemma looked up, caught me staring at her, and pulled a stupid face. Still adorable. "We can sit at the table and it'll be like us having a conversation, so answer with whatever feels right. Some of the questions might seem a bit dumb because I'll already know the answer, but it's things people will be interested in hearing about."

"Are you putting your voice in too?" I asked.

Gem laughed and passed over a tiny microphone and a thin strip of cloth strapping tape. "Nope, the mic will be on you, and

I'll edit myself out. Just clip it to your shirt and tape the cord to your skin..." She pointed at her cleavage, and I tried not to look. "Please don't break it or I'll have to pay the school to replace it."

"I promise I won't." I turned away and slid the microphone under my shirt, clipping it above the first closed button and taping it just above my bra. "How's this?"

Her voice squeaked. "Great." Gem took the cable and plugged it into a black box about the size of a phone, which she shoved into my back pocket. As Gem tugged the back of my shirt down, an unexpected surge of anxiety made my stomach flutter. I'd done so many interviews, and even a round of media training, and I'd never been nervous before. But I so did not want to screw this up for her. Gemma must have caught something in my expression, because she brushed her fingers over my forearm. "Relax. Think casual, just friends chatting. The camera will be rolling, but I'm mostly just interested in audio for this, okay?"

I exhaled slowly. "Got it. Okay, I guess I'm ready when you are."

She pulled on a headset. "Can you say some stuff, please?"

I tried to think of something funny, and all I managed was, "Skiing, skiing, one, two, three."

"Got you loud and clear." She fiddled with the video camera for a few minutes, checking the light and other stuff before she said, "Okay, we're recording." Gem slipped around and sat opposite me.

"Aren't you going to say action?"

Gem rolled her eyes, but she was smiling. "Action!" After a moment she asked, "Can you tell me what your goals are, long-term, bigtime? If you were wishing on a star for your racing career, what would that wish be?"

"To always ski the best race I can. Because if I do that, then I feel I have a good chance of being rewarded with a podium finish, or some World Cup points, or another Olympic medal."

"What do you love about skiing?"

I thought for a moment, wanting to give her a really good answer. "I love the freedom of skiing. And I love the...paradox,

I guess would be the best way to describe it. Every run, if it's training or off-the-clock skiing or a race, is different but it's always the same."

"What do you mean?"

"It's the same equipment, I have the same feeling on my skis, the same training behind me, and the same confidence in myself. So you'd think that would result in the same outcome each time. But it doesn't. I don't always ski the same race, even if it's on the same course. Because I can't control the weather or the slope or my competitors. All I can control is myself and how well I ski."

We chatted for another half hour, and I tried my best to be articulate and give her good footage and soundbites, until she said she thought that would be enough. Probably because my stomach had growled audibly.

Gem stood up. "You were utterly fantastic. Who knew you were so quoteworthy?"

"Uh, me?" I jumped up too. "Have you even read my social media? I am a wellspring of cool quotes and interesting stuff."

"A wellspring. Wow. Big word. Sometimes I wonder how all that ego fits inside your body." Her eyes flicked downward, as if they'd decided to check out that body. My body. Just as quickly, they moved back to make eye contact with me. Gem's expression was neutral, and if I hadn't seen her checking me out, I wouldn't have known what she'd just done.

I fought down the flood of heat. It would be so much easier to pretend I was perfectly happy with being just friends with Gem if I didn't get so excited all the time. I put on my cheesiest grin. "It's not ego. It's confidence. A necessary trait in my profession."

A smile quirked the edges of her mouth. "Mmm." She moved away to relocate the camera into the kitchen, did something to test the lights, then told me I could keep the mic on while I prepared dinner in case I said something good.

I rubbed the back of my head. "My hair okay?"

"It's perfect." Gemma winked. "Action."

I moved to the fridge, pulling out chicken breasts, a prepackaged bag of mixed vegetables to steam, gnocchi, and ingredients for a creamy, garlicky, lemony sauce. Gem watched on, pretending she was monitoring the camera and therefore super busy and important and unable to help. I halved two chicken breasts and put them into a pan to grill before dealing with veggies and gnocchi.

I paused before I added my usual generous few teaspoons of garlic to the pan. "Are you planning on kissing anyone anytime soon?"

"Not on my agenda," she said lightly, but I caught the underlying tension in her words.

"What about Noah? I thought he was trying to get back together with you?" My questions were appropriately friend neutral-but-caring.

"Trying, yes." Her mouth twisted in annoyance. "You'd think being broken up for ten months after barely dating would be enough of a hint, but not in his world. He accosted me at lunch, and he was waiting by my locker after my last period, trying to get me to hang out this weekend."

I smiled over at her. "Can't blame him for trying." She'd dated a few people—guys and girls both—in the last couple of years, but had never seemed particularly enamored with any of them. Not that I was any great benchmark of judging everlasting love. My main feeling about my girlfriend's apathy was relief, because at the moment I didn't have the mental stamina to deal with someone who was trying to get more from me than I could give. That was one of the best things about Gem—she took what she needed from our friendship and gave me what I needed. But she never demanded anything of me that I didn't give voluntarily. We'd found the perfect symbiosis.

Gem gestured to the pan. "I'm guessing Bree doesn't mind garlic breath..." She sounded as friend neutral-but-caring as I had.

"Bree hasn't bothered to change her plans so we can spend time together, so...right now, I don't really care if she doesn't like garlic breath." I added another teaspoon then poured in the cream and turned the gas down to low.

"Oh." Gem chewed the inside of her lower lip. "You wanna talk about it?"

"Nothing to talk about," I said honestly. "She's just doing her thing, the way she always does, and I'm here doing my thing."

Gem was silent as I concentrated on my sauce, adding some grated lemon rind, tasting and adjusting the seasoning and watching for my glorious little potato puffs to start popping to the surface of the boiling water. I noted her worried expression. "Seriously, it's fine. Situation normal, which I guess is telling, right?"

Gemma shrugged. She'd never said a bad word about Bree. In fact, she hardly said any words about her, which was fair enough given they barely knew one another. It wasn't exactly a conscious effort to keep them apart, but I knew deep down that I'd made no real attempts to have the two of them socialize so they could get to know one another better. Partly because I knew they'd never be close, and I didn't see the point in trying to force it when Bree wasn't going to be around forever.

I tasted the sauce, checked my chicken, dumped all the gnocchi into the pan, and declared, "Dinner is served! Or... well, dinner is ready."

Gem's stomach answered for her with a loud grumble that told me I was just in time. She turned off the camera and hooked the headphones around the tripod. "You need help serving up?"

"I've got you, Director Archer. But can you set out some water and cutlery please?"

While Gem set the table, I served the meal, making a smaller portion for Gemma who didn't have to inhale a million calories burned every day like I did. I'd never forgotten the hilarious bug-eyed look I'd received the first time I'd cooked us dinner and unthinkingly dished up the amount I usually ate for her as well.

I'd just set the plates down when she grabbed my arm. "Let me get that mic off you so you can sit comfortably for dinner." She unclipped it from my shirt, the unintentional touch of her hand against the top of my chest making my heart race.

I raised my arms, twisting to find the little box thing and cord stuff. "Yeah, it's gotten a little tangled under my shirt." We both reached for my shirt buttons at the same time, our hands brushing.

Gem pulled her hands back so quickly I wondered if my skin had turned to acid. "You get it," she said.

I kept my eyes down as I reached up under my shirt to rip off the tape, and carefully threaded the mic and cable down until everything appeared from under my shirt. She took it carefully from me instead of just grabbing it. So carefully that she didn't touch me at all. Then, with the same care, Gem moved around behind me, raised my shirt at the back, and pulled the box from my butt pocket. "All done," she said quietly.

I exhaled, forcing myself to calm down. "Great. Let's eat."

CHAPTER EIGHT

Gemma

With the promise of a beautiful day, I'd been given permission
to take a morning off school to film Stacey's on-snow training
session. I'd have to make up the missed morning classes but it
was worth it to finally nail down some of the last footage from
my shots list. The perfect weather was great timing, because I
had film club after school and could start playing around with
things that afternoon.

Stace always trained really early so the course was not only
pristine, but icy and super-fast. As someone who preferred soft
groomers and forgiving powder, it sounded horrible to me. Even
though I'd set an alarm, Aspen knocked on my closed door as she
walked past to go down and start the coffee machine. I'd barely
stretched and thrown back the covers when a message from
Stacey pinged through. I carried my phone to the bathroom
and opened up our message exchange.

*Yay! Filming day! I even remembered to put on my Captain
Marvel race suit for CONTINUITY. I learneded a big movie word
from you.*

The U.S. Alpine Ski Team had worn Marvel Legends race suits a while back, when Stace hadn't been on the team. But she'd wanted them so badly and when she'd found some barely used suits from an official used-gear site, we'd had a two-hour discussion about whether she should get Captain America or Captain Marvel. In the end she'd just bought both.

So clever. Nice to know you're listening to me.

I know. And I always listen. Heart emoji. Kiss emoji.

Those harmless little pictures on my phone screen sent a flutter of excitement through me. It was just Stacey being Stacey, I reminded myself. Nothing more. I really wished me knowing that would stop my stupid wishful thinking. I stuffed down my feelings and texted back: *Fuel up, racing genius. I'll see you soon.*

Stacey arrived less than thirty seconds after Aspen and I had pulled into a parking space, and jumped out of her car to come rushing over. She wore a U.S. Team Spyder jacket and black ski pants, but I knew she'd have that Captain Marvel race suit underneath. My heart tripped at the thought. There was plenty of padding, not to mention the body protector vest she wore under the suit, but that body-hugging material would leave nothing to my already overactive imagination.

She said a casual, "Morning, coach" to Aspen before picking me up and spinning me around. I could feel her face against my neck as she murmured, "Hey, you." Stacey set me down and blurted, "Damn, I'm so excited for this training session."

Aspen unlocked the ski racks on top of her Land Rover. "You're excited for every training session."

"Well yeah, but I'm super excited for this one. I get to ski for Gemma's movie, the snow is prime, and it's gonna be a bluebird day. Couldn't ask for better."

I took my skis from Aspen and rested them carefully against the spare tire on the back of the SUV. "Don't be so excited that you don't train properly," I said. Or worse, so excited that she crashed. I kept that thought to myself.

She pressed her hand over her heart. "I won't, pinkie swear. 'Kay, I'd better grab my shit. Don't wanna keep everyone waiting." Stace grinned at me. "Or make those of us who have to go to school afterward late."

"Don't remind me," I grumbled as I pulled out my equipment cases.

Stace leaned close to tell me, "You know, I even washed the race suit for this."

"You're so thoughtful." After a pause, I sniffed her shoulder. "They were probably all due for laundry day anyway."

She put on a drawly southern accent. "You sayin' I stink?"

"Only in the best way," I said earnestly. And honestly. My stomach twisted at the thought. I'd learned about pheromones in biology and had instantly concluded that could be the only logical explanation for the fact being around Stacey made me want to press my face against any body part I could, and just breathe her in. Totally not creepy…

She booped my nose, then jumped back before I could poke her in the stomach. With a manic grin, Stacey jogged to her car and popped the trunk to retrieve her bag of gear. Once all three of us had our stuff, we trudged up to where Mike, Aspen's second-in-command, as well as another of the assistant coaches sat with idling snowmobiles, ready to zip us up the mountain. Ski racers didn't have time to wait in lift lines.

As soon as Mike spotted us, he came over to help with the gear. He was a cheerful dude probably in his early thirties—it was hard to tell because I only ever saw him hidden under a helmet and behind goggles—and he greeted us all with fist-bumps. Once he'd helped Aspen and I stash our skis—all Stacey's racing skis would already be up top waiting for her—and secure my filming equipment and Stacey's bag to the snowmobiles, he rubbed his hands together. "So, who's riding with who?"

Stacey got in first with, "Gem and I can come with you on the three-seater."

Aspen smiled, nodded, climbed onto the back of the not-Mike's snowmobile, and started up the mountain. Mike got set in the driver's position of his mobile while I just stood there, wondering where I was supposed to sit.

Stacey touched my back. "Hop in the middle, Gemmy. You're the smallest."

I climbed in behind Mike, and Stace hopped lithely up and swung her leg over to settle behind me, sliding back until she was pressed into the backrest. She lightly gripped my hips and pulled me toward her and into a more comfortable position where I wasn't so close to Mike. He was a nice guy, but I felt weird about practically hugging his back.

Stacey's arms came around my waist and I felt the press of her against my back a moment before her arms tightened even more. My heart tripped stupidly. This wasn't the first time we'd touched this way, but tell my body that. And when I turned back to tell her I'd been on a snowmobile before and wouldn't fall off, Stacey grinned. "Just keeping you safe."

Who was I to argue? I relaxed into her, grabbed the handgrip with one hand and with the other, held on to her forearm around my waist. We stayed like that the whole ride up the mountain, and I kept chanting to myself that it meant nothing, she was just being Stacey.

Everyone else was already up the top of the training course, assembled in a three-sided mesh-fenced-off area with "Race Training in Progress" signs dotted around. Stacey wriggled out from behind me then held on to me until both my feet were firmly on snow. Because of Aspen, I knew the people in Stacey's coaching team pretty well, and how things worked, which eased my introvert discomfort. As well as Aspen—her head coach—for her on-snow sessions, Stace always had Mike and her ski tech, Christina, as well as a handful of assistant coaches whose jobs were to do all the other things that came with Stacey's on-snow training. Her team was essential to keeping things running smoothly, and Stace spoke about all of them as if they were gods and goddesses.

While they went through the morning's schedule, I noted the most unobtrusive yet suitable spot for my tripod and started setting up my gear for the first shots on my list. "Shots list" was a generous term. I had ideas of what I wanted to film but I wasn't going to intrude upon Stacey's training or make her do anything she wouldn't normally do in an on-snow session.

Aspen came over and handed me a walkie-talkie. "Here you go. Make sure you get the all-clear before you move down near the course. And keep an ear on the radio chatter so you know where she is at all times. I don't want her crashing into you on the course, because then I'd have to explain that to both your mom and Stacey's parents."

I saluted. "Yes, coach."

Grinning, Aspen swatted me.

I'd gotten consent from everyone in Stacey's team to have them in the documentary, and started off by filming Christina laying out eight sets of bright red Atomic Redster race skis in a row. Apparently each pair was tuned differently, and after they'd been down the course to check it out, they'd decide which set to run with, and possibly change them up during training. It was about constantly fine-tuning how the different skis performed in different conditions to gain the most speed and control.

I filmed Stacey warming up with stretches and band exercises, catching a small rubber ball thrown by Mike which was for reflex and eye training, talking and laughing with Aspen, gearing up, catching gummy bears in her mouth thrown by Aspen—good for morale and energy apparently—pulling off her outer layers, and running through her pre-run routine.

Before every run, whether she was training or racing, Stacey would check all her gear, always in the same order from feet to head. Then she'd twist her torso side to side, and stretch left and right to touch the snow with her fingertips. Then fist-bumps with her team. This time, she slid over to me and grinning, fist-bumped the camera too. The only change in her routine was when she was racing, she'd listen to music while she was warming up and would pull out her headphones after she'd clipped in to whichever pair of skis she and her team had decided would be the best for the race.

Stacey lifted her leg perpendicular to the ground so the tail of her ski rested on the snow, and almost on autopilot, Christina wiped down the base of the ski. Standing beside me, Aspen directed everyone, from those up top to Mike who always followed her down the course with a GoPro, to the snowmobile driver who'd go down to wait for Stacey and Mike at the bottom of the run, to the three assistants dotted along the course in case something happened—I always tried not to think about that— to prep for Stacey's first run.

A second after Stacey pushed through the timing wand, Aspen's voice echoed through the radio clipped to my waistband. "Stacey is on course, Stacey is on course." A chorus of confirmations echoed through the radios.

I adjusted my focus, and panned to film Aspen watching the footage being streamed directly from Mike's GoPro to her iPad as she dictated her thoughts into her phone. I'd get copies of the GoPro footage from each training run, even though I already had drone footage from a previous filming session. Drones were forbidden in pretty much every ski resort, but at the start of Stacey's training late last year, Aspen had sweet-talked the mountain management team into letting me use mine, pointing out that technically it was media use, not the no-no recreational use.

Returning to the top again, Stacey climbed off the snowmobile and grabbed her skis off the back. "Phew! That was wild. And so much fun! She's fast this morning, coach!"

"So I saw," Aspen said. "Tight lines are good. Clipping a gate or losing your edge and spilling is not good."

"Aye-aye," Stacey agreed. "Balance."

"Exactly."

I felt like a kid at Watch Your Parent At Work Day. I'd attended weekend race training sessions before, as well as the other one where I'd been filming, but watching Aspen in work mode was always weird. Obviously I knew she was a ski coach, but my main experience of it was from when we first met and I was just a noob trying to stay upright, and she was fun and funny and patient and kind. She was all those things with Stacey as well, but watching her telling Stacey to remember her calmness and focus but to also attack! and that respecting the hill too much slows you down, and to get out there and give the course a bit of disrespect felt totally unlike the Coach Aspen I knew.

They went through the routine again, and then off Stace went for run number two. She finished the course. She came back. While I tried to keep my camera batteries warm, Stacey stood off to the side with Aspen, hydrating while she went over the run. Apparently Aspen still wanted her to attack the course more. It looked to me like Stacey had already attacked and *killed* the course, but who was I to have an opinion?

Once I'd filmed another start and Stacey had disappeared out of sight, I checked I was clear to go on course and skied very slowly and sideslippy down to set up on the second turn. The light there was amazing at this time of morning and I had space for a long, sweeping pan shot. And then I regretted my life choices when I had to carry all my gear back up after filming a few takes, because no snowmobile was coming to get me and there was *no way* I was going to ski down that course, especially not carrying camera equipment.

And so it went for almost two hours before they took a break and Stacey clipped out of her skis. She ate an energy bar while discussing something with Aspen, so I busied myself checking my footage. Mike came over. "How does my GoPro stuff look to you, Director?"

"Really good, thanks."

He tilted his head, grinning down at me. "But...?"

Dammit. I was so bad at hiding my thoughts. Smiling, I said, "But nothing. It's great. From a coaching perspective. From a filmmaking perspective, not quite so much."

"Gotcha. Tell me what you're looking for, and I'll do my best to get it."

"What you've done so far is really great, but if you could try to follow more directly behind her line and keep her more squarely in the frame, that would be *amazing*."

Mike's mouth quirked, and I hastened to add, "If you can. I know you're doing your best just to keep up with her and stay upright."

"You know it. But I'll see what I can do for you without taking a tumble myself."

"Thanks very much."

"No problemo." He grinned. "You know how to spell my name for producer credit, right?"

I kicked a toeful of snow at him, and he bent as if he was going to grab a handful to toss back. Thankfully, instead of starting a snowball war, he laughed and skied off. I returned to checking my footage.

A sly hand snuck around my waist. "Bored yet?" Stacey murmured near my ear.

I took a deep breath to push down the spine tingle of having her so close. "Course not," I assured her.

"Good, because it ain't over yet." She hugged me quickly, then awkward ski-boot jogged back to get ready again. Before she took her place at the timing arm, Stacey glanced at me and winked before pulling her goggles down.

There was no point in filming Aspen watching the iPad again, so I moved over to stand beside her, holding the iPad for both of us which freed up her hands for phone dictation. The next run was much better from a film perspective, with Mike doing as I'd requested and keeping Stacey more centered in the frame. And to my semi-trained eye, it was a good training run too. She had so much angle, was so balanced and fast in her turns, that the side of her thigh and butt were brushing the snow.

I wasn't a ski racer by any stretch of my imagination, but I'd watched enough races to know what looked controlled and fast and what was borderline a wipeout. And what I saw on the iPad made my breath catch. Stacey flew over the jump, landed and was already positioned to make the next gate. From Mike's position behind her I could see she was taking the tightest line possible and realized at the last moment it was really tight. Maybe too tight. She skidded slightly in the turn and a millisecond later, slipped over onto her side, tumbling over and over and down and down, dense puffs of snow kicking up behind her.

I thought I was going to throw up.

"Fuck!" Aspen cursed beside me. Aspen hardly ever swore, which told me she thought it was as bad as I'd thought it looked. She picked up her radio and blurted, "Mike, is she okay?"

And I just stared at the iPad, almost too afraid to watch what Mike's GoPro was sending back to us. He raced down to where Stacey lay about twenty feet away from the blue dye that marked the edge of the course, and I could hear his breathing over the sound of skis and the rushing air. The footage was that maddeningly annoying type of shaky and unfocused and at everything except what I wanted to look at. Finally, he focused down on Stacey who had rolled over and was moving to get up.

A moment of static. Then, "Mike here. Stacey's already on her feet, moving all limbs and seems fine."

"Copy that. Still, run through the protocol please."

I knew the protocol, which was basically judging: Is she conscious, is she hurt, is she acting like herself? Stacey was often evasive when questioned about her pain but if you asked her outright, she was incapable of lying in the face of a direct question. And if she seemed not like herself, then we'd worry about a brain thing. My stomach churned.

The sound through the GoPro stream was muffled, but I could see Stacey moving around, laughing, seeming her usual self. The radio buzzed before, "Mike here. All good, I'm happy she's alert and moving normally, but she says her hand is painful, so I'll take her down to the medics."

Aspen raised the radio to her mouth. "Good. Keep me updated."

"Will do. Just a sec, Aspen, Stacey wants to talk to you."

After a few seconds' silence, Stacey's voice came over the radio. She sounded fine, just breathless as usual after a run. "I'm okay, guys, just caught an edge on something and went down awkwardly. It's just a bruised hand or finger or something."

"Have you taken the glove off? Are you a medical professional?" Aspen didn't wait for Stacey to answer before she went on. "No, you haven't removed the glove to look and no you're not a medical professional. It could also be a broken hand or finger," Aspen said dryly.

After a pause, Stacey mumbled, "Yeah, my pointer looks kinda not normal." On the iPad she held up her left hand, studying the angle of her still-gloved fingers. My stomach turned when I saw the weirdness of her left forefinger.

Aspen turned purple. "Go down to the medics now and if they say you need to go to the ER, then you're done for the day."

"Oh-kaaaaaaay, coach," Stacey sang. After a pause, she came back again with, "I'm really sorry, Gemmy Gem. Did you get enough footage?"

Aspen nodded at me, and I nabbed the radio from my waistband. After a deep breath to settle the upset bouncing around in my stomach, I said, as cheerfully as I could manage, "I got plenty. You're a superstar. Now go see the medics."

I could hear the grin in her voice when she agreed, "Yes, boss. See you soon."

Aspen gently extracted the radio from my tight-knuckled grip. Her arm around my shoulder startled me. "You okay, Gem?"

"Mhmm. Of course," I lied. My legs felt wobbly, like I'd just trudged from the bottom of the mountain to the top, and I could feel cool sweat under my warm jacket.

She held me closer, rubbing up and down my arm. "You sure? You're shaking a little."

It would have been so easy to tell her I was just cold, but we always talked out things that upset us. I spoke to the snow. "Just...I don't like seeing her get hurt."

"Me either. Luckily she doesn't do it much, right?"

"Right," I agreed, though the thought of how often I'd seen Stacey wipe out made my agreement feel teary.

Aspen let me have a few quiet moments to calm myself, still hugging me to her side, before she said, "Come on, let's get set up in case she comes back. I'm pretty sure we're done for the day, but she might surprise me."

"She usually does."

Aspen laughed. "She sure does."

Stacey didn't come back up. The medics said they thought she might have dislocated or broken her finger, and she and Mike were already enroute to the ER to get her checked out. My phone buzzed in my pocket. Text from Stacey. *I'm totally fine, it's just sprained or something. Maybe dislocated. NOT BROKEN. Stupid cautions. Come around tonight? I'll buy dinner.* Then a handful of kiss emojis and the tongue-pokey wild-eyes one too.

I texted back that I was in for dinner and to hang out, and that I'd come straight after film club. The sick upset feeling hadn't eased, but I knew by now that it was my normal reaction to her getting hurt. Aspen interrupted me packing up the camera gear into cases. "I've just called the snowmobile back up to grab your stuff. You want to ride down or ski down?" Instead of cruising down the course the way Aspen and the rest of Stacey's training team did when her training session was over, I'd always chained together a bunch of green and blue runs to get back down to the bottom, which took me longer than them.

"I might just jump on the snowmobile. Make sure my gear is safe." I made myself smile. "You should thank her. Now you have the rest of your morning free."

Aspen huffed out a laugh. "You know, I would thank her, but then she'd probably just take it as an invitation to be reckless and then wipe out even more. And then it'll be broken bones, or worse."

Wipeout. I hated that word. And what was worse than broken bones? Actually, scratch that thought. I didn't want to think about it. I swallowed hard, and nodded.

Aspen tilted her head, but didn't say anything more. After a quick hug she patted the top of my helmet. "See you down at the base."

Once I'd unloaded all my gear at the bottom of the mountain and changed from skiwear into school clothes, Aspen helped me carry my stuff to her car. I was almost at school when Stacey texted again. *At ER. So begins the long wait.* Eye roll emoji. *Have fun at school, see you later this afternoon.*

You bet. I'll bring ice.

Stacey's response was a couple of red-heart emojis.

And my heart cracked a little more. I knew it was my problem. I couldn't help thinking of what those hearts could mean. *Could…* If only things were different. If only Stacey felt that way about me, the same way I felt about her. If only I wasn't so afraid.

CHAPTER NINE

Stacey

Stupid dislocated finger. When I'd called Aspen with the news on the way home from the ER she'd declared the next two days non-training days for both snow and gym, to give my finger a chance to chill out. She would have made it longer if I hadn't complained and assured her I could ski *and* work out with a fixed-up dislocated finger and that I'd be super very careful, pinky swear, cross my heart, to not injure it further. The thought of stopping training at this time of year when we were racing the Northern Hemisphere snow clock made me so anxious.

Anxiety was a rare emotion for me, but I knew exactly what had triggered this bout because I'd had it at the end of every season when I was moving from competition mode into training mode. A dose of end-of-season mehs. My whole self was tied up in being a ski racer, so not racing—even when I was training my ass off—always made me feel a bit…wrong. I knew this case of the mehs was probably being exacerbated by yet another bout of enforced rest.

The mehs wasn't sadness. It wasn't annoyance. It was…a weird feeling of aimlessness when I usually felt so focused. And then when I added the anxiety of cramming in as much on-snow time as I could, while I could, I just felt a bit wonky. Thankfully the mehs usually only lasted a week or so, but it was horrible to feel like I wasn't quite sure what I was doing as I transitioned from one focus to another, especially because I was also waiting to hear if I'd been nominated to the U.S. Alpine Ski Team for the new season. Making the team was pretty much guaranteed, given my performance. But there was always a niggle of doubt…

As I pulled into my driveway after my unwanted ER trip I saw Bree's Jeep in the turnaround. Total honesty: my heart sank. Of all the days for her to practice spontaneity, today was quite possibly the worst. Once I'd parked, I slipped under the closing garage door and wandered out to meet her, trying to ignore my frustration about leaving all my gear unpacked.

I smiled as she hopped out of her car. Maybe my smile was a little tight, but it was still a smile. "Hey," I said lightly. "Didn't expect to see you today."

"I had the afternoon off so thought I'd come see you." There was a definite "I made the effort and you didn't" vibe in her tone.

I should have said "I'm glad you did" or something else that conveyed being pleased to see her, but I just couldn't make the words come out of my mouth. If I hadn't injured myself, I would have been at the gym for the afternoon as usual, which made me think her gesture was more thoughtless than thoughtful. I would have loved a comforting hug, but unlike Gem—and Gem's family—Bree wasn't a hugger. So, I offered a kiss, which she accepted. I didn't push for more. And neither did Bree, which cemented my feeling that we were both just in a holding pattern with this relationship. "How was school?" I asked.

Bree drew herself up, and somehow managed to look down her nose at me despite my being three inches taller than her. "College, Stacey. I'm at *college*, not high school."

"I know that, but it's still school, isn't it?" Gem always referred to college as school.

Bree's exasperated inhalation was her only response, and I had to bite back my "What?" at her pedantic reaction.

She gestured at the contraption on my left hand. "What's up with your hand?"

I held up my splinted pointer finger. Thankfully it was a simple treatment of putting it back into place, immobilization, anti-inflammatories and analgesics, and then some PT when the swelling went down. Oh, and of course—the dreaded rest… "Dislocated my finger at training this morning." Frowning, I added, "It's more annoying than anything."

I'd expected some sympathy. Instead, I got…indifference. "Oh. Well I guess that won't bother you too much," Bree said, and I caught the innuendo. But it wasn't teasing. It was mean, like "who cares because those fingers aren't doing anything to help me anyway." And I wondered, *really* wondered, why I was dating her.

I mean, Bree could be funny and charming, when she wanted to be. She was a good listener, when she wanted to be. She had ambition. But lately it seemed like all her good qualities had run off and hidden somewhere, leaving a not-so-nice person behind. We'd been together for three months and I really had nothing to show for it—I hadn't grown as a person because of her, I wasn't desperate to see her every day, and I had no desire to give her a part of myself nobody had been given. So what did it say about me that I was with her, that I was settling for someone who had as many, or maybe even more, bad qualities as she did good?

I made myself smile, ignoring her snarky undertone. "Nope, I can still train. So I'm not too worried."

"Right. As long as you can train." The sarcasm wasn't lost on me, and confirmed she was only worried about herself and the benefits she thought she should be getting from me.

And I wondered what benefits I was getting from her too. Not many, it seemed. "Are you staying?" I asked. She'd driven from Boulder, so it was logical she would.

"Do you want me to? Or do you have something more important to do?" As usual when asking about my time, the questions felt more like accusations.

"Other than putting away my gear and taking a shower, I'm all yours for the afternoon." I crossed mental fingers that she wouldn't try to join me in the shower.

Her smile seemed forced. "Lucky me."

* * *

Bree lasted exactly two hours and forty minutes before she declared she had to go. Given we'd been sitting stiffly on the couch watching a movie while she talked me through everything she thought wrong with the lead actress's performance, I wasn't saddened by her declaration. And Gemma was due to come round soon anyways. There was no contest for who I wanted to hang out with.

I walked Bree out. "I'm still coming to Boulder on Monday to have lunch with you and your friends, right?"

She shrugged. "Maybe. Not sure if something will come up before then."

Something more important than spending time with me when I'd made time for her... "Okay," I said as calmly as I could. "Well, it's my day off training, remember? So I'll be free, regardless."

"Mhmm."

"Let me know so I can plan, or let me know if you want to do something else."

"Sure."

Gem's arrival saved me from forcing myself to kiss Bree goodbye. She pulled in beside the Jeep, leaped out and slammed the door, casually holding her keys behind herself to lock her car. Not wanting to seem nasty, I held back my relief at my best friend's arrival, though inside I was doing backflips at the arrival of some relief from the past three hours of awkwardness.

Bree muttered something under her breath when Gem waved and said, "Heya."

And instead of saying hi back, or waving, or doing something most polite people do, Bree stared at Gemma and offered a withering, "Oh, it's you."

Gem's eyes widened. "Yep…it's me."

Bree executed a hair flip that would make a model jealous. "I guess I'm not needed then." Before I could point out "You *wanted* to go," she kissed me. The kiss was surprisingly rough, unpleasantly so.

Once she'd finished her possessive display, Bree flashed me a smile that I saw right through. And I realized that not only did I not want to be touching her, but I didn't want her touching me. Her arm around my waist felt heavy, sickening. So I ignored it and focused on Gemma, who had on my favorite pair of her jeans—the dark skinny ones that accentuated all her gorgeous curves. All her gorgeous curves that, as her best friend, I really shouldn't be admiring. But they were right there, and so were my feelings.

"Hey, you." I squirmed out of Bree's heavy grip and as soon as Gem was in reach, I hugged her.

Gem's return hug was tight, and after a squeeze she released me. She took a tiny step back, but was still close enough to touch. "How's the finger?"

I displayed it for her. "Annoying. But fine. Two days off training."

"Ah shit. That really sucks, Stace. But it needs to heal."

As I nodded my agreement and enjoyed the dose of sympathy, Gem looked from me to Bree. "Sorry, I didn't realize you were here, Bree. I can come back later. Or tomorrow?"

Bree sniffed. "I was just leaving. So you've got her all to yourself," she said snidely.

Gem paused, confusion plainly written on her face. "What do you mean?"

Bree's expression contorted into something ugly. "Gemma, look. This"—she gestured between Gem and me—"is ridiculous, and embarrassing for you. Why are you always hanging out with my girlfriend? Don't you have a life? Shouldn't you be thinking about other things, like…you know, graduating high school?" She could not have sounded any crueler or more condescending.

My brain was totally stuck. Had she really just said that? And my immediate thought, after *WTF?*, was disbelief that anyone would actually say something so deliberately rude and nasty. I saw red. Fiery, fuming, frustrated red. I couldn't look at Bree, so I watched Gem's expression run through about ten different emotions. She wasn't quite able to hide her devastation, and it made me just as devastated for her.

I took a deep breath, ready to let loose at my girlfriend for her unforgivable display of bitchiness. "Bree—"

But Gem interrupted me. "It's fine, Stace. Bree's right, I should really be studying for finals. So I'm just gonna go." But she'd only been here a minute, not even enough time to come inside, so she was obviously just being the better person and extracting herself from the situation. The situation my girlfriend had created.

Oh it was so not fine. I turned back to her. "Gem—"

Gemma gave me a forced, fleeting smile. "I'll see you later." After what seemed like a monumental effort, Gem quietly said, "Bye, Bree," turned around, and walked to her car. Her head was up, shoulders back, but her walk was stiff like she was trying hard to not sprint away from us.

I wanted to call after her, to tell her to come back, then to send Bree away. Send Bree away for good. But I was so utterly stunned by what'd just happened that I couldn't do or say anything. Then it was too late because Gemma was in her car and driving away.

I inhaled slowly before whirling back around. Anger made my skin feel hot and it took an enormous amount of control to not lose my temper. "That was totally uncalled for. She's my best friend, and she's been my best friend for years, long before you and I started dating. Of course we hang out. And she's been nothing but nice to you since you first met."

Bree crossed her arms over her chest. "Why do you hang around her? She's just a kid."

I held back my urge to snap and said with a calmness that made me want to pat myself on the back, "She's eighteen, she's not a kid. And you know what? In a lot of ways, she's more mature than either of us."

"That's true for you, but not me," she scoffed.

I frowned, trying to decipher exactly what she meant.

But I didn't get a chance to ask, because Bree threw me a bone. "You know, when I first met you, I thought you were so cool, so grown-up, off racing overseas all the time, moved out of home, got your whole life figured out. But deep down, you're just childish little Stacey who still plays with her Legos and paints her little orcs and knights and wizards."

The barb didn't penetrate the way she probably thought it would. "Like you don't have relaxing hobbies to take your mind off the stress of your college classes?" I asked bitingly. Give me a break. I'd burn out if I had to spend my whole life with the laser-sharp focus I allocated to racing. So who the hell cared if in my free time, the time where I was supposed to be relaxing and recovering, I turned into a big kid who played with Lego?

"Whatever." Bree's pout got even poutier. "You know Gemma's got a huge crush on you, right?"

I did know that, obviously. And also obviously, that crush was reflected right back at Gem. But acknowledging it would just stoke the flames of Bree's fire that I was trying desperately to extinguish. So I said nothing. I didn't need to say anything, because Bree was on a roll and just kept on talking. "That day me and the girls met you up on the mountain, Gemma was giving you the biggest puppy-dog eyes."

I kept quiet. Letting Bree get it all out of her system was the best course of action. And, a tiny voice said, letting her get it all out is showing you exactly who she is—a jealous, and maybe also delusional, bitch.

Still pouting, Bree continued her rant. "And I thought she was going to snap at me for touching you and kissing you. Like, you're my girlfriend, right? I'm allowed to kiss you. She's just so jealous of me."

Okay. That was it. Gem was many wonderful things, and some annoying things, but one thing she wasn't was mean. She would *never* say anything rude, or even look like she wanted to "snap at" someone. And I doubted she was jealous of Bree, because I knew Gem well enough to know that she didn't aspire to be anything like Bree. The two of them were as different as salt and pepper. I straightened up, feeling more certain about what I was about to say than I had about almost anything. "You know what? I get the feeling you're not all that excited about this relationship anymore. And if I'm honest, neither am I."

"What do you mean?" she asked flatly.

"I think we should break up."

Bree's mouth fell open, and I had to hold back my laugh at how ridiculously clichéd she looked, like she'd trawled through expressions from acting class and landed on *incredulous*. "Are you serious? You're breaking up with me?"

Wasn't that what I'd just said? I didn't hesitate, and I made sure to speak clearly. "Yes, I'm breaking up with you." The second the words left my mouth I was flooded with relief. What the hell had I been doing with her, a vapid, thoughtless piece of arm candy? Yep, that's it, Stacey. She was arm candy, nothing more, and that's what you focused on above everything else. Time to grow up. I felt even more relief as the certainty hit me and when I spoke, it was completely steady. "I'm sorry, I just don't think we're compatible, and I don't think you respect my personal or professional life."

"What the fuck would you know?" She sneered, and the look was so ugly on her pretty face that I almost recoiled. "All you think about is skiing."

"That's not true. I've tried to think about you, but you're never available. I feel like I barely even know you, like we're just new friends, even after three months. I haven't even met your parents." She'd met mine and had been suitably polite, yet also distant.

Bree scoffed, "It's not like you ever made any effort for my friends or family."

I bit back my response of "Neither did you" and tried to remain neutral. It wasn't true—I wanted, and had tried, to involve myself in her friend things, but it was like she deliberately scheduled them to be during my training times. And her parents lived in New York so we couldn't just pop around for dinner one night. After Bree met my parents, my mom had twice invited us out to dinner with them, but Bree had declined each invitation, citing a huge school workload. Mom took the hint. But not before she'd sent me a text that didn't explicitly say it, but let me know exactly what she thought of my new girlfriend.

"You make it very hard," I said, as evenly as I could, "for me to join in with you guys when all your activities are at a time I just can't attend. Skiing is my *job*, Bree. I'm not a socialite out skiing all day because I love it. If I worked in an office, I wouldn't be able to leave for three hours in the middle of the workday, and I can't just stop training early or skip half my gym time to be with you."

Bree's tone became biting and unsurprisingly, she turned her focus to attacking me. "I'm sick of scheduling to see you. Like I can have an hour here or there and then it's on to your next thing. You don't give a shit about me."

"This is my *life*. I'm a professional athlete. And you knew what my schedule was like when we started dating because I made it very clear. But lately, I feel like you're constantly pissed off at me because I can't make time to see you when it suits you, because I'm busy training. But…you liked the results of that training when you could tell Insta that it was your girlfriend getting that medal at the Olympics, or when you anticipated you might be on TV if you came to my races. You can't have it both ways, can't be pissed at me but want the benefits." I inhaled a slow, deep breath. "And I'm around in the evenings if you'd wanted to spend time together."

"Yeah, for about three hours before you go to bed so you can get up before dawn to train. There's more to life than just a job. It's all you think about."

Not true. Her accusations made me realize there was no reason for me to tiptoe around the truth anymore. "And all you think about is yourself. And you know what? The person I just saw being so rude and so cruel to my best friend, one of the most important people in my life, isn't someone I want a relationship with." It wasn't the first time she'd been weird to Gemma, and at first I'd thought I was maybe misreading it, and I hadn't stepped up. Stupid me. But now I knew what I was seeing and hearing and I wasn't going to let her get away with it. Bree was nasty to

Gemma, simple as that. And if I had to choose between my best friend and this girlfriend, Gem would win every single time. No contest.

Bree's jaw tensed, and she declined to answer, so I pointed out, "And, you know what? I actually think it's you who's jealous of her."

She scoffed, and her words dripped with forced incredulity. "Why would I be jealous of Gemma?"

I could have listed all the reasons, but it wouldn't have done anything except antagonize her. I didn't want that. I just wanted her to leave. "There's no point discussing this anymore, because you refuse to see anyone else's point of view. Take care. And drive home safely." Like, right now.

I walked away before she could respond, not because I was set on having the last word but because I couldn't stand being near her a moment longer, and I needed to go check on Gem, whose expression had torn my heart. Bree called something after me but I ignored her, jogged up my front steps and pushed inside the house, closing the door behind me, locking Bree out. Out of my house. Out of my life.

I made a quick stop to grab a peace offering or an icebreaker or an apology gift or a "Hey you're my best friend and I love you so here's an iced latte" or whatever it was called. Gem was one of those weird people who drank iced coffee even during blizzards, and it was sure to break the ice. So to speak. Aspen didn't seem particularly surprised to see me, and after scrutinizing my splinted finger and giving me a twenty-questions grilling to make sure I really was taking it easy, she let me go upstairs.

Gem was at her desk, back to the door, working on her laptop. When I knocked on the doorframe, she muttered, "I still don't want to talk about it."

It was probably what had happened at my place. I pushed aside my distress that I'd had something to do with her feeling bad, and forced cheer into my, "Hey, Gemmy Gem."

She spun around, her mouth falling open. "Hey. Sorry, wasn't expecting you."

"Can I come in?"

"Of course."

I set the drink down on her desk. "Gotcha something."

She flashed me a smile. "Thanks."

Doing great so far. Not a stilted conversation at alllll. I dropped down onto her bed. "So…Bree's a Class-A Bitch, huh."

Gem huffed out a laugh around the straw. After a long swallow, she set the cup back down on her desk, turning it around and around. "What she said wasn't wrong, though. She's your girlfriend and should be your priority."

She said it so calmly, as if she'd resigned herself to the fact that I was going to side with Bree. Not a chance in hell. "Ex-girlfriend," I corrected. "And no, she shouldn't have been my priority. She's done nothing since we began dating to deserve being prioritized over important people like you."

"Pardon?" Gem squeaked.

"She's now my ex-girlfriend. I broke up with her. About a minute after you left." I lay back on the bed with my feet still on the floor. "God, I don't know why I didn't do it sooner."

"Wow. But…why?"

I stared up at the ceiling, grateful I didn't have to moderate my thoughts. "Because I realized that she's kind of a bitch. We have hardly anything in common. I don't love her, and after what she did to you today, I realized I didn't really even like her." I turned my head to look at Gem. "I'm so sorry she was nasty to you. And I'm also so ashamed of myself, and sorry that I didn't call her out on it sooner."

Gem shrugged. "You can't control the way people behave, and I get that she put you in an awkward position. I knew it wasn't personal. I think she hated that I know you better than she does."

"Right?" I exclaimed. "That's exactly what I told her, that she's jealous of you. The way she treated you wasn't cool at all. I'm sorry, Gem."

"S'okay, but thanks." She was letting me off too easily.

"It's not okay. I guess I'd just been accepting her attitude when it was only about me. But when it was about you, nastiness directed at you? That's not right and I'm not putting up with that. It's wrong, and you don't deserve it and I'm so sorry."

"You don't deserve that either, Stace," Gem said gently.

"I guess."

"You don't," she asserted. "You deserve someone who understands you and what's important to you."

Someone like you, I thought. But instead of saying that, I said, "And *who's* important to me." Aaand again, in case you weren't sure, that's you, Gemma.

Her ears went red, and I wondered if she was thinking the same thing I was. Gem drank half an inch of her iced coffee before asking, "Why not break up with her sooner if you knew you didn't really like her?"

"I dunno," I groaned. "Because it felt harder to deal with the fallout than to just keep trucking along the way we were." That said, the fallout had been minimal. Probably because I'd basically told her to go away and not given her a chance to go full screaming banshee on me. "I mean, I know it was barely a relationship at only three months long, and I've been away for a chunk of that time. But by the end, the bad outweighed the good, and I guess I just didn't want to acknowledge that because it would mean I'd have to look closely at why I was even dating her."

"And why was that?" she asked quietly.

I felt mortified at what I was going to admit, though I had always suspected Gemma knew why I chose the girlfriends I did—she'd basically confirmed as much during our talk about Bree at Beaver Creek. "For the same reason I've dated everyone else. Because I liked the way we looked together, and I liked that those social posts make my sponsors happy. I know it's shallow, you don't need to remind me."

Gem made a valiant attempt to hide her grin, but thankfully she just nodded instead of giving me an actual "Told you so."

"I mean, it's just…I feel like there's a certain expectation, from brand partners and even the public, that I have this image to maintain in and out of racing."

"The image of you with a hot woman hanging off your arm?"

I fought down a blush. "Right. That."

"I thought sponsors sponsored you because of your race results."

I coughed out a laugh. "The skiing ones do. But even then, I mean, we all know there's an image that goes with snow sports, and fitting that image makes me more attractive to the sponsor. The non-snow sports ones just want anything that draws attention to me with their brand, and let's be honest—me plus one gets more attention than just me." Managing public eye and sponsor expectations was something I'd found really hard when my racing career had taken off. Wasn't it enough to ski well and put up the occasional social media posts that included my sponsors? Apparently not, but thankfully Brick knew how to tread those uncharted waters, as did Aspen.

"I think you do what you need to do so you can race, and race well."

"Yeah," I muttered. It was so hard to manage all the weird stupidity I had to deal with alongside the skiing. If only it could just be skiing. I rolled onto my side and propped my head on my hand. "Listen, can you pause your studying or editing or whatever you're doing and we'll go out and catch an early movie and dinner? I know things got weird, but we were going to hang out tonight, right?" I pushed out my lower lip and tried to sound mopey. "I just broke up with my girlfriend and I need to spend time with my best friend."

"Yeah, and you seem really heartbroken about it," she drawled.

I was about to jump off the bed and tackle her, until my brain ran through what would happen after I did that. We'd end up back on the bed with one of us pinned beneath the other one. We'd be close together, pressed full length against each other. We'd be— I bit my lower lip and pushed the images from my brain. Okay, maybe not completely from my brain, but to the back where they'd be accessible when I'd want them later.

Gem looking at me like I'd grown a second head made me realize I'd spent too much mental time with my fantasy. Instead of grabbing her and kissing her the way I'd just imagined, I sat up. "I'm heartbroken about the fact I now have to find another hot woman to date."

That funny look morphed into an expression I couldn't read, and I wondered if she'd been thinking the same as me. That I had a beautiful woman right in front of me. Someone who would be so easy to date. Someone who already knew me and my life and loved me as I was. Someone I could trust. But I'd already put that thought into a box a long time ago, back when I'd first realized I was attracted to Gem and had then run through all the ramifications of acting upon that attraction.

Gem acquiesced with an exaggerated sigh. "Okay, fine, you win. Let's see what's on." She tapped some keys then turned her MacBook in my direction. Her background was a professional photograph of us from her parents' wedding a few years ago. I'd been her "date," and staring at the photo made me remember how nervous I'd been about looking good for her.

I'd seen it before but for some reason it hadn't twigged, until that very moment, that Gem and I looked even better together than Bree and I. Bree had a face you'd see in a current blockbuster movie—gorgeous, but not standing out. But Gemma was stunning, eye-catching, unique. She looked a lot like Mrs. Archer, with the same elegant bone structure, straight nose, plump lips, and light blue-gray eyes (no, I didn't think my coach's wife was hot). And Gem's body. Oh help. We'd never seen each other naked, but definitely in bathing suits and also in underwear while changing, and Gem had the kind of body that made my mouth dry and my stomach fluttery—soft and feminine, with hips and boobs and curves and a million places I wanted to sink into.

Oh don't say it, Stacey. Don't ruin everything by being a horndog. I swallowed hard then forced a bright smile. "Your choice."

She unplugged the MacBook and sat beside me. I shuffled until I was leaning back against the wall and Gem snuggled in beside me, resting the laptop between us. "*Ambulance, Sonic the Hedgehog 2, The Lost City*, or *Morbius*." She chewed the inside of her lower lip, fingertip tapping beside the scroll pad. "I don't think I'm in the mood for serious or action, and I don't want to see *Sonic*. How about *The Lost City*? Rom-com, Sandra Bullock, Channing Tatum, and Brad Pitt." She turned to grin at me. "Something for everyone."

"Sure," I agreed, grateful for the chance to think about something other than the hotness of my best friend.

"Okay, well, we have no minutes to spare if we want to get there before it starts." Gem slapped the laptop closed. "So I'm driving, Grandma."

CHAPTER TEN

Gemma

I wasn't sure how I felt about Stacey breaking up with Bree. Aside from so thankful that I'd been worried I'd give away my relief, that is. My thankful relief wasn't just about my feelings toward Stace, or how hard I found it to be around Bree in the fortunately brief time we'd spent in each other's company. My relief was because she really wasn't good for Stacey. Stacey didn't seem miserable around Bree, kinda the opposite really. It was almost like Bree just didn't exist. So if that's how Stace felt about her, then she wasn't getting anything out of their relationship, right?

I'd meant it when I'd told Stacey the night before that she deserved someone better, someone who understood and accepted her as she was, because she was amazing. And I'd hoped she hadn't caught the blush I'd felt as I'd said that, because of course I'd been thinking about me. Being in love with someone who didn't love you back that way was so hard.

I dragged myself through my school day, then dragged myself home to drag some more with study and editing, though study was definitely draggier than editing. It wasn't just my usual excitement about a project this time—now I had the added excitement of working on a project featuring Stacey. I said hi to Aspen, who was grumbling at the TV—*Call of Duty* woes—then took Taylor out for a quick jog before I came back to fit in some work before dinner.

As I stared at the background on my MacBook I felt the same funny fluttering in my stomach that I always did when I looked at that picture. I'd noticed last night how much attention Stacey had paid the photo, even though I knew she'd seen it before and had a copy, which made me wonder why she was suddenly so focused on it. The photo was from Mom and Aspen's wedding three years ago. I was in the wedding party, and of course Stacey had been invited, so we'd decided to just be each other's dates. I'd had to wear a light purple sleeveless gown, and Stacey had turned up wearing a three-piece suit and some swagger. She'd matched her pocket square to the color of my dress, done her hair in its usual quiff, and her makeup brought out the angularity of her face but not in a harsh way.

She was stunning, and even if I was objective, which I totally could be, we looked stunning together. We had arms around each other's waists and were touching all along the length of our body. Stace and I touched a lot, we always had, ever since we'd become good friends and then best friends. We touched to get each other's attention, snuggling while we watched TV, during skiing when she was showing me something or we were excited about finding a fresh stash of powder.

But this touch had been different. I remembered how Stacey's hand on my waist had felt almost possessive. As if she was telling people I was hers. I was hers…but only her friend. And I wanted to be so much more than that, that it almost hurt to think it.

I sighed. Maybe it was time I learned to get over my crush. The worst thing was, aside from Erin at school, I didn't really have anyone I could talk to about it. Obviously I couldn't talk to my best friend about it, which was shitty because Stace was the perfect person with whom to work through such a problem.

And while I knew I could—and did—talk to Mom and Aspen about anything, it would be beyond weird to confess that I had a massive crush on the person Aspen was responsible for shaping into the best ski racer she could be.

I put my headset on and cued up the audio I'd recorded at Stacey's the other night. I'd just listen all the way through first and try to concentrate on the art of it, not the Stacey of it. Then I could make notes about standout lines and start thinking about their best placement. She'd said so many great things, it was going to be tricky to choose, but a couple stood out right away.

"Some women have closets full of dresses and shoes." A deep, happy laugh. *"Not me. I have ski boots and race suits."*

"I spend my whole life training for just ninety seconds on a racecourse. That's all it is, like my medal-winning Downhill time in Beijing was 1:32.16. Then it's over and there's nothing more I can do about it. Except look forward to the next race, go back up the mountain and start training again."

I'd just scrubbed back to the start of the audio for another playback when loud knocking on my doorframe penetrated my headset. I turned around to see Aspen leaning against the frame.

"Hey," she said once I'd pulled the headset off. "Your turn to make dinner, in case you'd forgotten."

Shit, I had forgotten. "Sure, no problem." A quick glance at the time told me I'd have to start soon if I wanted it to be ready close to when Mom got home from work. Ever since she'd started her own PT practice here in town, catering to the endless stream of injured athletes, Aspen and I had tried to take some of Mom's houseworky stuff off her plate.

"May I come in?" They always asked, even when the door was open and even though I always said yes. Apparently they'd read some parenting book or something about respecting a child's privacy and boundaries.

"Sure."

Aspen glanced at my screen, which was paused on a frame of Stacey grinning at the camera as she stirred the sauce in the pan. "How's it coming along?"

I leaned back in my chair. "Pretty good. I've just got one more training session to film at the gym the day after tomorrow and then I'm done with my visual list. Might need a little more audio for overlay. Then there's effects, and the score, and…" Puffing out a breath, I admitted, "A lot more shit. It'll be so much easier when I have teams for audio production and editing, and I'm not running a one-woman-show."

"Way over my head, but I'm sure you know that." Smiling, she plonked down on my bed. "Everyone on the team was very impressed with how professional you were. Your mom and I are too, and also really proud."

"Thanks." Nice to know I at least looked the part of a filmmaker, even if I still felt like I was fumbling through everything.

"We're also proud of how dedicated you are to this, and how much you've learned in just a few years."

I grinned. "Helps when your parents are so supportive and let you go to summer film schools and every photography course in a hundred-mile radius." Again, beyond lucky to have such great parents.

Laughing, Aspen agreed, "I guess it does." She stretched out her legs, crossing her ankles, and watched me in that intense but not uncomfortably stare-y way she had, the way that made me sure she had some clairvoyant abilities. "You okay?" she asked.

I quickly looked up and made myself smile. "Yeah, I am. Just a lot going on right now." Understatement, and not just the end-of-school looming, and film-project stuff, and waiting to hear on my few remaining college applications.

"I know. But you seem to be handling it all okay. Is there anything you want to talk about?"

I spun around in my chair so I was face-to-face with her. "Do you think I hang around Stacey too much? Like…in a way that's bad for her?"

Aspen gaped before spluttering, "What? No, of course not. Why would you ask that? Do you really think that?"

Though I was sure Stacey would have told Aspen about her breakup with Bree, I still felt uncomfortable bringing it up. But breakup aside, Bree had been horrible to me, and I really wanted to get it all off my chest. I could have talked to Stace, of course, but she was tangled up in it, and it felt weird to point out that a person she had dated made me feel like absolute shit every time we'd interacted.

"Just something Bree said to me yesterday. Did Stace tell you they broke up?"

"Oh yeah, she sent me a text this morning, said they weren't together anymore." I couldn't read her expression. "Just so I knew if Bree contacted the team for whatever reason she was to be told politely to go away." Aspen inhaled slowly. "What did Bree say to you?"

I recounted those uncomfortable few minutes from yesterday, and with every new fact I relayed, Aspen looked like she was about to suit up and go to battle for me. I was surprised at how easy it was to tell the story again, and though I felt a little of the hurt and humiliation I had yesterday, it was less choking than it had been. Once I was done, I raised my hands. "So yeah. It's made me self-conscious, thinking I might be acting like a fool with a—" I just stopped myself from saying *planet-sized crush*.

"Bree's an idiot. A rude one at that. Aside from whatever issues she and Stacey were having, I think she's just jealous of how close you and Stacey are."

How close we are… Super close, but I wanted closer. And now Bree was gone… That thought dominoed into the next. Stacey was single and so was I and I loved her and wouldn't it be amazing if— Nope. Nope. Too risky. My anxiety spiked and I glanced at the laptop screen, feeling instantly calmer seeing Stacey's face. "That's what Stace said." I fiddled with the mouse. "Bree just hit a raw nerve I guess. Especially now when everything's in this weird kid-adult space and she was basically saying I'm just a kid hanger-on'er."

"Do you feel like a kid? Or do you feel like an adult?"

Shrugging, I said, "Neither, really. Maybe more adult? But still not like you and Mom."

"Some days, Gem, I don't feel like an adult either." Her expression softened from goofy to caring. "It'll all work out, I promise."

I wondered exactly what *all* was, but decided not to ask. Hopefully it really was an all-encompassing all. "I know. It's just all that shitty stuff before the good stuff I guess."

"You gotta have the shitty stuff so you recognize and appreciate the amazing stuff. Trust me." She pushed herself up and reached over to lovingly rub my back. "See you down in the kitchen." A gentle hint.

"Yep, be down in ten."

I decided to check my emails before starting dinner and got instantly sweaty palms and a racing pulse when I saw one about my application to the University of Southern California. I logged in to the applications portal, simultaneous disappointment and relief rushing through me when I realized it was a rejection. A not-unexpected rejection because the USC Cinematic Arts program was one of my reach applications. I wasn't naïve enough to think I could just waltz into one of the best film schools in the country with my sparse portfolio, but it'd been worth a shot. Aim high and all that.

This whole becoming-a-documentary-filmmaker thing would probably have been easier if I'd realized earlier that this was what I wanted to do, and had started my portfolio sooner. No matter. I'd get my bachelor's degree somewhere, learn as much as I could, build my portfolio, then see where it took me and if I needed to apply to the American Film Institute or just... start making films.

I jogged down the stairs, almost tripping over Taylor who apparently thought it was playtime. At the sound of the garage door rolling up, she shot past the kitchen toward the laundry to greet Mom and escort her inside. After dumping her coat and bags on the kitchen table, Mom hugged me and kissed my forehead, then gave Aspen the same treatment except lips not forehead. Aspen opened a bottle of pinot noir and left it on the counter to breathe.

"May I please have a glass?" I asked. Once I'd turned eighteen, they'd agreed if I wanted one, it was no big deal for me to have a cold beer or a glass of the few wines that I liked when I was home with them. I sometimes went to my friends' parties but I really wasn't a partier, out every weekend drinking and stuff. Way too much social for me.

"Sure," Aspen agreed, grabbing a third wineglass.

As if she knew what I'd been thinking, Mom groaned, "God, I still can't believe I have an eighteen-year-old. I feel so old."

"You don't look it," Aspen and I said together, then exchanged a grin.

It wasn't to appease Mom, who really didn't look old at all, even next to Aspen who was nine years younger than her, which I didn't think mattered at all because they didn't seem to care about the age thing. Aspen was mature and parenty in some ways, and teen-like in others, and she and Mom were *totally* compatible. So the two-and-a-bit years between Stace and me was nothing and screw what Bree had implied about me being a kid.

After a small sip of wine, I decided to delay dinner for a few minutes to tell them my latest news. Get it out of the way, or whatever. "So, I, um, had a rejection from USC just now."

Mom set her glass back onto the counter, her shoulders dropping. "Oh, honey. I'm so sorry." She pulled me in for a hug.

"It's fine," I said against her shoulder, patting her back reassuringly. And it really was. "That one was a bit out of my reach I think for my filmmaking experience."

Mom released me slightly, pulling me against her side, rubbing my back the way she always did when I was sick or upset, even though I was neither of those things.

"Nothing's out of your reach, Gem," Aspen said seriously.

"I know." I grinned and added, "Not once I've got a bachelor's degree and a portfolio full of amazing short films that is."

They both nodded their agreement, support written solidly on both their faces. Mom pressed her lips together to hide her frown before asking, "Are you *sure* you're okay?"

"Absolutely," I said honestly. "I knew this one was unlikely, and I've already got acceptances to some great schools, so it's not like I don't have solid options."

Aspen's nod was so vigorous, she could have given herself concussion. "You do. And we're so proud of you."

"Me too." I exhaled a long breath and pushed down the general college anxiety. College. Adulting. Bah. Of course I wanted to grow up and move on and achieve things, but why did it have to be so hard and overwhelming?

CHAPTER ELEVEN

Stacey

Charlie had okayed Gem coming to film our training session on Sunday afternoon, and when he strode into the gym, I could tell he'd dressed for the occasion. He'd done his hair so it was extra swiffy, and wore his most muscle showing-off tank. After noting a conspicuous shine to his bronzed skin, I had to ask, "Did you oil your bare skin?"

Charlie flexed. "Maybe."

"You are such a peacock."

He graced me with a withering look. "Please, Stacey. Isn't Gemma Family?" They'd met a handful of times when Gem had come by at the end of a workout, or to have a workout of her own in the public section of the gym, and seemed to get along well.

I had no idea why that was relevant, but, "Well, yeah, she is." Gem had never explicitly declared her sexuality, but she'd dated guys and girls and when we watched *Avengers* movies, she swooned over Scarlett Johansson and Chris Evans equally.

"Right. So when she's a famous filmmaker, she's going to have our people flocking to watch her work. Including her old stuff. And I don't want anyone seeing me looking less than my best." He flicked the brim of my ball cap. "You're wearing your nicest workout gear. You've even replaced your regular gross, sweaty hat."

"Course I did. She's my friend and I wanna look good for her movie."

He raised an eyebrow, and drawled, "Her movie. Okay then. Sure." Charlie's raised eyebrows whenever Gemma was around were the stuff of legends, as if he was trying *so* hard to tell me something. I knew exactly what he was attempting to convey with his wide eyes and wiggly eyebrow bounces, and tried my damnedest to ignore him. I had no idea how he saw the thing I was trying to hide, but he did.

I was about to punch his arm when Gem strolled in, dragging a rolling hardcase of her equipment. Her smile was the sweet one she always had when she was feeling a little shy, and after a finger wave for me, she turned to my trainer. "Hey, Charlie. Nice to see you again."

"You too, Gemma. You're looking gorgeous, as always."

She smiled, and I watched the blush creep over her cheeks as she said, "Thanks. I try."

I gave myself a pat on the back for not contributing to this part of the conversation. Verbally at least. Mentally, I was skipping around yelling, "Yep! She's gorgeous! My best friend is hot!" And right then, I wanted nothing more than to call her my girlfriend as well as my best friend. I bent down and checked my shoelaces, just so I wouldn't have to look at Gemma.

Charlie saved me from myself by rubbing gleeful hands together as he asked Gem, "So, want me to make her puke for you?"

Gem declined with a laughing, "Not sure that'll appeal to my audience. But don't go soft on her on my account."

He placed hand on his chest. "Oh I would *never*. I'll give you a few minutes to get set up, then we'll have to get started."

Grinning, he jerked his thumb at the spin bike in the corner. "Stacey, on your bike."

I snapped my heels together and saluted. "Yes, drill sergeant!"

He rolled his eyes at me and turned away to talk to Gem. "See what I put up with?"

"Oh this is nothing," I heard Gem say as I jogged to the spin bike.

By the time I'd finished my ten-minute heart-rate-pumping warmup on the bike, Gemma had set up her camera in an out-of-the-way spot and Charlie was signing a piece of paper I recognized as a permission thingy to use him for the film. He smiled as he passed it back to Gem. "Don't tell anyone my middle name is Athol. English parents," he explained with a wry grin.

Gem bit down on a smile. "You have my word, Charles Athol."

They probably would have continued bantering if I hadn't come back, pumped to start my workout. And work out I did. Charlie wasn't kidding when he'd told Gem he wasn't going to be soft on me—though the workout was slightly amended to accommodate my splinted finger—and within fifteen minutes I was gulping down air and trying to ignore my rapidly fatiguing muscles. I almost puked, but managed to swallow it back down before I ruined Gem's footage. The life of a pro athlete was so glamorous.

When Charlie was done torturing me, and I'd finished my cooldown, I collapsed on the mat to stretch. The torture of his training sessions was worth it for the way he helped me stretch all my overworked muscles then helped me hang upside down from the pull-up bar with my arms dangling because I loved the way it felt.

Once he'd helped me back upright again, Charlie clapped his hands decisively. "Right," he said, "I'm out."

Gem said shyly, "Thanks, Charlie. I appreciate you letting me butt into your workspace."

"My pleasure," he chirped. With a wink, he added, "Hope you got my good side."

"Every side is your good side," she assured him with a smile.

Charlie's laugh echoed through the room. "Oh, you're going to go far in this business, I can tell. It was great to see you again, Gemma. Don't forget, Athol is our little secret." He patted me on the back. "Great work today, so proud of you. See you tomorrow. Refuel, rehydrate, and rest." After a wave, Charlie slung his bag over his shoulder and swaggered out of the gym. Yep, peacock.

Despite the fact I was disgustingly sweaty, Gem hugged me, leaning her cheek against my shoulder. "And thank you for letting me crash your workout."

I tried so hard not to smell her hair, and was mostly successful. My throat felt tight when I said, "Anytime. Hope it was what you were after."

"Sure was. You looked great. I mean, you did great." Gem relaxed her grip but stayed close. She looked up at me with an expression I couldn't work out, before she grinned and pulled off the cap I used to keep my too-short-to-ponytail hair out of my face during workouts, and turned it back-to-front. "You all done? Ready to head out?"

"Yes," I breathed. My post-workout endorphin high was quickly being overtaken by a post-workout need-to-replace-everything-I'd-burned low.

I ate a banana while I slipped into sweatpants and a hoodie—I felt weird about showering at the gym so always did it when I got home—and once I was dressed, Gem handed me my shaker bottle. During my cooldown and stretch, she'd prepared my post-workout shake for me. God, I loved her. Like, really loved her, not just in the "because she was the most thoughtful sweetheart on the planet" way. Actually, maybe that was part of it. Wasn't feeling loved and cared-for part of being in love?

Gemma nudged me. "You okay?"

"Totally. Just zoned out thinking about how hungry I am." Not exactly a lie. After a huge gulp of chocolate-flavored heaven, I slung the strap of my gym duffel across my body, and grabbed the handle of Gem's equipment case. Chivalry and all that. Plus, I just liked doing stuff for people, Gem especially, even if it was awkward with my still-splinted finger.

She rolled her eyes. "If you're going to pretend you're a pack mule, then at least give me your shaker bottle to carry or something."

"Can't," I said as soon as I'd gulped down another mouthful. "I'll die if I don't drink it now. I can juggle everything." To end the discussion, I started walking, swigging shake as I went. "We still on for dinner and a movie at my place tonight?"

"Sure. What are we watching?"

"I still haven't seen *Black Widow*." I shouldered open the door and used my back to keep it open for her.

"I'm appalled," Gem deadpanned as she slipped past me, lightly brushing against my front in the cramped doorway.

I ignored the goose bumps that'd appeared at her touch and squeaked out, "And I'm busy. Plus, watching movies without you is boring."

She smiled at that and resumed pretending I wasn't struggling with both my duffel and her rolling hardcase getting in the way of me exiting after her. After my second fumble, Gem hooked her toe under the case to pull it through the door.

Once all bodies and bags had escaped the building, I pouted at Gem. "I totally had it."

"Mhmm, I could see that by the way you nearly tripped and dropped everything. Are you just ignoring the fact you dislocated your finger a few days ago?"

"Pretty much, yeah." I stared at it. "Doesn't bother me, just annoys me."

"Of course it does." She blew me a kiss, then took custody of her equipment as a cute twenty-something brunette approached us. Not wanting to be seen as rude for just standing there, I hastily dragged the door open to let her exit.

"Thank you," the stranger said silkily as she slipped past me, but unlike Gemma she didn't touch me. Thankfully.

I smiled and deliberately did not follow her with my eyes.

Gemma's eye roll was legendary.

"What?" I asked.

"You. You've been single for how long and you're already checking out every hot stranger."

Not really, and not just strangers… I shrugged, and fought the urge to defend myself and the fact Gem seemed to think I was a shallow player. Nothing was further from the truth. "It's not like Bree was my soulmate and breaking up with her has broken my heart."

Smiling, Gem just shook her head then walked off, leaving me to follow. Behind her was not a bad place to be, and unlike with the stranger, I didn't bother disciplining my eyes, taking a few sneaky peeks at Gem's butt. I mean, yeah, I was as guilty as anyone of enjoying attractive people and Gem was right up there on my list, but her gorgeous outside was just a bonus to her amazing inside.

We'd met up at the gym, and after I'd helped her stow all her equipment in her car, Gem said she'd see me back at my place. Being in separate cars gave me time to refocus my thoughts from "La-la-la, I'm in love with my best friend." Refocus, not eliminate, because those thoughts were always there, lingering pleasantly in the background. The least I could do was put them someplace out of the way so I wouldn't act like a moony idiot around her when we were snuggled up on my couch watching a movie.

I showered off my workout, and together we made a quick oven-baked salmon with steamed veggies. Gem was unusually quiet during dinner—not upset or annoyed, but more introspective. And I knew her well enough to know that pushing would make her self-conscious and that she'd tell me if she thought it was something I should know or that she wanted to share.

Once we'd eaten, we sprawled on the couch, leaning into and entwined around each other for maximum comfort. The movie was brilliant, and doubly hilarious with Gem's muttered adoration of the female leads. I shared her enjoyment, but was finding it hard to concentrate with her so close, and my uncomfortable shoulder which felt like someone had stuck a rock under the skin, right on my scapula—that old bastard. It was a recurring tightness and usually I just ignored it until a PT session, but now it was making it too hard to relax and enjoy the movie. Shifting a little eased the discomfort, but only slightly.

Gemma poked my stomach. "What's up, Squirmo?"

I twisted from where I was lying half in Gem's lap so I could look at her. "Shoulder knot. I'd do anything if you'd massage it out for me."

She paused the movie then peered down at me, her mouth twitching the way it did when she wanted to laugh but was trying to be serious. "Didn't you get your weekly massage two days ago?"

"Yes, but it's back. And this time, it brought friends. Please. I'll do anything," I said again, hoping my pathetic desperation wasn't too pathetic. If my massage therapist and I could fit it into my schedule, I'd have a massage every day. But Gemma was a great interim masseuse. And, she never really seemed to mind digging into all the spots that were inevitably sore or tight after training.

Gem did her thing with one eyebrow. Her thing that always made me tingle inside. This time, though, the tingle was more like a rumble when Gem drawled, "Anything?"

I should have laughed and said something like "Within reason" but instead, I just nodded and managed to squeak out, "Mhmm, anything."

Gem's smile was kinda mysterious. "You know I'll hold you to that." Before I could say anything, she murmured, "Get on the floor."

I slid from the couch and nestled myself so I was leaning back against Gem's legs. She started the movie again, then her fingers brushed the back of my neck before settling on my shoulders. As she kneaded the tops of my shoulders, she asked, "Usual spot?" Her fingers trailed down to my scapula before she dug in.

"Ohmygod, that feels so good. I love you." The sensation of her fingers had turned me to goo, and she wasn't even massaging properly. And of course my brain immediately went to how it might feel if her fingers were touching my bare skin and in other places. Yep, doing a great job of not thinking about being in love with her. Doing an even better job of not being a moony idiot.

Her fingers paused for the briefest moment before she answered, "I know you do."

As Gem worked at the knot on my shoulder blade, her feet rubbed along the outside of my thighs like she was soothing me. Or herself. I knew she didn't even know she was doing it, because she often squirmed her feet against the floor, the couch, or me, while we were chilling. But it didn't stop me enjoying the sensation.

"Can you go…" I reached back and moved her hand, barely holding in my groan when she got the spot.

Gem laughed as she massaged the knot. "Did I get it?"

I let my head fall backward. "Mhmmm, you did. You're a genius. A goddess. A genius goddess."

"You really don't pay me enough, you know."

"Right now, I'd pay you anything you asked for."

Her fingers were utter magic, lulling me into the dopey massaged-out state where I was so relaxed my brain went to mush. Mush, and free to wander. Underneath the sensation of Gem lovingly working at my icky spots was me still wondering how it might be if she touched me in other places. Places that would have me worked up instead of chilled out.

She spent half an hour working at the knot while we watched the movie, and I tried—and thankfully managed—to keep myself where I was. It was only when I'd let out a long, relaxed exhalation that Gem paused her kneading to ask, "How's that feel?"

Instead of answering, I just gurgled.

Gem laughed. "Good." She patted the top of my head.

I twisted in place and slung my arm over the top of her thighs. Resting my chin on my forearm, I gazed up at her, utterly unable to think of anything except how content I was. And how much I wanted to kiss her.

Our gazes locked. Gem's mouth fell open before she snapped it closed again. "I'm just gonna grab some chips." Her voice sounded kinda rough. "You need another drink?"

"I'm good, thanks," I said, grateful that she'd broken the crackly tension between us.

While she was messing about in my kitchen, I climbed back up onto the couch and tried to ignore the lingering sensation in my body that had nothing to do with the massage. I was so relaxed and pliant that my brain had followed suit and was feeling particularly unfiltered. She set a bowl of chips between us, then restarted the movie.

After a few minutes I got distracted watching Gem lick the flavoring off each one of the salt and vinegar chips before she ate it, as she always did, her lips puckering more and more as she got further through the bowl. She had so many endearing habits. So did I (though how many were weird and how many were endearing I didn't know) and I loved how completely unashamed she was of being herself around me. And of course I felt the same being around her. I could just be totally myself and know she'd accept and never judge me for being a dork who thought about skiing ninety percent of the time.

There was so much trust and love between us. And I wanted to screw that up by admitting that I loved her as more than just a friend? Good one, Stacey. That's the best way to risk everything. Guaranteed.

CHAPTER TWELVE

Gemma

By some miracle of planning, my final period on Wednesday afternoons was free, which meant I could get into film club early, take my favorite station in the corner where I wouldn't be surrounded on all sides by people, and work for an hour in silence. I liked my film club pals well enough, and we were all friendly in that absorbed-in-our-projects kind of way, but I also liked my space where I could bury myself without having to stop and talk all the time.

Because of course, now, layered over all the usual college chatter was the talk of finals and graduation in a few weeks. I was so saturated by it all that my brain had reached switch-off point every time I heard the words *college*, *finals*, or *graduation*.

Mr. Williams, our film club guru and supervisor, came in and said hi to me, then assumed his position at the desk up front and in the corner. He mostly just sat there playing around on his laptop with something—the rumor was it was porn, but we all knew he was actually editing videos of his son who'd just learned to walk—unless we needed him to help or give advice. His main message to me was to focus on one portion of the editing process, like getting all the visuals put together from start to finish, then move to audio or VO from start to finish, instead of completing little sections and then doing final continuity edits at the end. He was probably right, and maybe college would make me change my ways, but for now I knew what I wanted in my head and the way I worked, worked for me.

I spent almost three hours in the video lab playing around with slo-mo shots, trying to get them at the exact speed and length so it didn't look like a gimmick. Of course, the slo-mo just accentuated Stacey and all her insane skill and hotness. Maybe this project was a bad idea, considering I could barely get through a filming or editing session without drooling. Little bit late to abandon it now, Gemma... Move on, be an adult, accept that to Stacey you're just her best friend.

A flurry of movement outside the room caught my eye, and I looked up to see Erin waving and pulling stupid faces through the huge fishbowl windows along the top half of the wall. I discreetly waved and motioned she should come in. She slipped through the lab with the stealth of a spy, murmuring greetings to some of the other film nerds before she pulled out the chair beside mine. "Hey."

"Hey. What're you doing here?"

She leaned back. "Enjoying the peace. My options were to study here where headphones block out the noise of everyone talking about sports and sex, or study at home where *nothing* blocks out Mom and Dad."

I really didn't know what to say. When I'd first found out how unpleasant her home situation was, I'd said right away that she was welcome at my house any afternoon after school to study. It was a no-go apparently. School was okay, going to a friend's house where she might have fun instead of actually studying like she was supposed to was not okay. Her parents seemed like real dicks, and I was always amazed that Erin was so freaking normal and also managed to be at the top of the class every year with that hanging over her head. Mom and Aspen had always wanted me to do my best, gave me little nudges here and there, and supported me. But they weren't pushing me with study-study-study no fun no play for Gemma, even with finals so close. Sure, finals were important like most exams were, but I'd already laid down all the groundwork for my academic future, and unless I just didn't show up to any of my finals, I couldn't ruin anything now.

I nodded. "Got it."

Erin leaned closer the monitor I had hooked up to my laptop so I could work with dual screens. "So this is the big project, huh? The get-you-into-the-LA-film-school masterpiece? Assuming that's the route you take."

"Yep, this is it." The American Film Institute in LA. The big dream. After I'd done my double degree of course—Bachelor in Film Studies plus Bachelor in Ecology and/or Biology.

Mr. Williams had apparently clocked the fact he had an extra someone in the room and abandoned playing around with the footage of his kid to loom over us. He sounded mildly exasperated, but not angry when he pointed out, "Ms. Lawson. You're not part of film club."

Erin flashed him a smile that would win over even the grumpiest of teachers. "No, Mr. Williams. But Gemma asked me to research the legality of showing brands on film, and I was just following up with that."

I pressed my lips together to stop myself laughing. She was so clever.

Erin continued, "So I'm just checking this footage to make sure she's compliant with federal trademark laws." She was going to be an amazing lawyer.

He looked like he didn't believe her but was so impressed with her ability to spin bullshit that he let it go. "All right then. Don't break anything."

This smile was eyelash-flutteringly sweet. "Of course not." Once Mr. Williams left to resume his kid-film, Erin turned back to me. "Okay, show me what you've got."

"Really?" I was unexpectedly nervous about letting someone who wasn't part of film club and therefore used to half-finished projects see my work, and my voice squeaked as I hurried to explain, "It's nowhere near done. I only have like...three and a half minutes completed. And it's still just a rough edit. And I haven't sweetened the audio, okay? There's just a little voiceover."

"Okay," she said cheerfully. "I have no idea what you're talking about, but okay."

"And it might change, and I'm not set on the title. And what I have edited probably isn't finished-finished, but—"

Erin slung an arm around my shoulders, shaking me gently. "Gemma. Chill. No judging. I just want to see what awesome thing my awesome friend has made."

"Okay..." I handed her one of my earbuds, opened up the master file, took a deep breath and pressed Play.

The film started with an establishing early-morning drone shot, pulling back from the sun-dappled snow to reveal the racecourse lined by trees. Then from the top of the frame, Stacey came into view and the shot pulled back further and further and lower and lower down the mountain to show a full twenty seconds of her carving through the course as a small, speedy dot.

Stacey's VO came in over the footage. *I love the freedom of skiing, the feeling of giving myself completely to the mountain.*

Title overlay—*1:32.16*. I'd agonized over the title, her medal-winning time from Beijing and a reference to Stacey saying she trained so hard and so long for a minute and a half of racing. I still wasn't sure I'd stick with it. But it was an okay working title for now.

Transition to dark screen. The sound of gravel crunching. Then slow fade in on Stacey walking to her car in the predawn light, travel coffee mug in hand and gear bags on shoulders and in her other hand. We'd moved her car out of the garage for that early-morning shot because I wanted the gravel crunch and the steaming breath in the illumination from the security lights on her house. She'd been so eager to please, to do whatever was needed to get the shots I wanted, including pretending to go to training on a morning she wasn't training.

Transition to Stacey lacing up her racing boot liners, putting on boots, clipping in to skis, stamping skis in the snow stained a pinkish orange from the sunrise. She'd laughed about having out-of-camera-view mics taped to her boots to capture the unmistakable sound of clipping in and snow stamping. She looked up, grinning at the camera before she pulled her goggles down, settling them carefully over her eyes. *"When I step into skis, I feel like I can do anything."*

Then stuttery, every-two-seconds footage of her pushing off repeatedly through a timing arm, until she finally went down the course. The shot panned to follow her from the top to bottom of the frame. I hit Pause. "That's it for now."

Erin leaned back in her chair, and let her mouth fall open. "Wow. So pro. I'm impressed."

"It's a start," I said, still feeling extra shy about the project.

"How long does that all take to do? The editing stuff?"

"Professional editors take an hour or two for each completed minute. But me? At least three hours." I glanced at the time. "On that note, I think I'm done. You going home?"

"Can't put it off forever, right?"

"Right." I triple-saved my work then packed up and said bye to everyone. As I shrugged into my backpack and jammed on my beanie, I asked Erin, "You want to go grab an early dinner with me?" I knew it was a pointless invitation but I couldn't help asking.

"I do, honestly. But I can't." Her disheartened shrug was all the explanation I needed. "Thanks for asking, though. And thanks for letting me hang out. Your film project looks amazing."

"Thanks," I said as I pushed open the door to the film lab.

"Know what else looks amazing?"

"What?"

"Stacey Evans…" She fanned herself with both hands. "She is so hot. So much swagger. And that's my opinion as a person who is mostly into guys. I don't understand how you haven't just jumped her yet." Under her breath Erin muttered, "The sex would be so hot."

I was overwhelmed by a mix of mild annoyance and resignation, the sensation a by-product of knowing she was right to question my inaction. "Are you ever going to give me a break about that?" I asked, ignoring her mutterings, because if I let myself acknowledge them, even to myself, I wouldn't be able to think.

She shrugged, but was smiling. "If you really want me to. Otherwise I'm just going to keep gently guiding you in the obvious direction."

"Which is?" We started walking toward the doors and freedom.

"She's single now, right? You're single. You've got a serious dose of the in-loves for her and I'd bet that she'd go for it if you so much as hinted you wanted to jump on her."

"But I don't want her to just go for it because why the hell not. I want her to go for it because she feels the same. Or even kinda the same."

Erin stopped abruptly, turning to face me. She grabbed me by both shoulders, shaking me lightly. "You're a freaking catch, my friend. And if she has half a brain, which I'm sure she does, then trust me, she feels the same."

"I dunno," I mumbled.

She used the backs of her fingers to slap my arm. "Get your laptop out, I want to see that project again."

"Right here? In the parking lot?"

"Mhmm. There's something I need to show you."

I set my laptop on the hood of my car and opened up the project. Erin said, "Okay, now take it to the bit right after she puts her skis on."

I did as I was told.

Erin pointed at the screen. "There. You see that?"

"What?"

"Who filmed this?" she asked in exasperation.

"Me, obviously."

"Right, so you're behind the camera?" When I nodded, she said, "So there's nobody else that look could be aimed at."

"What look?"

"Oh, Captain Oblivious, you are *killing* me." She moved the video back a little to just before Stacey pulled her goggles down. "Where's she looking, Gemma?"

I couldn't believe that in all the times I'd watched this footage, I'd never seen it. Stacey's gaze moved slightly out of frame to where I would have been standing. Her grin softened into more of a wistful smile as her gaze moved up and down. Up and down...*me*. She was checking me out. "Oh, shit. Oh my god."

When I looked up at Erin again, at a total loss about what to say, she was smiling smugly at me. Both eyebrows slowly rose before she said, "Told you."

Aspen was getting an early start on a rib roast when I came home from school, with ever-hopeful Taylor standing by. I let my backpack melt to the floor beside the breakfast bar, gave my dog some love and Aspen a quick side-on hug. "Hey."

"Hey, hon. How was your day?"

"Long," I breathed. "But I have almost four minutes of perfectly edited footage for my project, with VO as well. So there's only...eighteen more minutes to produce." And, you know, I just realized that my best friend who I've been crushing on for years was checking me out in a way that was more than merely friendly. I rummaged in the fridge, hoping to pull out a ready-made meal that I could devour before dinner and was disappointed, but not really surprised, when the only suitable quick-eat I found was grapes.

"That's awesome, Gem. I'm so proud of you and so excited to see what you've created."

"Me too..." Because at the moment, I still wasn't sure how it'd come out. I'd always been so methodical with my school work—homework, assignments, study—but for some reason filmmaking and photography felt more visceral and less logical, like I went purely on gut-feel.

When I emerged from my fridge expedition, Aspen asked neutrally, "Has Stacey called or texted you today?"

The question immediately got my antennae up. Frowning, I answered, "No, why?"

Aspen blew out a huffy breath, and held up placating hands. "She's fine, but she had a training accident on the course, and I sent her to the ER."

I felt like I'd just jumped through a hole in the ice into freezing water. My voice sounded like someone else's asking, "What happened? What sort of accident?"

"She was pushing everything to the limit and beyond, as usual, and she clipped a gate. With her face. We think she's broken her nose." Aspen glanced at her watch. "The last I heard about three hours ago was she was still waiting to be seen by a doctor."

I leaned against the fridge door, my legs having suddenly turned to jelly. Geez, Gemma, it's just a maybe-broken nose. Not like she's broken her spine or cracked her skull, or—devastating for Stacey because it'd impede her off-season training and leech into next season—broken a leg or something. I knew the inevitability of Stacey getting injured, because ski racing was a high-risk sport, especially her speed events, and that no matter the skill someone had and training they put in and all the precautious taken, nobody escaped injury. Aspen was a walking example with her grocery list of crashes and massive injuries. And I trusted Aspen and Stace to manage those risks and lessen the impact, so to speak, but I'd never been able to be not-upset about it. "It's just…I know ski racers sometimes get hurt. But two so close together? It's just—"

First her dislocated finger, and now a possibly broken nose. Two injuries within a week of each other, and just in training rather than competition when Stace would *really* let loose and take risks to shave milliseconds from her race times. It made me feel sick. She'd had dozens of injuries over the years—most of them minor, but some major enough to keep her out of competition, or need rehabbing and even requiring surgery. Skiing was dangerous as a hobby, and even more dangerous as a career, and even knowing that everyone involved did everything to manage and mitigate the risks, the idea that Stace could be seriously injured or even killed was always there in the back of my mind. The world's worst and most upsetting earworm. And when she hurt herself, those thoughts in the back of my mind made their way to the front.

"I know," Aspen sympathized kindly.

I put both hands over my stomach, trying to quell the nausea. "Are you sure she's okay?"

Aspen laughed. "I'm sure. I mean, as okay as she can be with a maybe-broken nose that is."

I nodded, unable to find my voice again for even a basic "Okay."

"Gem?" When I looked up, Aspen continued gently, "You know…maybe it's time you told her how you feel."

My words felt stuck and I had to force them out. "And how's that?" I hoped desperately she wasn't about to say what I thought she was going to say.

"That you're in love with her. Or…something that looks a lot like that."

My whole stomach felt like I'd just taken a fall on a black run, tumbling my way down the mountain. First Erin, now Aspen? The universe was ganging up on me. Or maybe I just had a gigantic I LOVE STACEY EVANS sign above my head. I wilted. "Is it that obvious?"

"To people who know you as well as me and your mom, yeah, a little."

"Great." I had to blink back tears. "That's not embarrassing at all."

Aspen's expression softened, and she pulled me in for a quick hug. "No, hon. It's not. What's embarrassing about having feelings for someone?"

"Because she's my best friend and she's never even hinted that she thinks we're anything other than friends. And what if she finds out? What if she thinks I'm an idiot? What if she doesn't feel the same?"

She laughed. "We are talking about Stacey, right? She would never think you're an idiot." Aspen's eyebrows came together. "And as for the feeling the same, you might be surprised."

That stopped my panicky embarrassed upset in its tracks. "What do you mean?"

"Let's just say, when your job is to watch Stacey, you notice things." Aspen paused, and I could tell she was debating whether to say more. After a few moments, she seemed to make a choice and said, "Like the way she looks at you for example."

That pulled me right up, especially on the back of what Erin had pointed out to me in the school parking lot. The way Stacey looked at me? More than just the quick checking-out that I'd seen in my footage? I mean, yeah, sometimes she did look at me in a way that made me feel excited and nervous. But I was sure that was just me, wanting it so badly I was imagining her seeing me in a way she didn't, right? I'd never let myself think of it as anything more than just her being Stacey, because Stacey just… loved. She loved everything she did, even the hard or scary stuff, and she loved everyone special in her life with all of herself. It was just who she was. I cleared my throat so I could ask, "How's that?"

My question made Aspen squirm, and when she hedged, I realized she was stuck in an awkward spot. "Look, it's not really my place to say. But I will say that I think if you stopped and took a breath and removed the filter you've been applying to her then you'd see what I see."

A filter? What the heck did she mean? I didn't filter Stacey into the version of her I most wanted to see. Did I? If I did filter Stacey, then every time I saw her she'd be a clichéd dream sequence, bathed in light, asking if she could kiss me. Or did Aspen mean that I was filtering out some sort of truth?

"So maybe you should tell her how you really feel," Aspen said again.

If Aspen thought I should jump into the deep end, then maybe I should. I felt all shuddery and sick inside, and when I didn't answer, she quietly asked, "What have you got to lose?"

I bit my lower lip, trying desperately to hold back my tears. Overwhelmed tears, not upset tears. "Everything," I whispered. "My dignity if I tell her and she doesn't feel the same. My best friend if she gets freaked out and thinks I'm a desperate pervert kid." Just like Bree had said.

She pulled me into another calming hug, squeezing some of my anxiety away as she rubbed my back. "Hey, come on. I really, truly, honestly don't think that would happen, Gem. I think you could also gain everything." Aspen released me, still holding me by the shoulders. "Let's stop those brain gremlins, yeah? It's normal and okay to be afraid. Wanting something badly doesn't immediately mean you have no fear about it."

"I know. It's just…you know." I was usually pretty good at articulating things, but trying to explain how terrified I was of ruining the best friendship I'd ever had made me completely tongue-tied.

Aspen grinned. "Yeah, I do. I've been afraid many, many times in my life, Gem, and afraid of a lot of things. But the one thing I've learned about fear is that ignoring it doesn't make it go away and it doesn't make it easier to deal with. It just gets bigger and bigger until you literally can't hold it anymore."

"I guess." Slumping against the counter, I asked, "You really think I should do it? Tell her?"

"I do. But the decision is ultimately yours. What I really think is you should do what can bring you the greatest amount of joy."

Well the answer to that was obvious, but only if it worked out. "What about you guys?"

Her eyebrows scrunched. "What about us?"

"What if me and Stacey…" I swallowed. "What if us dating changes your coaching relationship with her?"

Aspen leaned against the counter beside me, her arms loosely folded over her chest. She took a few moments to answer, and when she did, she was calm. "I think the only thing that would change how I felt about Stacey would be if she deliberately hurt you. And I know her well enough by now to know that's not who she is, that she wouldn't do that." She tucked some of my hair back, lingering to gently cup my cheek. "I acknowledge that it's a risk, but Stacey and I both know how important our coaching relationship is to her success, and it would take *a lot* of distrust on both sides for either of us to want to split. I don't think there's anything about you two dating that would make that happen."

I leaned into her, thinking about what she said. Before I could answer, Aspen gestured at the roast, still waiting to go into the oven. "This won't be ready for a while, so if you have to go somewhere, like over to see Stacey and maybe have a chat, then it's fine."

"Are you trying to matchmake me?"

Aspen's laugh filled the kitchen. "Of course not. I'm just… trying to help you see what could make you happy."

I hugged her tight around the waist. "I love you."

She kissed the top of my head. "Love you too, Gem."

Upstairs, I flopped down on my bed and texted Stacey. *Did you break your nose today and forget to mention it to me?*

Halo emoji. *Course not. And I didn't break my nose, just walloped it good, as confirmed by the ER which I only left half an hour ago. There was a huge pile-up that was more important than my nose, so it took hours to get seen by a doc. Didn't want to bother you at school. Not a big deal.* Huge grin emoji.

Idiot. As if she'd ever bother me. *It is a big deal. You hurt yourself. Can I come round tonight? Keep you company?* Tell you I'm in love with you, you know, no big deal.

The response was an almost instantaneous *Yes please.*

Be there soon.

I let my phone fall onto the bed and rolled onto my back. Was I brave enough to do what I wanted to do? Brave enough to let myself see what I thought was there? Maybe. But I wasn't brave like Stacey. I didn't just jump in with the absolute confidence that I could deal with whatever happened. And all the bad things that could happen, all those negative thoughts, hit me like an out-of-control skier.

Why would Stacey even want *me* when she could have anyone she wanted—models, influencers, rich people, worldly ski racers. What if she didn't think I was hot enough? What if she was into it, and we started dating but even us being close in that way didn't change how Stace approached relationships, and she kept me at an emotional arm's length the way she had with all her other girlfriends? What if after three, four, five months, she decided to toss me aside too?

I took a deep breath and squished down each of those thoughts. Stacey didn't *want* any of those other women or she would still be in a relationship with one of them. I'd seen the expression in her eyes, and there was definitely a level of thinking I was hot in her expression. Why would she suddenly one-eighty on how close, how emotionally open we were with each other if we started dating? And if we were sharing our feelings openly, then there was no reason she'd suddenly panic and dump me after a few months. And most importantly, unlike her previous girlfriends, I understood and accepted how much of her life was focused on skiing.

Being scared was totally understandable. But…wasn't this the time in my life when I was supposed to be taking chances, doing new things, making life changes so I could move forward into being an adult? And telling Stacey how I felt was the biggest taking-a-chance of all. I knew that what we shared was unlike anything either of us had shared with anyone else, and I wasn't an idiot—I knew what attraction looked like. Maybe all this time I'd just been too scared to let myself hope that maybe she might really feel the same.

So I'd tell her, admit how I felt and take whatever happened and hope what we shared was strong enough to weather this bombshell. Still, the thought of finally admitting to Stace that I was in love with her had my guts twisting. Because I knew with absolute certainty that she loved me as her best friend. But could she ever love me as her girlfriend?

CHAPTER THIRTEEN

Stacey

For a nose that wasn't technically broken, mine really hurt like a broken nose.

Aside from analgesics and shoving an icepack against my face, there was basically nothing I could do except wait for the swelling to go down. And I was so great at waiting. It wasn't my first nose ouch—I'd broken it in a crash when I was eighteen and had had surgery to fix the sidewaysness of it—and maybe give me a slightly better nose—and I'd landed face-first at high speed plenty of times. And honestly, in the scheme of things, a broken nose was preferable to a broken other bone.

But it still sucked.

After I'd responded pitifully to Gem's text telling her, like a sad little kid, that I wanted her to come around and keep me and my nose company, I'd texted Aspen to tell her the news. Then I texted Mom to fill her in on my latest injury. Mom was suitably worried and sympathetic, which just made me desperate for a hug. Living alone really sucked, especially when your parents were off enjoying some well-deserved relaxation.

Once I'd assured Mom that Gemma was on her way around right now to make sure I was okay, and to provide me with my hug, I collapsed back onto the couch with my feet on the coffee table and the baggie of ice against my nose. After being stuck at the ER for over five hours and skipping my post-snow training nutrition, I was beyond hungry. And Mike's hospital vending-food deliveries—I'd convinced him that me eating was more important than fasting in case my nose needed surgerizing—had barely made a dent.

I was too tired and sore to make myself anything to eat, and even a handful of nuts felt beyond my capabilities. Hashtag pathetic. Food delivery it is! But I'd wait for Gem in case she wanted to stay for dinner and maybe a movie and just making me feel better by being here. Even the thought of seeing Gem boosted my kind-of-sour mood. I was in a sulky funk. Why couldn't I stop hurting myself in training and giving myself my own enforced training breaks? Injuries were inevitable, but having two so close together was frustrating as heck. So, I'd do what I'd done with my still-healing finger—as soon as the swelling eased up, I was going to be back training. Who cared if I looked goofy, as long as I could breathe enough to make it down a racecourse or through a gym workout.

Gemma drove into my turnaround ten minutes after our text exchange. My icepack and I stood in the doorway while she parked, surprised when instead of her usual sonic-boom car door slam, she pushed it quietly closed.

As she jogged up to my front door, Gem stuffed her hands in her pockets, and kept her head bent down against the light sprinkle of rain. Oddly, when she finally raised her gaze to make eye contact, I saw something unexpected in her eyes.

Fear.

I had no idea why she was afraid, and it sent a ripple of unease through me. When I held out my hand, Gemma took it, squeezing as I pulled her inside. "Hey, Gemmy Gem," I mumbled from behind my icebag as I closed the door.

The fear seemed to melt from her as she slipped her shoes off. She took her time hanging her coat and camera bag before turning to face me. "Hey." She looked up at me, eyes narrowing as she studied me. But it wasn't an angry expression, more like she was trying to figure it out. "What have you done to yourself, Stace?"

"Clipped a gate, same-same, no big deal, right? Maybe the pole snapped back and cracked me right in the nose. Or I just hit it super hard." I still wasn't quite sure how it'd all happened in such a split second, but the proof I'd run face-first into a gate pole was on my face. "It's worse than it looks."

Her left eyebrow shot up. "Really? Well that's a nice change from your usual Ms. Macho 'It's not as bad as it looks' response."

I smiled at her and regretted it. Time to practice Botox face to protect my nose. "Yeah. I'm learning." I pulled the icebag away, leaning down so she could get her inspection out of the way.

Gemma's face fell. "Oh, Stace. Ouch. It looks so painful." She reached for me, then thankfully dropped her hands before she made contact with my swollen nose.

I exhaled slowly. "Yeah." I gingerly touched my cheekbones under my eyes, which had started to turn purple the last I'd checked. "But, thankfully it's only really freakin' sore, not actually broken or anything, so my good looks are intact. Lucky Instagram."

She laughed, but it sounded forced. "They sure are. And yeah, lucky Instagram." She took a tiny step forward and carefully, as if checking to see if I'd move, took my face in her hands. Her palms were gentle and warm against my cheeks and she turned my head slowly from side to side to study my nose. "Yep," she whispered. "As hot as ever." For once, she wasn't masking her expression, and the open desire in her eyes, the unmistakable look of lust or love or whatever it was, made my stomach clench.

Once I'd deciphered Gemma's expression, my response barely squeaked out around the tightness in my throat and the sudden excitement rushing through me. "Thanks." Lame. Inadequate. But it was the only thing I could think to say.

She hugged me again, catching me off-guard, and I felt the deep inhalation as she squeezed me. I probably would have just kept hugging her, absorbing her comfort and love if Gem hadn't said, "I'm glad you're okay." She pulled back, and I lost myself in the blue of her eyes. "You *are* okay, right?" she asked quietly, almost like she was afraid I'd say no, I wasn't okay.

And yeah, I was so not okay, but not in the way she must have thought. "Mhmm, I am. Aside from the fact I'm starving and I can't find the energy to create food. You wanna order some dinner?"

Gem's teeth brushed her lower lip. "Oh. Aspen's cooking and she's expecting me back in a bit for dinner, so I probably shouldn't. But I don't mind if you order in now while I'm here. Or I could make you something?"

"You'd cook for me?"

She paused for a few seconds. "I'd do anything for you."

The way she said it was different. Instead of the teasing or pretend exasperated vibe she'd usually use for such an utterance, this time it felt...intimate, and I realized immediately that something had shifted. Something between us.

"I know. And me too. For you, obvs." I almost blurted out more, told her my feelings right there and then—it seemed kinda like she'd be okay with it—but the thought of putting that out in the open made me suddenly panicked.

Smiling, Gem repeated my, "I know."

We just stared at each other with this weird, charged vibe crackling between us. But apparently, neither of us knew what to do with it, and an unspoken agreement seemed to pass between us, and we just...let it go.

Gem's expression was forced calm as I settled at my breakfast bar, leaning an elbow on the counter to prop my ice bag against my nose as she made me a ham and cheese sandwich to tide me over while she cooked pasta for my dinner.

As I ate my sandwich, I kept watching her. She moved around my kitchen like it was hers. She belonged in my house, and I had to keep pushing aside the intrusive thought that I should just tell her that I was in love with her, put it all out in the open and wear the consequences. Or, maybe I should ask her what was up and open up the space for her to tell me what was on her mind.

I finished my sandwich in record time, dropped the ice bag on the counter, slid from the stool and went around to put my plate in the sink. She didn't move, didn't look up at me, didn't say anything. It was like she was doing everything she could to pretend I wasn't right there beside her. I lightly touched her back. "Gemmy?"

She didn't look up from chopping vegetables. "Yeah?"

"What's up? You seem like something's bothering you, or maybe you're upset about something?"

She avoided eye contact, instead focusing on the red pepper she was dicing. "Nope, not upset. But—" She let a shrug finish the sentence for her, which really didn't tell me anything.

I rubbed her back. "Hey, come on. You can just say it, you can tell me anything, right?"

"I know, it's just…" Gem swallowed hard and finally, finally looked me in the eyes. She set the knife down and turned to face me fully. "Stace."

I grinned. "Gemmy Gem."

Smiling back at me, she shoved at my shoulder. "How do you always do that?"

"Do what?"

She said something completely unexpected. "Totally disarm me. Take away my fears and make everything seem like it's going to be okay." She took a deep, slow breath. "I've been thinking about this from the minute I first saw you. Almost every day, every time we're together, when we're not together, it's just always there."

The implication of what she was thinking, what she might be about to say, made my mouth go dry. "Thinking about what? What's there?"

She didn't hesitate for even microsecond. "That I love you."

My heart was galloping, and again, instead of saying something clever, or asking if she was saying what I thought she might be saying, what I knew she was saying, I just smiled stupidly and said, "I know, I love you too."

Her expression turned helpless, as if she couldn't understand how I was being so dense. She jiggled her shoulders, the way she did when she was nervous before we skied a run she found hard. "No, I mean, I *love* you." Gem's eyes were wide, searching mine, begging me to listen to her. "I'm *in* love with you, Stacey. I have been for years. And I've just been trying to ignore it, because I didn't think you felt anything like that for me, and you've had girlfriends, and we're the bestest of friends and I've been terrified of screwing all that up by telling you that I'm in love with you."

"Oh," I said dumbly. Yup, I was so stupid.

She inhaled slowly and took my hand. "Now...I think I've seen some things that make me think it's not just one-sided, things I kinda think I've been pretending aren't there because I was scared to see them. But I don't want to pretend anymore." She traced gentle circles on my palm. "Am I imagining it?"

"You're not," I whispered.

"Good," she exhaled.

The realization of what was happening between us had my entire body quivering with anticipation. "What changed?" I asked hoarsely.

Her mouth quirked into a smile. "I decided to stop being scared of what might happen if I told you. And I decided to stop pretending that I wasn't seeing the way you're looking at me now." Gem leaned closer, her eyes never leaving mine.

Then she kissed me.

It wasn't a complete surprise, but she still caught me off-guard and it took me a moment to recover, to realize I was kissing Gemma. *Gemma*. My best friend. My sweet, gorgeous, wonderful best friend. *Finally*. I was kissing Gemma.

She was gentle, but not tentative, as soft, warm lips carefully caressed mine. The sensation was unlike anything I'd ever experienced, sending a rush of warmth through me. Then her lips went suddenly still and I felt her pull back, as if she suddenly regretted kissing me. Regret was the last thing on my mind, and I wrapped an arm around her waist and held her against me.

Gem made a quiet sound, a whimper and a groan in one, gripping the front of my hoodie to pull herself closer to me. And it was Gem who opened her mouth and invited me even deeper. I would have obliged, except my nose bumped against her cheek, and all my focus moved from the sensation of kissing Gem, of the rightness of that feeling, of the pleasure and the safety of the kiss, to the pain in my face. I pulled back, blinking hard to get rid of the avalanche of tears.

Gemma, adorable, sweet, thoughtful Gemma was so flustered she barely managed to say, "I'm so sorry. I didn't mean to kiss you. I was just going to tell you how I felt and then just—"

I held up my hand, unable to articulate anything except, "Ohhhh oww, owwwww." I managed some vague gestures—a stop sign, an extended forefinger, weak finger flapping—as I tried to tell her without words that the kiss was amazing, but I'd bumped my nose and that was so not amazing.

"Oh, *oh*, it's your nose." Gem's hands came to her mouth. "Oh, Stace, I'm so sorry." Thankfully her apology seemed to be for the nose bump, not the kiss. I wasn't sorry about the kiss either.

"It's okay." The choked whisper of my response wasn't exactly convincing, but it really was okay. I took a slow breath through my mouth, trying to focus on something other than the pain. "Ahhh. Ouch."

Gemma's tender hands came back to my face and she gently wiped under my eyes to clear the tears. "It's not bleeding."

"No? Good." I took a few more slow, deep breaths through my mouth. "It really is okay, I just need a moment to get my breath back."

"Is that your way of saying the kiss made you breathless?"

"Wow. Corny. But yes, it did." I brushed the stray piece of her bangs out of her eyes, tucking it behind her ear, where it immediately escaped again. "Love, huh?"

Her expression turned serious. "Yes. Love. I love you. And I'm in love with you."

"Me too. And I'm so scared," I admitted in a near-whisper.

She widened her eyes, her mouth twitching into a smile. "What, you? Never."

"I know, hard to believe." I took a few more slow, shallow breaths. "Because what if this doesn't work and then things are weird between us? Not that I don't think it will work, or that we're suddenly going to start fighting if we're dating, but what if it changes things somehow?"

"I'm always going to be your best friend, Stace." She drew back, suddenly super-serious. "Do you really think we'd have a fight all of a sudden just because we're dating?"

"Well, no, but…" I shrugged, and finally admitted, "I can't control any of this. It's all variables."

"Not true. You can control how you approach dating me, and I'll control how I approach dating you, and we trust each other the way we always have." She rubbed the outside of my biceps, and lightly squeezed. "I'm scared too. I've been trying to hide it because I didn't want to push it onto you, and I was worried that things might change, same as you are. But Aspen made me realize some things are too important to ignore forever."

"She's good at that."

Laughing, Gem agreed, "She is."

"Speaking of Aspen…what about Aspen?"

"What about her?"

"She's my coach, she's your mom. Do you think this might be a conflict for her?" My relationship with my coach was key to my success, and I would never do anything to jeopardize that.

Her eyebrows scrunched in. "No, I don't think so. She knows how to put everything in its proper compartment. You could talk to her if you're worried, but it was Aspen who told me to tell you how I really felt, so I don't think she's that worried. She made me realize that never telling you how I felt, maybe never having the opportunity to try a relationship with you, maybe always wondering 'what if?' would be way worse than anything bad"—she air-quoted—"that might happen."

"Bad like what?"

"Like you freaking out instead of telling me you loved me back. That maybe if it doesn't work out then we can't find a way to be friends again. That maybe—"

"I don't think that's going to happen," I interrupted, not wanting to think about how we might ruin things. Because how could we ruin something so solid? I had to believe that we couldn't, wouldn't. "I mean, we're best friends, Gemmy. We already know each other so well, and this friendship is the most important thing to me. I won't jeopardize that and I'll do everything to protect it. Even if we decide that for some stupid reason we're not meant to date."

"I know. It's—" She cut herself off, shaking her head. "I love you," she repeated. "And that's not going to change." Gem wrapped her arms around my waist, pulling us together, and it felt so natural that I did the same, my fingertips tracing up and down the small of her back. She smiled, a shy, secretive smile like she couldn't quite believe what had happened in the last five minutes. "Stacey, I fell head over heels in love with you that first day we skied together. Remember? It was the week after you guys were in that avalanche at A-Basin, and Aspen had her broken wrist. And you came with me for some runs after your training. Just little baby blue runs. And I was so scared and freaked by the avalanche thing, even though we were on a different mountain, and I was so embarrassed about being scared and not being a pro skier like you. But you literally held my hand and made it seem like no big deal that I just hockey-stop skied the whole way down. And you've taken me on so many other ski runs since then and I've trusted you every single time to keep me safe on the mountain. And I trust you now, off the mountain, to love me back and do everything you can, same as I will, to make this work out."

I tilted my head and softly kissed each of her cheeks, but kept myself from kissing her mouth again. I knew once I did that, I wouldn't be able to stop, and I wanted us to talk, wanted her to hear me out too. "I love you too, Gem, and same…I've been in love with you for ages but I've been doing the pretending thing too. I've been too scared to say anything because I didn't want this to change our friendship. I value that so much and I was scared of scaring you away."

"You'd never scare me away," she said quietly.

"I hope not." I traced my thumb over the soft fullness of her lower lip. The thought of pushing her away was more frightening than anything I could think of, scarier than the gnarliest of ski runs, the most important of races. "Thanks for being the brave one."

Gem drew in a quick breath, her words coming out unevenly. "Me the brave one for once. Shocking."

"I don't think so. You've always been brave." I leaned in, the anticipation of kissing her again making my stomach flutter. "Now, kiss me again, but please…let's be very careful of my nose."

CHAPTER FOURTEEN

Gemma

I mean, I'd thought for sure I'd still have a best friend after I told Stacey how I felt, but the idea of maybe having a girlfriend too had felt like…fries with a burger. Just a bonus. But a really good bonus.

We'd talked while Stacey ate dinner, not really about us except for confirming that we really were dating. It was just a regular easy conversation like we'd had B.G.—before girlfriends—but mostly we just kinda stared at each other, both of us smiling like goofy idiots. And I couldn't stop thinking about how light I felt after getting that off my chest, how relaxed, as if I'd been holding on to it as a sort of hidden emotional weight. Then there'd been the mental forehead slap that we'd taken so long to finally admit it to each other. Fear was so dumb.

Stacey and I agreed that each of us should speak with Aspen separately because she was different things to each of us, and while us dating wasn't really anyone's business, it kind of was given how entwined we all were. Stacey would mention it to Brick, for the same reason and because she wanted him to be prepared for the new social media stuff that would mention me. She'd smiled as she'd said that, but it was a tight, forced smile. But when I asked what she'd meant, she just shook her head and changed the subject.

I knew her public persona was somewhat controlled, and that she hated having to think about every post she put on social media. But I'd always assumed she just accepted it as part of her job, because I'd never really been involved aside from on the periphery in posts about friend stuff—mostly skiing related— over the years.

When I'd reluctantly said I had to leave, only because I knew I had to get home for dinner, she'd smiled and pulled me against her. As I melted into her, Stacey's arms slid low around my waist, her fingers slipping under my jacket to caress the small of my back. "Bravest person I know," she murmured, before dipping her head and kissing me carefully but not softly. I was really looking forward to her nose healing so we could be less careful with each other…

While I'd been out, Mom had come home from work and had given me a knowing smile before her usual hug and forehead-kiss greeting. Yep, Aspen had definitely told her where I'd been and why. And aside from asking me if everything had gone well, Aspen had also been conspicuously silent about asking what had happened at Stacey's. We were a talking-it-out family, so the silence was unusual. We'd eaten dinner, I'd tried not to grin like a fool the whole time because I couldn't stop thinking about Stacey, and then I'd excused myself to study.

Study, brain. Not daydreaming. I'd caught myself staring dreamily at my desktop background, thinking of all the photos we could take together as girlfriends. Right. I had to focus. Homework. Finals. Film project. Thinking about Stacey and me. Later. I managed to focus on study for a solid hour before I took a break and checked my emails. There was just one. From CU Boulder.

My heart was pounding as I logged in to the portal to check the status of my final college application. Then I carefully closed the browser and went downstairs to talk to my parents. I was a quarter of the way down when I heard some of Mom and Aspen's conversation.

Aspen said, "You know the first thing I thought when we were talking about it this afternoon, aside from how thrilled I was that they might finally admit how they feel, and that I love the idea of them being together, was that I was worried for them."

"Why?" Mom asked.

Aspen took a few moments to answer. "I don't want either of them to get hurt. When I first saw Stacey again right before we began working together, she was so confident and cocky, the kind of kid I would have been jealous of as a teenager, and she was only sixteen. And one of the first thoughts I had right then was she's going to be such a heartbreaker when she's older. I just don't want her breaking our daughter's heart. I know Stacey and I know she's a good person and she'd never do it intentionally, but what if it happens?"

"As much as it kills me to even think it, someone is probably going to break our daughter's heart at some point in her life. Few of us get away without that happening."

"I know, but she's *Gemma* and I don't want that. And I also don't want Stacey to get hurt if they break up."

Break up? That was the last thing on my mind. I mean, yeah, *maybe* it'd happen, but who started a relationship and immediately thought about breaking up?

Mom laughed quietly. "I don't want that either, but it's not going to kill them to experience life in all its messy glory, including everything that comes from being in love."

There was some quiet murmuring I couldn't quite make out, and I snuck down another few stairs to try and hear the rest of what they were saying.

"Aspen, we both know Stacey. She doesn't have a malicious bone in her body. She would never deliberately do anything to hurt Gem. And we also know Gemma. She's not going to deliberately hurt Stacey. If something happens, it'll just be regular relationship stuff. And I hope—no, I think I *know*—that their friendship is strong enough to withstand whatever might happen."

"I know that, god I know it. It's just…" Aspen sounded frustrated. "And I know she's going to have sex, I mean, shit… maybe she already has, and she'll maybe have kids and get married and do all of that grown up stuff, but…"

"But what?"

"But it's different."

"Why?"

"Because she's *our* daughter, Cate. Of course I want her to grow up and live a fabulous life and experience everything she possibly can, but I also just want to bundle her up and protect her from everything."

"That's just parenthood, honey. It's been happening for years, remember? We can't stop her from growing up and experiencing life. *All* of life, including sex and marriage and maybe kids."

"Are you *sure* we can't?" Aspen asked, but it wasn't serious.

Unable to keep quiet anymore, I called down the stairs, "I'm not a nun, you know."

There was a pause before a quiet laugh. "Yet!" Aspen called back, though it was with the teasing voice she used when we were messing around.

Mom's sigh was audible even from where I was. "Gemma, stop eavesdropping on the stairs and come down here, please."

I clomped down into the living room where Mom and Aspen were on the couch facing each other, holding hands, knees touching. Taylor acknowledged me with a brief tail wag before returning to her important napping business. Mom looked kinda neutral, kinda alarmed, kinda pleased. Aspen was trying very hard to not smile.

Aspen held out her hand to me and tugged me to sit on the couch between her and Mom. I snuggled against Mom, hating that I now had to squirm to get comfy when I used to fit so easily. Getting old sucked. Mom wrapped both arms around me, hugging me tight like she was trying to squeeze any upset out of me. But I wasn't upset. How could I be?

"We're so happy for you, sweetheart," Mom said. "But we're also just being parents. We're always going to worry about you, even when you're doing something we know makes you happy."

I twisted to look up at her. "It does make me happy. And I know you guys are worried, but if I just keep avoiding things for the rest of my life because I might get hurt, then I'll never do anything." It'd taken me eighteen years to realize that sometimes I'd just have to cross my fingers and take the leap. Better late than never.

"Yes, you're right," Mom said.

I asked Aspen, "Are you *sure* it's not really a problem for you? Like, a conflict of interest because I'm your daughter and you're Stacey's coach?"

She took a few moments to answer. "I know both of you can be mature about it. And I can be professional. You're always going to be my priority, Gem. Always. We'll just take it a day at a time and whatever happens, happens. And if I wasn't sure, would I have told you to be honest with her and tell her how you felt?"

"I guess not." I thought back to what Aspen had said earlier. "She won't break my heart. So you won't have to be tough with her." I squirmed so I could sit up in between them.

Aspen burst into laughter. "You think I'm going to be a thug to Stacey? 'Treat my girl right or else'?" She could barely get the words out around her laughter.

The idea was pretty funny, and Mom and I joined in with the hilarity.

When we'd stopped giggling, Mom started playing with my hair. "We just want you to be careful, and take things slowly."

"Right," Aspen agreed. "We know you love her, and that your friendship is solid and amazing. Just…don't schuss down the relationship hill before you've had a chance to check out the terrain first."

"Don't do *what*?" Schuss was a bar at Thredbo, the ski resort where we'd met in Australia. I only remembered that because it was a strange word. It made no sense in this context.

"Schuss," Aspen repeated, frowning. "Have I really never taught you that term?" The frown got frownier. "You haven't even heard it from Stacey?" When I shook my head, she almost choked. "That might count as parental neglect! I'm the worst ski instructor in the world, and I know, because I've coached all around the globe. It means to ski straight down the fall line, skis parallel, super-fast, no turns, no brakes."

"Ohhhh, right. You could have just said that in normal-people language. You know, maybe 'Don't rush into things, Gemma'?"

She grinned. "Can't, brain's always in ski mode."

"Like Stacey," I said dryly.

"Exactly." Aspen rubbed my shoulder. "All I'm saying is take some time, make some turns, snowplow if you need to, and get to know her as your girlfriend as well as your friend before you jump into something, uh, more serious."

I bit my lower lip, thinking. "But what if I'm already at the bottom of the run though? Like…I got there a while ago, years maybe." Because we already knew each other so well, were so comfortable with each other, shared so much trust. And now that there was something else there too, wouldn't the natural progression be to sex?

Aspen let out a long breath as she glanced at Mom, who shrugged, laughing. "You keep going, darling. This ski metaphor talk you've started is all yours."

Aspen inhaled slowly. "Then I'd say…take a break before you get on the chairlift again."

Mom and Aspen exchanged A Look and I braced myself for A Discussion. Mom said calmly, "We just want you to be careful with your heart and with…doing…other stuff."

"Are you trying to tell me I shouldn't be having sex?"

The pause was so long, I thought I might have broken both of them with my question. Both Mom and Aspen sat there, as if my question just didn't compute. It was Mom who seemed to snap back into consciousness first. "You're legally an adult, Gem, and if you think you're ready, then we trust you." Despite her assertion, she looked almost like she was telling me it was okay to go do something illegal. I knew she didn't think me having sex with Stacey, or anyone, was actually a crime, but it was more that she was having a hard time imagining the whole thing.

"It's not like either of us can get pregnant," I said. They both smiled, but the mutual lip-tightness told me my joke had fallen flat in the face of parents worrying about their kid having sex. Sigh.

"No," Mom agreed, "but once you've done this, it's different. And we just want you to be sure."

"I am sure. And I'm sure she's sure, not that we've actually talked about it, because we literally just started dating three hours ago. But I love her and I know she loves me, and we're not strangers, so why wouldn't we go the next step? When we decide we're ready," I added hastily in an attempt to keep their brains inside their heads.

"I know that, sweetie. And love is a wonderful foundation to take that next step of having sex. But there's no rush. If you're sure, then you're sure and we trust you," Mom said again. "But…"

"But," Aspen picked up where Mom had faltered, "we can't stop you from having sex, and we wouldn't want to. We just want you to be prepared for what it might mean for you beyond just the um, physical enjoyment of it. We know you've got hormones and we're well aware of what that's like."

Mom coughed out a sound like she was choking, her eyes wide and begging Aspen to not say anything more about their *awareness*, and I silently begged that this was as far as they'd go with the whole parents-having-sex thing. Thankfully it was.

Laughing, I poked Aspen in the ribs. "Is it as bad as you thought it'd be? The S-E-X talk with your kid?" We'd already talked about it years ago, of course, but it'd been a "Hey this might happen when you're older" thing, not a "This is imminent" thing.

Aspen grinned. "Ohhh, no, *this* wasn't the sex talk. But we can have that again if you wan—"

"No, thank you," I interrupted. I knew how things worked, and was happy with keeping it all unembarrassing like this. "So what talk was this then?"

"This was the…make sure you do a course inspection so you know what to expect before you rush down the hill talk."

Mom groaned as I jabbed Aspen in the arm with my forefingers. "Again with the ski metaphors."

"Oh I've barely dipped into my repertoire, pal. Just you wait."

I slumped back into the couch. "That's just it. I don't want to wait. I've waited years for this."

Mom made a garbled strangled sound. Aspen rubbed her shoulder and picked up where Mom seemed unable. "There's no rush, Gem. Like you said, you guys only just started dating. It's okay to give yourself some time to get used to your new normal."

Tell that to my hormones and the crush I'd been holding on to for four years. "But what if she decides she doesn't want to wait until I'm ready or that I'm not worth it?" Stace was twenty, almost twenty-one, and she'd had girlfriends—sex would be part of her expectation for sure. It was part of my expectation too, but I also had no idea what to expect with my expectation. I'd never really considered sex with anyone I'd dated, and not because I didn't feel ready or because I was worried about it, but because none of them were people I wanted to sleep with, just for the sake of getting it over with.

Mom tapped in to give Aspen a breather. "Then is she worthy of giving that to? Is she that special then?"

I knew she didn't mean it like it'd come out, that Stacey wasn't special, but it still made me bristle. "She is to me," I said indignantly. "Because beyond the fact of how I feel about her, I keep thinking what if we break up, and I've just been sitting on this for ages, waiting and waiting just because I think I should wait for…whatever reason, and then it never happens?" And I so wanted it to happen with her.

"If you're worried about breaking up already, then maybe you two need to have a talk about your expectations and where you think this relationship is going," Mom said carefully.

"I'm not worried about it," I grumbled. "And I think we know it's going as far as we both want to take it. It's just a stupid anxiety thought with all the others because you guys are making me think about it." I'd given up the anxiety of actually telling Stacey and now I had another anxiety focus.

Mom exhaled a long breath. "Right. Okay. Well, it's normal to be anxious about something new. And as Aspen said, there's no rush. If you think the time is right, then just see what happens."

"That's our plan." I left off that it felt like the right time was now. "Sooo…to take the conversation away from my impending sexual revelation"—I swear they both choked when I said that—"I just got my final response from my college applications. An acceptance from CU Boulder."

They couldn't have looked more pleased. Aspen was closer and she hugged me tightly, kissed the top of my hair, hugged me more tightly. "That's amazing, we're so proud of you! You are *so* clever."

She released me so I could get a Mom-hug too, which then turned into an all-of-us hug. Mom was obviously both proud and emotional, because all she kept saying was, "So proud of you, we love you so much," just over and over like a glitching audio file. When we finally separated, she sneakily wiped under her eyes. Aspen looked like she'd just won a billion dollars.

"Now you've had responses from all your applications, have you thought any more about which one you're going to accept?" Mom tried to feign indifference, but she was such a mom that she failed.

I gently dissuaded Taylor, rallied by the excitement, from trying to get onto a couch that was already full. "I'm pretty sure CU. It's a good school with good programs." I knew before I said it that I was going to be met with some resistance.

"It is a good school," Mom agreed, but her tone was careful. I knew what she was holding back on.

Both of Aspen's hands came to her chest, fingers pointing at herself. "Hey, I went to CU Boulder. It's a great school. I have a degree in engineering physics, magna cum laude, remember? It's a great school!"

"Yes, darling," Mom said, patting Aspen's shoulder while I held back my snort. "We remember." She turned her focus on me before turning to face Aspen, who raised her eyebrows at Mom in that expression that meant "This one's all yours, babe."

I got in first. "I know what you're both going to say. But CU is in the top twenty-five film programs in the country, and their science programs are great. And like Aspen keeps saying, they're a really good school and their focus is more on independent and experimental film, which is what I'm interested in, not doing SFX of a mutant mouse eating a car. And I mean, let's face it, as much as Stanford and USC would have been amazing, they were my reach applications and so, I'm happy with my choice." I wanted to make documentaries about science and nature, work for Nat Geo maybe, be the next Sir David Attenborough. The Michael Bay action blockbuster stuff just wasn't me and CU Boulder felt like the best choice for everything I wanted for school and my personal life.

"It's also close to us. And to Stacey," Mom said, as if she'd read my mind.

"That doesn't change the fact it's a good school with programs that align with my aspirations to be a documentary filmmaker," I rebutted. "We already talked to my Advisor about all my options, remember? And you guys supported each of my college applications and said you were happy with every one of them."

"Yes, we did. We do support your choices," Mom said. "And we're not just saying that."

"And CU is one of the cheaper schools," I pointed out.

Aspen almost choked in her haste to tell me, "You know money for your education isn't an issue, Gem."

She was right, and I was extremely lucky that Mom had saved for my college and that Aspen's life aspirations were be a pro alpine ski racer, get married, and have kids—not necessarily in that order. I knew she'd been saving to pay for college for her offspring right from her first race-win paycheck and it just so happened she'd absorbed me and Mom as her family and I was now her offspring.

Mom took a deep breath and I braced myself. Thankfully, she went the softer route. "Gem, we just want you to have the best opportunities you can possibly have. To make the right choices for your life, your *whole* life, not just the right now. I know how close you and Stacey are, and that you've just started something wonderful and exciting, an emphasis on the just, but—"

"Mom—"

Aspen pulled me into a hug. "Let her finish, sweetie."

Mom shot her a grateful look. "But is that very new relationship worth sacrificing your chance to build your dream, just to be closer to her when she's home training?" I caught the unspoken, that Stacey traveled for five or six months of the year for competitions and training camps, ping-ponging from home to somewhere in the States to back home and some other country, and during the race season she wouldn't even be in Colorado for most of the US time.

That had definitely factored into my thoughts, but why wouldn't I want to be as close to Stacey—and my family for that matter—as I could be, when we could be? Why would I choose to go to school across the country where I'd maybe see her for a day once a month, and then hardly at all for half the year? Studying in Boulder meant a two-hour drive instead of a long flight. I could come back to Edwards whenever my classes let me, and Stacey could even come visit me if she wanted. It was a no-brainer.

I held back my sigh. "A sacrifice? Dramatic, much? No school is going to tick all the boxes for education and the whole student, living in a dorm, learning to be an adult, experience." Not that I really wanted that whole student party life. "Didn't you say I should do what makes me happy, which will make my study easiest and most fulfilling?"

"I did," Aspen agreed, though she looked like she regretted our previous conversation at the start of last month.

"This is what's going to make me happy," I asserted.

They glanced at each other, Aspen nodded, but it was Mom who answered. She actually seemed more relaxed now, as if she'd accepted what I wanted. "Then we're happy for you. And so proud," she snuck in.

"Yeah, I kinda got that part, all the million times you've said it."

"Smartass," Aspen drawled.

"I love you guys." I snuggled into them, trying to hold back the sudden onslaught of tears. Totally not sad tears. Excited tears. This decision was the start of the rest of my life. And judging by everything that'd happened today, my life was going to be amazing.

CHAPTER FIFTEEN

Stacey

Thanks to some epic spring dumps, we'd been able to keep training at Copper Mountain after it had officially closed for the season. Having the snow almost to ourselves was awesome, as was the amusement of the mountain prepping for the summer hikers and mountain bikers while I was racing down some amazing training snow on another part.

Aspen had grumbled about me training with both busted finger and nose, but there was *no way* I was going to sit on the couch while I still had all this on my doorstep. Neither nose nor finger were unskiable injuries—I could breathe, I could hold my pole, and I was being careful to not injure either of them further, which would mean I'd really have to wrap up my on-snow training. And my training was going way too well to end it early.

Once we were done for the morning, I helped pack up the racing gates, course dye sprayers and tools, and my many pairs of racing skis into Christina's Secret Service level of care, then rode the snowmobiles up onto their trailers, the only time I ever got to pilot one. After saying bye to the team and thanking them all, I walked with Aspen back to the practically empty parking lot where we'd parked side by side.

Now was as good a time as any to tell her about Gemma and me, though I was sure she already knew what had happened last night. I still couldn't quite believe it, and every time I thought about the look Gem had given me right before she kissed me, my stomach did backflips. But I was still surprisingly nervous about telling my coach about us. Aspen and Mrs. Archer were both really cool women, but there was a difference between "best friends cool" and "girlfriends cool."

"Can I talk to you about something?"

Aspen stopped wiping down her skis and straightened up, her whole focus now on me. "Of course. What's up?"

"I'm sure you already know but I just wanted you to hear it from me too, that Gem and I are dating. Officially."

Aside from a flicker at the edge of her mouth, her expression didn't change. "Yes, Gemma mentioned it." She patted my shoulder fondly. "I'm really happy for both of you, Stacey. Truly." Aspen resumed cleaning snow from her skis.

"Thanks. I mean, it's only just happened but I think we're pretty happy too. I can't believe it took us so long to finally admit it, you know?"

"Neither can I," she said dryly. "Cate and I had almost accepted that you two were just going to feign oblivion for the rest of your lives."

"Well, in this case, I'm glad to not live up to your expectations."

Smiling, Aspen nodded. But she remained silent as she strapped her skis together and secured them to the racks on top of her car.

"You look like something's bugging you," I observed, almost afraid of what she'd say in response.

After a few moments, during which I held my breath waiting, Aspen quietly said, "Stacey, Cate and I just want you and Gem to be happy, you know that, right?"

Oh shit. This was so going to turn into a "but" conversation. "Right."

"And me as your coach is completely separate to me being Gemma's mom."

"Mhmm." Now I really had a sinking feeling about where this conversation was heading.

"So how I think about her being your girlfriend is different to how I think about you being her girlfriend, if that makes sense." Aspen let out a long breath. "But it *is* something I have to think about."

"I know."

"Because things you experience away from the racecourse can affect what happens on the racecourse, right?" Without waiting for me to agree with anything more than a nod, Aspen barreled on. "And I hope you know it's not going to change our coaching relationship, but at the same time I also have to think about eventualities with you and Gemma and…this."

I knew Aspen wasn't implying she thought Gem and I would break up and that it would be messy and horrible and mean, but there was a definite vibe of "what if this doesn't work?" I inhaled slowly and let the cool air calm me. "I love her. And look, I get this is probably super awkward for you with the mom *and* coach thing, but—"

She gently gripped my shoulder, and started massaging with her fingertips. "Hey, chill. I don't want you two to break up. I know how important your friendship is to both of you, and now the relationship as well. I know how good you both are for each other and how supportive you guys are. But I'd be a bad coach and a bad mom if I didn't think about the implications of you two dating. And if you and Gem decide you're better off as friends, then I want to be sure that neither of you is hurt by that decision."

"I don't think we will be." I leaned against my car. "Gemma as my best friend is probably the most important non-family relationship to me, maybe tied with my coaching relationship with you, and I'll do anything to keep that friendship, even if we end up deciding girlfriends just doesn't work for us. But I think it will. I mean…it's us, you know?"

"Yeah, I know. And I'm really happy for you two, and also so relieved that it's *you* so we don't have to worry about her dating someone we don't know at all."

I grinned at her. "No 'hurt her and I'm coming for you' speech?"

She feigned horror. "Of course not. Cate and I, and Gemma, know you'd never deliberately hurt Gemma. You're a good person, Stace. And Gem is beyond lucky to have someone like you in her life as both her friend and girlfriend."

"You're real sweet, coach."

Aspen came back with the same response she'd given me ever since I'd first said that to her. "I have been told that a time or two before."

"Or two hundred…" I opened the front passenger door of my car and sat down, facing her, so I could exchange my snow boots for sneakers for the drive home. "Look, I don't know what's going to happen, but obviously we're looking long term and we're going to do everything we can to make it work."

"I know you both are, and you both will." She mirrored my posture in her driver's seat, sitting sideways and pulling her feet up to rest on the running board. Her expression told me she wanted to say more, but was either trying to figure out how, or she was rethinking saying anything at all.

I stretched my foot out and nudged her shin with the tips of my toes. "Spill it, coach."

Aspen looked like what she was about to say pained her. "I know we haven't encountered this problem before with your other girlfriends, you being cut up about a breakup, and then your training or racing suffering, but as an outsider looking in, I think that's because you didn't, uh…care about them the way you do Gemma."

Ah. Yeah. "No, I didn't," I admitted. "I mean I cared about them in some way I guess, but I've never loved any of them." I held up a hand. "And yeah, I know it makes me sound like a selfish dick."

Aspen's expression softened. "It makes you sound like a twenty-year-old who's just trying things and figuring life stuff out."

I supposed she was right. I hadn't been cruel or unavailable—except when I had to be unavailable for racing—or given any of my previous girlfriends an unrealistic expectation of what dating me would be like. Was it really my fault if they didn't listen to what I'd so clearly laid out? "I guess. I thought I was supposed to have a pretty good idea of myself by now. I already have my career all figured out, those goals are set, but everything else feels like it's lagging."

Laughing, Aspen reminded me, "You're twenty, Stace. When I was twenty I was in exactly the same position as you—my whole focus was racing, racing, racing. With some college and even some girls on the side. You don't need to have it all figured out right now. You're a good person, kind and smart and caring. You'll get there."

I felt suddenly, and unusually, emotional about her gentle pep talk. "Thanks," I said quietly.

"We really are happy for you guys. We support you and Gemma dating. I just want you to be aware of the consequences relating to racing, good and not so good."

"I am aware of them. And so is Gemma." I huffed out a long breath. "I think having her as my partner is perfect. I mean, come on, who else aside from my team and my family understands me so well? Knows how hard I have to work, gets that I'm away a lot, supports my dreams? It's like having the best of everything in one person, right?"

"Right," she agreed.

I bit my lower lip. Aspen sounded like she was okay with it, but some of what she'd said made me worried. She'd been right when she'd said I didn't really care about my other girlfriends, didn't really immerse myself in those relationships. Maybe it had been a little like reverse psychology—the more they demanded from me, the less I wanted to give to them? I didn't know exactly why I'd behaved like I had; I wasn't a shrink. But I *did* know that I loved Gemma and she had never demanded anything unrealistic of me, so surely I wouldn't be distant and withhold from her like I had with other girlfriends? God, I hoped not. Shit. But…what if Bree was right? What if I was a horrible, selfish girlfriend who only thought about skiing?

As if sensing I'd gone totally into my head, Aspen sighed loudly. "I'm sorry, Stace. I didn't mean to put a downer on something that's so exciting."

I shrugged. "You didn't. Well, not much."

"I want this to be the best thing that's ever happened to Gemma and to you. Just…remember what I said at our first-ever session together? I need you to talk to me. And if you don't think you can talk to me about this, then talk to your therapist. Let's keep it as the best thing ever, okay?"

"Okay."

"Good. Now get your butt home and rest before you hit the gym."

I saluted. "Aye aye, coach."

"Smartass."

As if Charlie sensed I was all over the place emotionally with excitement and then the bombardment of "I hope you've thought about this" and "Don't screw it up and ruin your focus," he busted my ass at the gym until my brain was empty of all thoughts except how I barely had the energy to get in my car and drive home. And as my brain finally un-mushed, I had an idea. A brilliant idea. I was going to take Gemma on a date. We deserved dates, hanging out as a couple instead of as BFFs.

I'd just stepped out of the shower and was toweling off when a text from Gem arrived. *Leaving school now. Be at your place in 10 min.*

Perfect timing. Just jumped out of the shower.

As soon as I'd sent the text, I second-guessed it. Was it too forward? Too "Hey I'm naked right now, hint-hint maybe we could be naked together sometime"? I would have sent the same thing B.G., so maybe it wasn't. But everything felt innuendo-y now, especially because I knew that Gemma was someone I really wanted to get naked with. And you know, do stuff that usually came when you were naked with someone.

I braced my hands on the bathroom sink and tried to calm my nervous excitement at the thought of sex with Gem. She was the only person that I'd ever come close to considering sharing that with, and for a few seconds I closed my eyes and let myself imagine it. Of course it was perfect, no clumsy fumbling and no awkwardness. Though given how close Gem and I were, how much we trusted each other, maybe all that new stuff we might explore with each other, all that intimacy that required trust we already had, would just click into place.

Gemma. Naked. I'd thought about it so many times, imagined what she might look like, but I knew the real thing would be so much better. I wanted to touch and taste her skin. I wanted to hear what she sounded like when she came. Oh, fuck. What if I couldn't make her come? What if I was a complete sex noob? That worry turned into an irrational one about whether Gem found me sexy. I mean, I was in peak athletic shape, which I knew appealed to a lot of people but I wasn't sure if it appealed to Gemma. My hair was a beast with a mind of its own and my face wasn't model-hot, though some people called me hot on social media, as had a couple of girls I'd dated. But they weren't the one who mattered.

This insecurity and uncertainty was new, and really freaking unpleasant. But hadn't Gemma called me hot just a few days ago? And the look as she'd said it had made me shiver inside. She'd told me with her eyes, her words, her touch, that she found me physically attractive as well as all the inside, character stuff.

I might have stood at the bathroom mirror debating with myself for hours if Gem wasn't on her way over. I was just struggling into a hoodie when the "Hey, someone's here" alert sounded at my front door.

Seeing Gemma felt like the sun coming out to promise a bluebird day. "You know, I really should have given you a key months ago. Remind me to do that."

"You should give me a key," she said.

"Funny," I drawled. "So, you've been here for almost thirty seconds and I haven't touched you yet."

"You should fix that."

Hugging her, I kissed her cheek quickly, then again and again, and when she started laughing I kept going, planting rapid-fire cheek kisses and mumbling, "Mwah-mwah-mwah-mwah-mwah" against her skin until we were both giggling.

I stopped the giggling with a proper kiss, lingering against Gemma's lips until I felt breathless. Thankfully my nose had chilled out and didn't scream too loudly at me when we accidentally bumped noses. I'd had no idea Gem kissed like that, and now I knew, I was addicted to it.

"Mmm," she mumbled against my neck. "You smell good." Gem pulled back. "I missed you today."

I raised my eyebrows. "More than you usually do?"

"No. But now I can tell you how much I miss you when we're not together."

"It's kinda nice, isn't it? Not having to hold back."

"Super nice." She cupped my face with her hands and kissed me slowly. "So is this."

I relaxed into her touch, and my hands wandered with a mind of their own until they found the deliciousness that was Gemma's ass. "I'm not sure I've said it yet, everything's been kind of a blur since we started this—"

"It has," she interrupted, her teeth grazing her lower lip.

"I mean, I think *I love you* is"—I made a dome-y covering type motion with my hands—"a blanket thing that it's all of you I love. But, Gemmy, I want you to know I think you're gorgeous, inside and out. I'm not sure you know how hard it's been to not just stare at you all the time for the last few years."

She grinned. "Oh, no, I know how hard it's been to not stare."

"Phew. Because I think you're freaking hot." And I wanted her to be utterly sure of how I felt about her, didn't want her to feel an ounce of the stupid uncertainty I had before. "And I really wish I was articulate enough to say that in a smarter or sexier way, but you've fritzed my brain." I let my hands wander upward, stopping short of cupping her boobs. Instead, I satisfied myself with stroking up and down her stomach.

Gemma exhaled a shuddering sigh. "Maybe we should go sit down."

I bounced my eyebrows. "You're saying you wanna get more comfortable?"

Laughing, Gem slapped my chest. But she didn't say no…

When I sat at the end of the couch, propped against the arm the way I usually did, Gem motioned for me to put my legs up. Then she sat down, snuggled in between them, leaning back against me. Once Gem settled my arms around her, she sighed deeply, prompting me to ask, "What's up?"

"Nothing. Nothing at all. I was just thinking...*finally*. Us being close like this isn't new, but this feeling is."

"What feeling?" I asked, even though I had a pretty good idea.

"Openness."

"Mmm." I bent down so I could kiss her temple, and Gem turned her head so my kiss landed on her mouth.

"How did your mom and Aspen take the news last night?" I asked when we pulled away. It was so tedious that you couldn't just spend your whole life kissing someone without breaks.

Gem's smile came with a little eye roll. "It went as expected. They're *really* happy for us. But there was A Talk."

"Oh. Was it bad?"

"Nah, just...parenty. And Aspen told me not to schuss our relationship."

"Ha! That's the best definition ever." Oh, but I wanted to schuss it, right to the bottom, right into bed with her.

As if Gem had seen into my brain, she said, "The whole conversation was basically don't rush into things, which was really a coded message for you don't need to have sex with Stacey unless you're ready."

"Oh."

Gemma turned back to look at me and the moment we made eye contact, she grinned. "Oh? That's all you have to say about it?"

I swallowed, desperately trying to get my brain and my mouth to function as a unit instead of my mouth just blurting things before my brain had the chance to approve. "I—" I cleared my throat and my voice was embarrassingly high and squeaky when I asked, "Is that...something you'd like to do with me?"

"Yes," she said immediately. "Very much."

I let out my breath, trying to not let it sound like a rush of relief. Which it totally was. "Okay, good. I mean great. Me too.

Like, I really do. But whenever you're ready, no rush. I can wait. I—"

She sat up and I pulled my legs down so she could turn and sit cross-legged on the couch facing me. "Stace."

"Yeah?"

"I say this with love, but shut up." Then she kissed me to make sure I did just that.

Kissing led to a make-out session where we both remained fully clothed, but I managed to determine that Gem's boobs fit really nicely in my hands, and she figured out that when she sucked my neck I turned to absolute mush.

After what felt like an eternity of amazingness, we both pulled back to take a breather. And maybe to settle down. I'd never been so turned-on, and was this close to asking if she wanted to stay the night. But it still felt too soon to be doing that. Too soon, but I still wanted to do it soon. It seemed Gem had read my body language, or felt the same, because she tucked herself against me and made a timely subject change. "So I got an acceptance last night from CU Boulder. My last one."

"Holy shit, Gemmy!" I scrambled off the couch, dislodging her in the process. She'd barely stood up before I picked her up and swung her around, only just missing whacking her legs against the couch and coffee table. I kissed her hard, then carefully set her down. "Another acceptance! That's amazing! You're amazing."

She shrugged, feigning nonchalance, but I could tell how pleased she was. Once we'd settled back on the couch, I asked, "So now you've got all your replies, have you decided where you'll go?" I almost didn't want to know the answer. I was sure she'd pick Syracuse which, based on my Googling and her information, seemed to be the best of the colleges she'd received acceptances from. And the thought of it made my stomach churn because it was in New York, which meant we'd hardly see each other.

"Mhmm. No brainer. I'm going to CU Boulder." Gem ran her fingertips up my inner thigh. "It ticks all my boxes academically, and it's the closest to home."

I tried to sound stoked, but was pretty sure I fell short with my, "Oh. Cool."

Her fingers stilled. "That doesn't sound like a very excited 'oh cool,' Stace." Gemma shifted backward until we were no longer touching, and I felt the coolness of the gap. "I thought you'd be happy that I'll be close by. We can see each other most weekends, and maybe during the week too."

"I am, Gemmy, I *really* am. That part makes me so freaking happy."

"So what parts make you not so freaking happy?" she asked dryly. She was trying very hard to mask how hurt she was and I wished I was better at explaining emotional things. Ask me to describe a race I'd just skied and I was a Nobel Laureate poet, but talking about feelings was so hard. But Gem deserved me at least trying to tell her why I wasn't turning cartwheels at her news.

Eventually I managed, "I guess it's just you not choosing the best school to pursue your filmmaking career."

"This is the best school for me, right now," she said tightly. "And if I'm in New York or Chicago then it's going to be super hard for me to see you, and my parents, regularly." She looked down, fidgeting with the bottom of her tee. "And…I don't really want to move so far away my first time living away from home. It'd suck to be ages away from Mom and Aspen, *and* you."

I took my time trying to frame my answer in a way that wasn't going to upset her. "I get that. I don't want to be apart from you either, and I know what it's like to not have your parents right there anymore. It sucks." I took a deep breath and dove in. "But you and me? We already spend time apart when I'm competing, so we can cope with whatever happens when you're at college. I just don't think you should completely rule out the other colleges just because they're farther away."

Her mouth twisted the way it always did when she was shitty about something, and trying not to cry. "You sound like Mom and Aspen. They basically said do whatever you want and what makes you happy and that gives you a good education. But only if it's at the best school out of all of them."

"Maybe they have a point," I said carefully.

She swiped hastily under her eyes. "Are you saying you don't want me to be close by while I'm at college?"

"That's *not* what I'm saying at all," I said emphatically, ashamed that I'd upset her. "If I had it my way then you'd be with me every morning when I wake up. I want us to finish our days and come home to each other and then go to bed and do it all again. But that's not practical with my racing and you going to college...wherever you go."

"Really? It doesn't sound that way to me."

"I'm sorry that's how it sounds. I love you, and I don't want you to go away. But I also don't want you to regret your college choice." I slid closer, relieved when she didn't pull back, and took her hands in mine. "I never even went to college, you know that. I dunno, Gemmy, maybe my perspective is warped because I'm a competitive athlete. Do everything the best you can. My point of view is always that if you're aiming for something then you should aim beyond the stars. I wouldn't race with untuned skis or without training and preparation, without dedicating all of myself to it. I wouldn't half-ass it, and I feel like you shouldn't just pick the college that feels the easiest for you."

"No college is going to be easy. It's going to be hard and scary and I'm terrified of it all. So what does it matter if I choose one that's academically comparable to other colleges, but that's going to make it easier to deal with the school stuff?"

She was right, and I was a dick for trying to push her into something she didn't want to do. "I want you to be happy *and* successful. That's just my point of view. Can you see that?"

"I can. Can you see my point of view? If they're all going to give me a similar education, then what does it matter where I am?"

I had an uneasy sensation in the pit of my stomach. We weren't arguing, exactly. But we were definitely having a disagreement. We'd had them before, but it felt different now, bigger, more important, like it could fracture everything.

She pulled me closer, held my face in both her hands, and kissed me. "I love you. And I want to stay close by. And CU will give me everything I need for my education right now. Simple as that."

"Okay. It's your decision. And I'll support whatever you do."

"Thank you." She kissed me again. "Did we just have a fight and make up?"

My grin felt wobbly. "Nah, that wasn't a fight. Just an honest discussion." I took a steadying breath and carefully pulled her into me, relaxing into the body contact as she wrapped her arm around my waist. We stayed like that for a little while, just quietly sitting together, and when I didn't feel so antsy about our "discussion," I said, "I had an idea this afternoon."

"Did it hurt?"

"Ha ha." I leaned in and kissed her, gently biting her lower lip. "I want to take you on a date on Saturday. All day." And maybe all night too, my brain oh-so-helpfully pointed out. "If you've got time. I know your finals are coming up and you need to study and stuff." I knew she *had* been studying and doing all the groundwork through the year to sail through these exams the way she always did, but I wanted to make sure she was comfortable and not worried about ignoring study in favor of more fun things.

Gemma's eyes lit up. "Our first real date?" She took my hand and pulled it into her chest. "Of course I can make time for it. Are you sure? It's your day off. Shouldn't you be relaxing or something?"

"Of course I'm sure. Can't think of a better way to spend my day than with you."

"Then I'm in. Of course I'm in." Her cheeks pinked. "What are we doing?"

"I thought we could go for a hike. Then we could come back here, have dinner and just…hang out, watch a movie, paint some Warhammer or work on my new *Star Wars* Lego. Whatever we want." I wanted so badly to add, "And you're welcome to stay the night" but all my bravado deserted me, leaving me feeling like a timid mouse.

"Sounds great." Gem turned my right hand over, studying the fingers. She gently moved my forefinger and middle finger back and forth, stretching the knuckles pleasantly. Her voice was quiet, but steady when she asked, "What about *after* dinner? Should I bring an overnight bag?"

"Yes," I breathed, grateful that yet again she'd been brave enough to take the first step. I cleared my throat. "If you want. I mean, we don't have to do that yet if you're not ready, but I want to. With you. Have sex I mean." The thought made me feel tingly and tongue-tied. "Sorry, every time I think about it, I go to Ramble Town."

"I love it when you go to Ramble Town." Her mouth twitched. "And I love knowing the reason why you went there. I'll pack an overnight bag and we can just see what happens? No pressure."

"Sounds good," I said hoarsely.

We talked about what she should bring for the hike and she was incredulous that we weren't sharing the load as we usually did. "It's fine," I said. "I'll give you a few of the light things to carry, but I will be the pack mule." I flexed. Gem pretended to swoon. Swooning led to kissing.

Kissing Gemma was a revelation. Our friendship had always felt perfect, easy, but having everything remain the same—our silliness, our comfort with each other, our trust and honesty— while we added the amazingness that was being girlfriends, was such a relief. I hadn't really expected things to change drastically once we took that step, but the niggling worry had always been there and now that I realized how baseless the worry was, I knew how tightly I'd been holding on to it. Silly Stacey, you could have found some courage years ago and had all this amazingness back then instead of wasting your time with women who were all wrong for you.

When I pressed myself against her, wrapping my arms around her waist, Gemma groaned. And when I lightly swiped my tongue along her lower lip, she opened her mouth, drawing me in. Dammit. I so wanted to forget everything and ask her if she wanted to come to bed with me, right now. But it didn't feel like the right time, especially after our disagreement. As if on cue, my stomach protested audibly. I pulled back, running my hands up and down the outside of Gem's upper arms, and said something predictably dumb. "Well…I'm guess I'm hungry."

Both her eyebrows bounced. "So am I."

CHAPTER SIXTEEN

Gemma

The fact Mom was awake when I came down for breakfast just after dawn was particularly suspicious. She'd started the coffee machine and oatmeal for me, and was slumped by the stove, stirring in her usual "I hate mornings" way. I hugged her from the side. "Are we in an alternate universe where you're functional first thing in the morning?"

"What on earth did I do to get this smartass kid?" She kissed my forehead. "Couldn't sleep so I thought I'd send you off on your adventure with a nutritious breakfast."

"Thanks."

While she stirred, I double-checked I had everything I needed in my daypack. Once I'd settled at the breakfast bar with a coffee I asked, "Why couldn't you sleep?"

She shrugged, which was a pretty solid response from her this time of morning. Along with a steaming bowl of oatmeal, complete with raw sugar and a sliced banana on top, Mom pushed a twice-folded piece of paper across the counter toward me. "Here."

I eyed it suspiciously. "What's that?"

Mom blushed, which made me think I didn't want to read whatever it was. "These are just a few things that Aspen and I wish someone had told us before we'd first had sex. Not…tips, but just, uh, advice."

"Oh my god, Mom! Please no." I had a great relationship with my parents but there were just some things I didn't want to discuss.

Mom held up both hands. "Trust me, Gemma, this is not something I ever wanted to have to give you, but here we are. I think. Back in my day, you just read *Cosmopolitan* magazine and thought you knew everything you needed to about sex. With men that is." She shook herself. "So, just take this and we'll never ever have to talk about it again. Unless there's something you want talk about?"

I shook my head. "Nothing, no."

She let out a breath. "Great. But if you change your mind, Aspen and I are here to talk. Have a good day and be safe. You know the drill—call us if you need anything, at any time. Love you."

"I will. Love you too. I'll see you tomorrow."

Mom gave me a long, tight hug then left me by myself in the kitchen, both mortified and grateful to have such cool, loving parents. I heard Stacey pull into the driveway just as I was putting my dishes in the dishwasher, and after a quick deliberation, I stuffed the note into the inner pocket of my softshell jacket. When I opened the trunk of Stacey's 4Runner, she slung an arm around the passenger seat to look back at me. Her smile was brilliant, and I didn't miss the quick up-and-down of her eyes as she checked me out. That was a new thing. As was the flood of heat that went through me at the look in her eyes.

Apparently something on my face gave me away, because she grinned before her casual, "Hey. Got everything you need?"

"Hey yourself. And yep." I stuck my overnight duffel and pack next to hers, noting her daypack was full to almost bursting. Whatever hike she had planned, it required a whole bunch of supplies.

I climbed into the passenger seat and Stace leaned over, murmuring, "Hey."

Smiling, I told her, "You already said that."

"So I did." She slid a hand around behind my neck to pull me closer. "Something about being near you makes me forget how to do words." Stacey kissed me with the same care and skill she seemed to allocate to everything. The kiss began slowly but quickly became quick, and I had a fleeting thought of saying we should skip the hike and just go to her place. But it was clear she'd put a whole lot of thought into our date, so we'd hike and then later we could do the things I'd thought about as I'd fallen asleep last night.

Before we drove off, she reached around, pulled a small bag from the back seat, and set it in my lap. "Snacks for the drive. And"—she pointed to my cup holder—"coffee to keep you awake so you'll keep me company."

"How far away is this hike?"

"A little under two hours. I wanted to hike somewhere we don't usually go."

Once on the highway, I realized we were heading toward Denver. "Where exactly are we going?"

She flashed me a grin. "Secret. But I promise it'll be worth it."

Interesting. Given the direction and the drive time, and the fact I'd lived just outside Denver, I had a few ideas. But I didn't want to spoil her surprise. I turned slightly sideways in my seat and reached into my jacket pocket. "So, here's something fun. Before you came round to get me this morning, my mother gave me a sex hints list."

Our speed dipped for a second before picking up again. "Whaaaaaaaat?"

"Yep. And in case you're wondering, it was as weird as it sounds." I glanced at the note, written in both their handwriting, as if they'd had a brainstorming session last night once they'd gone to bed. The thought made me laugh, and took a fraction of the embarrassment away. "You want me to read it aloud?"

Stacey shifted back in the seat and after a pause said, "Sure. Why not."

I made a show of clearing my throat. "One, always pee soon afterward. Helps you not get a UTI. UTIs aren't fun. Two, it should feel good. If it doesn't you can stop. Or you can always stop at any time, you don't have to keep going just because you think you should. Three—" I cleared my throat again, this time because my voice really did feel like it was going to croak. It still did when I said, "Three, clean fingers and toys are also important and can help avoid a UTI. Four...do you want me to keep going?"

"I, um, think I get the idea," she said hoarsely.

After skimming the rest of the note, which was less mortifying than I'd thought it would be, I glanced over at Stacey. "So what I'm gathering from this, is that they're both just really worried about us getting a urinary tract infection."

"Sounds like it. Probably a good thing to be worried about." Her voice still sounded tight, and I couldn't tell if she was embarrassed, or what was going on.

I touched the back of her neck, rubbed my fingertips in the buzzed hair. "You okay?"

"Totally." She glanced over at me. "Honestly, I am. Just... now I'm thinking about it."

"It?"

"Mhmm. *It*. Us. Together. Sex. You know."

"Ohhh." I'd been trying not to think about it, because whenever I thought about it, it made my stomach feel knotted and excited in a way it usually didn't when I was just horny. I knew it would be different with someone else, but just how different, I wasn't sure. Now, I let myself think about it, imagine it. Knowing Stace was obviously as excited or nervous or whatever about us having sex made me feel a little less anxious, a little bolder. "So I shouldn't do...this?" I rested my hand on her thigh, sliding it up as far as I dared. As far as I dared while Stacey was driving, that is.

She inhaled shakily. "Unless you don't want to go hiking because I've crashed off the road."

I withdrew my hand, reluctantly. "Hmmm. Given you spent so much time arranging this date, I'd feel bad if we didn't go.

But if you think I'm not going to put my hand there when we get home, you're dead wrong."

"You'd better," she murmured.

The rest of the drive was uneventful, except that I kept thinking about what would happen when our mystery hike was done, when we were back at Stacey's. We crossed into Jefferson County, and it twigged where we might be going, but I kept my mouth shut until she turned onto a familiar road. We were heading into Alderfer/Three Sisters Park. I straightened up. "Ohhhh I love it here." I'd hiked the park in all seasons, and it was beautiful no matter what time of year you hit the trails.

"You do?"

"Yeah. Before we moved, Mom and I used to come here at least once a month for hiking or snowshoeing."

Stacey deflated. "Oh. I didn't know you'd been here before. You never mentioned it." Under her breath, she muttered, "Of course you've been here, you used to live nearby. Way to not think, Stacey."

I realized right away that I'd spoiled her surprise. Not intentionally obviously, but still... I rubbed her shoulder. "Heyyy. Babe. Don't be like that. I might have hiked here before, but I've never done it with you. And anything with you is special. Plus, there's like eleven hundred acres of park. There's a zillion trails and ways to link them together. I bet whatever you have planned is amazing."

"It really is," she admitted smugly. "Know what else is amazing?"

"What?"

"You calling me babe."

I grinned. "It kinda is, isn't it?"

I watched the scenery pass by as Stacey drove us to the east trailhead. We were still early enough that we easily found a parking space, and once I'd peed—yes, I'm one of those annoying "has to pee all the time" people—Stacey passed me a few dry sacks. "A secret" apparently, or so she said when I asked. Once I'd repacked my daypack to include my new loot, shrugged into it, and clipped my camera to the mount on my left shoulder strap, I held out my hand. Stacey immediately took it, entwining our fingers. After leaning in for a kiss, I used our joined hands to point forward. "Lead on."

We set a decent pace, not hoofing it but not dawdling as we made our way onto Hidden Fawn Trail. Though we both loved hiking, and hiked for fitness as well as fun, we had different hiking styles—Stace liked to push through, eating as she walked, jogging some parts and stopping only when absolutely necessary, whereas I preferred to enjoy the scenery, stop for photos, and sit down for lunch. Over the years we'd adopted a mash-up style for whenever we hiked together—sometimes fast, sometimes chill. But she'd always been great about me pausing and this hike, we detoured to every lookout and photo spot. I put her in as many photos as I could, wanting to remember this date forever.

The sun was shining, the wildflowers were blooming, and the birds singing in a perfect Disney scene as we made our way through forests and fields and over rocky outcrops. We joined up to the Bearberry Trail then onto the Mountain Muhly Trail, with Stace trickle feeding me snacks to keep the hike hangries away. We'd hiked almost four miles when she stopped and took a look around. "How's this for lunch?"

"Perfect." A little way off the trail, semi-private among the trees but not dense enough that we couldn't see the incredible views. Stacey extracted a rubber-backed picnic blanket and spread it on the ground before she began pulling dry sacks out of both our packs. She'd clearly done a heap of prep work, and took her time setting out a wooden cutting board with cheeses, an assortment of fruit, nuts, and veggie sticks. Instead of bringing the hiking stove to make hot drinks as we normally would, she had a thermos, which she set on top of a flat rock next to the blanket.

I asked the most obvious question, because my brain was completely stuck on how much care she'd gone to, and the stuff she'd lugged along on the hike. "You made us a picnic?"

"I did." She glanced up, smiling when she realized I had the camera focused on her. "Multiple cheeses, just to please you."

"I'm very pleased." After snapping a few shots, I put on a horrible French accent. "Ze camera loves you, darlink." After snapping off a few more to be certain, I stepped backward to adjust the framing.

It took a split second for me to realize three things—I'd just stepped into the only mud puddle around; this mud was not shallow mud; and as well as being sucky, it was slippery and I was both stuck *and* falling over. As best I could with the strap around my neck limiting its reach, I held my camera aloft, trying desperately to keep it from being broken or mud-bathed as I tried to yank my boot from the mud holding it in place. The moment I pulled my foot free, I realized my mistake. I'd thrown myself off-balance and with nowhere else to put my newly extracted foot except in more slippery mud, I went over on my ass, rolling onto my hip and thigh. Flailing with my camera had actually put me more off-balance, and had been the thing to send me over.

Worth it to save My Precious? Absolutely.

Thankfully I'd managed to keep my top half aloft, which was a blessing given the sensation of cool mud against my pants. They had a water-resistant coating and could deal with short rain showers and some snow, and now I knew they also repelled mud. Stacey stood on her mudless ground, mouth agape as she stared at me. "I—" She couldn't hide her snort-laugh, and after taking a moment to compose herself, she asked, "Are you okay?"

"Do I look okay?"

"New question. Are you hurt?"

"I am not." I wasn't hurt, but I was utterly paralyzed because I couldn't extract myself without using both hands and one hand was occupied keeping one of my most prized possessions safe.

"Good." Her mouth twitched. "Now, are we laughing, swearing, or crying?"

"The first two, but in reverse order." I shook my camera at her. "Can you put that somewhere safe please?"

Stace took it carefully from around my neck and after setting it down in a safe spot, held out her hand to help extract me from the muck. When I held out my muddied hand, she just stared at it. "Very funny."

Smiling, I held out my clean hand and Stace hauled me up. Once on two feet again, I glanced down. The mud was basically from butt to ankle on my left side, but thankfully just on the outside of my pants. And also thankfully it was just mud, and not bear shit. "Well. It hasn't soaked through, but I need to clean up."

"I guess you can just scrape the mud off. Or...you could take your pants off and use some of your water to wash them, and drape them in the sun to dry while we eat." She bounced her eyebrows, making it clear which option she preferred.

"And what would I wear while my pants dried?" We were sitting in a nice shaded spot, and I would soon be cold without pants.

"The picnic blanket?"

The picnic blanket which had an amazing picnic spread out on it. "And what will we sit on?"

"Our packs? The ground? Or...we could just snuggle up and I'll keep you warm until your pants dry."

"Mmm. Tempting."

I decided to just scrape the worst of the mud off with a stick and let it dry to be flicked off later. By the time I'd washed my hands, Stacey was done arranging the food. She'd set it out beautifully, artistically arranging things on and around the wooden board. Frowning, she stared at her handiwork, then without saying anything, opened bag after bag, peeking in each one before setting it down.

"What have you lost?" I asked.

Instead of answering me outright, she muttered, "Goddammit, where are they?"

"If I knew what you were looking for, I could help." At her look of frustration, I added, "But that would ruin the surprise?"

She huffed out a breath. "No...it wouldn't. It's just some crackers. Fancy ones. They're in a small plastic container with a red lid."

"Ah. Sorry, I haven't seen them." Stace was totally stressing about the missing crackers, and I flailed for a way to appease her upset, and also my grumbling stomach. "Hey, we can just use the veggie sticks and apple slices for the cheese. It's not the end of the world."

"But what about my precious carbs, Gemmy?" She was laughing as she said it, so I knew she wasn't totally serious.

"Are they in the dry sacks you gave to me?"

"No, that's just regular hike supplies," she fretted. "Goddammit. I know I packed everything." Stace glanced down at me. "I had lists and everything."

"I bet you did. This is incredible." I held out my hand. "Come on, sit down and eat."

After a quiet sigh, she abandoned her search and sat down beside me.

"Thank you for indulging my love of sitting down for a slow-hike meal." I eased a few grapes free and held them out to her.

Stacey bent toward me and carefully took them between her lips. "I'm realizing there's some benefits to taking your time."

"Yeah? Like what?"

"Like…" Stacey kissed me, leaning in and rolling us over until she was on top of me. The kiss was unhurried, which did nothing to ease the sudden rush of excitement. Everything tingled deliciously, and I took a deep breath, trying to prolong the sensation. She carefully unzipped my jacket and slid her hand under my shirt, its coolness making me shudder. Things escalated pretty quickly from there. I'd just determined that the sound she made when my thumbs touched her nipples through her sports bra made my stomach flutter, when the unmistakable sound of people conversing broke through my pleasure.

We pulled apart so quickly that Stacey rolled off the blanket onto the dirt. I yanked my shirt down and zipped up my jacket just as a pair of trail runners came by. Stacey mumbled something, and I fought the urge to look away as they came level with us. Thankfully, despite having clearly caught us mid make-out session, they seemed more amused than scandalized. "Afternoon!" one said cheerfully as they jogged past.

Stace raised a hand, and I returned their greeting with a hoarse, "Afternoon" as I tried not to blush. Stace crawled onto the blanket and flopped onto her back. She covered her eyes with a hand. "You've got to be freaking kidding me. We've seen hardly anyone at all this section of the hike, and this is a secluded spot, but somehow, suddenly, right at that moment, a couple of people decide to glide on by?"

I was too busy trying to calm both my excitement and my embarrassment to answer.

She sat up again and leaned back on her hands. After a mournful look over at me, she grabbed a small handful of nuts. "Okay, well…I guess it's time for part two?"

"Is part two less muddy and less embarrassing than part one?"

"Be quiet." She made sure I was with a long kiss.

We lingered over her picnic, then continued until we'd joined back onto Hidden Fawn Trail. Stacey dutifully stopped every time I needed to photograph something. She was so outwardly patient that I rewarded each photo with a kiss, which I think made her even more eager to stop for me. Whenever I had to go into the woods to pee, she stood in front of me to hide me from view and act as lookout. We'd always been pee-watch for each other and the fact that it didn't feel weird now we were dating was comforting. Our friendship consisted of so many tiny moving pieces, and with each discovery that those pieces were still intact, a little of my anxiety let go.

We made it back to the parking lot just after two p.m. and after we stashed our gear in the trunk, Stacey pressed me against the side of the car. "So. First official date was officially a disaster, huh?"

I pushed my hands into the back pockets of her pants, enjoying the sensation of her ass in my palms. "Could have been worse. We could have been totally undressed when those runners came past. I could have fallen face-first into mud. You could have forgotten the cheese or the thermos of tea."

"I guess. It's just I had this all planned out so perfectly, and none of that was part of it."

She looked so utterly devastated, even though it wasn't her fault, that I had to kiss her. "I'm teasing, Stace. We both know this is nowhere near the grubbiest I've been on a hike, and more importantly, I'm having so much fun. Mud bath and no crackers and all. I love this park, and sharing it with you is amazing." I kissed her again. "And remember that hike up to Booth Lake where I tripped into the lake?" Thankfully it'd been summer and a refreshing, though unplanned, dip.

Her forehead crinkled. "I do remember that. I also remember how hard it was not to look at your wet T-shirt, and then how I almost choked when you pulled your clothes off to dry, and were sitting on the rocks in just your sports bra and underwear."

"You know, if you'd said something then, we'd have gotten here a whole lot faster."

She grinned. "I know." Stacey reached up under the back of my shirt to stroke my skin. "I guess it's easy now to say we both should have pulled our heads out of our asses and just been honest."

I leaned into her caress, trying not to melt. "Yeah. But also think of all those years of building an amazing, solid friendship."

"That's true," she agreed thoughtfully.

"What are we doing now?"

"Now, we're making a stop to collect dinner before we drive home."

She cemented the status of best date ever by stopping in Evergreen for Beau Jo's pizza—only the best pizza in Colorado—and we drove home in an almost manic mood, singing along to her music, and playfully teasing each other about the date. And underneath the excitement bubbled another kind of excitement. One that'd been steadily building all day. One I couldn't wait to explore.

When we got home, we put the pizza in the oven to reheat and unpacked our daypacks, by far the most tedious part of hiking. I pulled out the dry sacks she'd given me that morning and set them on the table to unpack. Laughing, I held up a container that definitely wasn't part of the usual hiking kit and shook it, which made Stacey look up.

"Oh, hey," I said casually. "Are these the crackers you were looking for?"

Stacey's face fell. "Shit. How did I miss that? I'm an idiot. See? Worst date ever."

I slipped around to her side of the table and kissed her. "Nuh-uh. Best date ever." And judging by the way her hands immediately went to my butt and the desperation in Stacey's kiss, our first date was only going to get better...

CHAPTER SEVENTEEN

Stacey

We showered in separate bathrooms and I took my time making sure I was extra clean in all the important places, even brushing my teeth when we hadn't even had dinner. I'd just finished dressing when Gem appeared in my bedroom doorway, her still-wet hair down around her shoulders. "So...in my excitement to um, go hiking, I totally forgot to pack a hoodie for tonight. Can I please borrow one?"

"Sure." I rummaged around in my closet and passed her a clean sponsor-provided hoodie with ATOMIC across the chest. "Here you are, m'lady."

Gem didn't take it. "That one's nice. But...you *could* just give me the one you're wearing."

"Why?"

She stepped closer. "Because it'll be warm, and smell like you." Unlike my mom who thought house hoodies should be washed after every wear, Gem totally got that I liked to wear them for a week and get them super soft and comfortable.

If I'd been cooler, I'd have said, "No point in putting it on when I'm just going to take it off you soon," but thinking about doing that stuck my tongue to the roof of my mouth. So I held the Atomic sweatshirt between my knees, pulled my gray (also sponsor) Oakley hoodie over my head, and passed it to her.

"Thanks." Gem held it to her nose before shrugging into it. As she freed her hair, she said, "I might return it periodically for you to launder, then get it all Stacey-smelled-up again."

"You're weird." I slipped into the new sweatshirt. "Why don't *you* wash it if you're just going to steal it from me?"

"We use different laundry detergent than you. It won't smell right underneath the Stacey smell."

"I take it back. You're not weird. You're super weird."

Gem closed the space between us, resting her hands on my hips. "I think you kinda like it."

"Oh I definitely do." She looked so cute that I had to kiss her, and had intended it to be just a quick one before we went back out to the lounge to chill before dinner.

But Gem had other ideas, and her ideas gave me ideas. Without breaking the kiss, she guided me back until my legs hit the bed. She gave me a gentle push until I fell backward. I took the hint immediately, scrambling so I was fully on the bed. Gem wasted no time following me, lying on top of me and kissing me again. I could feel her desperation, her desire in the kiss, and matched it eagerly. She was almost frantic as she pushed my sweatshirt up, dragging my tee with it until she'd pulled both up and over my head. The moment my torso was bare she lay back down on top of me.

I moved with her, delighted in the confidence of her hands and mouth, hoped I didn't seem as hopelessly lost in her as I felt. It was more than a make-out session, and when Gem whispered how good my skin felt and tasted, I sat up, and without breaking the kiss, rolled us over and began to drag her hoodie up.

Gemma made a funny little moany groan sound that made me want to yank off all her clothing. But before I could do anything more than touch the soft, warm skin of her stomach, she broke the kiss to mumble, "What's that smell?"

It took me a few seconds to decipher what she'd asked and then another second to realize the smell she was asking about was the smell of our dinner burning. "Oh, shit!" I climbed awkwardly off her and sprinted into the kitchen a second before the smoke alarm started screaming. Gem was right behind me and helped me fling all the kitchen windows open and silence the alarm. She wordlessly handed me my hoodie to cover the fact I was completely topless. But not before she'd taken a good, long look that made my abs clench and almost made me forget about our ruined dinner.

Staring at the charred mess, I uttered the only words that would adequately convey my feelings about a. the ruined dinner, and b. the ruined dinner ruining what had been leading to sex. "Well…fuck."

"Yeah," Gem sighed, leaning into me. "Here lies our dinner. Or what's left of it. RIP, Beau Jo's, you would have been amazing." She laughed. "Second date can only get better, right?"

"Right," I said glumly as I extracted the lump of coal and dropped it into the sink. Gross. And so sad.

Gemma pressed herself to my back and kissed the back of my shoulder, her arms stealing around my waist. "So, what do you want to do about dinner?" She rubbed up and down my stomach. "This isn't going to stay quiet for long."

I turned my head to look back at her. "We could order another pizza? It's not going to be on the same level, but it'll still be good, right?"

In the end, we just ate the lost-then-found crackers which we dipped in ranch, a bowl of cereal, and a grilled cheese—or two in my case. Our mix 'n' match dinner was part apathy, and part unspoken need to get back to what we'd abandoned. Once we'd cleaned up, Gem turned to me. "So. About that thing we were doing when the pizza caught fire…"

I blew out a breath, stuffing my hands in my pockets. "Right. About that. Are we supposed to dance around it? Pretend we're tired?"

Gem laughed. "We could." She faked a yawn.

After a deep breath, I quietly said, "Or I could just be honest and tell you that I've thought about having sex with you so many times I can't even count, that I've waited for so long, and I don't want to think or wait anymore."

She silent-clapped me. "Wow. That was smooth."

I took her hand. "I thought so." I'd thought it would be me who'd lead her into the bedroom, but Gem moved ahead of me, almost dragging me down the hall. The anticipation had my heart hammering, and I paused in the doorway. Not stalling, just…taking a moment to breathe. "Lights on, or off? Or bedside lamp? Or curtains open for moonlight?"

"Lights on. I want to see you." She bit her lower lip. "All of you."

My mouth got suddenly so dry I could barely say, "Me too."

Gem stretched up on tiptoes and kissed me. This time when she gently walked me toward my bed, it was unhurried, as if she too had taken the time to breathe. I paused, glancing down at the rumpled covers from earlier. "I uh, I guess this could be the obligatory 'we can stop at any time, please tell me if you don't like it or you want something else' talk."

"Right. That sounds good." Her smile wavered. "And you're my first, so…"

"Me too," I said quietly. My voice shook a little as I elaborated, "I haven't done this before, not with anyone else."

Gem's eyes widened. "I thought you had. Lots."

"No. Never." I knew she believed me but I still felt I had to explain. "I just…wanted it to feel special. And it wouldn't have with any of those women. I mean, I *could have* if I'd wanted to but, I just didn't with them. I know it's silly and old-fashioned, but—"

She silenced me with a long, deep kiss, and when she pulled away again, Gem was smiling. "Here I was thinking you were the stud of the ski racing circuit."

"No way," I scoffed. Then I realized though she was smiling, she didn't seem happy. "Did it bother you, thinking that?"

"Yes. And it bothered me that I was bothered because I didn't have any right to be jealous of them."

"I felt weird about you dating too for the same reason. I wanted it to be me." I kissed her slowly, traced her lower lip with my tongue.

"Well now it is," she whispered. "I didn't want to either, it didn't feel right. Until now, with you."

We undressed each other around kisses, letting our clothes fall to the floor. Then she was naked, and the sensation of her skin against mine made my heart race. I took a step back, Gem followed, and I had to move back again, hurrying to explain, "I just want to look," before she could think I was pulling away from her. "If that's okay?"

Her left eyebrow went up slowly, and her expression turned mischievous. "Just look?"

"No, definitely not just look."

But first I looked. I looked at all of her, letting myself linger as long as I could before the desperation to touch her was too strong. My fingers followed the path of my eyes, taking in the beauty laid out before me. Naked, Gemma was even more gorgeous than the woman I'd seen in bathing suits or her underwear. Soft and curved, deliciously feminine with strength I found intoxicating. "Is this okay?" I asked as my hands roamed to places on her body I'd only dreamt of touching.

"Yes," she breathed. "You can touch me anywhere. I want you to touch me everywhere." As if emphasizing her point, she pulled my hands against her boobs, using her fingers to guide mine to how she wanted me to touch her. "I'll tell you if it's not okay."

"Are you scared?" I whispered, still lost in the smooth warmth of her skin.

Gem's voice was quiet, but without hesitation when she answered, "No. Maybe a little nervous but not scared."

"I'm a little nervous too." I never met a nervousness I couldn't wrangle, but this one was a slippery bucking bronco.

"What about?"

I took a deep breath, and shared my insecurity. "About you seeing me naked, if I'll know what to do, how to make it feel good for you. Just normal first-time worries I guess."

Gem kissed me lightly, lingering close to murmur, "You know, I've had pretty much those exact thoughts. So we're in the same boat. We can learn together."

"What if I told you that I think you're the sexiest thing I've ever put my eyes on?"

"Even a new pair of skis?"

"Way better than that."

Grinning, she dropped down onto the bed, tucking one leg underneath herself. "Are you worried I don't like what I'm seeing?" But instead of waiting for me to answer, she gripped my hips and pulled me forward until her mouth was a breath from my skin. Her kiss against my stomach was featherlight. "You're so beautiful," Gem whispered against me. She paused, drew back. "Is that okay? Beautiful?"

I laughed quietly. "Yes. It's okay."

Her fingertips and lips traced patterns on my stomach and my abs tensed at the light, teasing touch. Gem raised her head to find my eyes. "Stacey?"

"Yes?" I said around a sharp inhalation.

Her hands moved to my ass. "I know you know it, but you are so freakin' hot." She licked a path from my belly button up to just underneath my boobs.

That feeling alone sent a rush of goose bumps over my skin, but when she moved her hand between my thighs as her mouth loved my nipples, I nearly went into orbit. She kept pulling me forward and I finally got the hint that she wanted to be less vertical. We shifted clumsily and as Gem lay back on the bed, she smiled up at me shyly before I moved to lie on top of her. The feeling of full skin-on-skin was amazing, and I relaxed against her, trying not to lose myself completely as we explored each other with mouths and hands.

Gem paused her attention to my neck, laughing quietly. "My heart is beating so fast."

"I can feel it." I bent my head and kissed the silky soft skin on her boob, right over her heart. And of course then was the worst time to have a random thought. I raised my head, stupidly abandoning Gemma's skin. "Boobs? Or breasts? Breast feels kinda clinical, but boob feels kinda silly."

"Stacey," Gem breathed. "I don't care what we call them, I just want you to kiss mine again."

So I did. And as she held me against her breasts, I was careful not to press too hard and squish her. But every time I tried to take some of my weight from her, Gem wrapped her legs around the back of my thighs and held me close. As we moved together, my excitement and panic spun together until the panic disappeared. When I slid my hand down her belly, Gem shifted to help me, guiding my hand between her legs. But before I touched what I most wanted to touch, I asked, "Can you show me what you do when you're alone?"

"When I'm thinking of you?"

My anticipation skyrocketed. "Yes," I said hoarsely.

"That's really what you want?"

I nodded, and sat back on my heels so I could take in the incredible scene in front of me. Her hand moved down over her belly and disappeared between her slightly spread legs. Gem held eye contact with me, and the pleasure on her face made my body ache and throb in ways I hadn't thought possible. I watched her, trying to see how she touched herself, how I should touch her. I hadn't thought watching someone else do that could turn me on so much, but it was almost like she was touching me too.

Her breathing grew faster and faster, shallower, and I unconsciously matched it. Then she just...stopped. Gem reached her other hand out to me. "I want you to touch me. I want you on top of me," she said in a breathless whisper, and when I took her hand she pulled me until I lay full length on top of her. When I again tried to move some of my weight off her, she just pulled me back down.

"I don't want to crush you."

"You won't," she promised. "I love the way you feel."

She wrapped her legs around my hips and I could feel how much she wanted this, for us to be together this way. I wanted to touch *all* of her, wanted to feel the silky softness of her skin against my fingers and my lips. And I wanted her to explore my body, wanted to feel what it would be like to have someone else's hands on me. But first, I wanted to hear the sounds she'd make when she came. I shifted into a better position—nobody ever mentions how much movement and repositioning happens during sex—and after quietly asking if she was sure, and receiving an enthusiastic "Yes…please" in response, I dipped my hand between her legs.

Gem gasped at the first touch of my fingers to her silken heat, a good gasp, a gasp that made me want to keep touching her. So I did. "Is this okay?"

"Yes," she whispered, holding me closer. "It feels so good." Gem's back arched, her hips rising and falling as she sought more from me.

We were clumsy then certain. Shy then bold. Awkward then confident. We laughed our way through things that just…didn't quite work, and then that laughter faded as pleasure took over. All my fears had left the moment I'd first touched her most intimate places. Because how could there be fear when there was so much love and trust between us?

And Gem…always sweet, sometimes shy, telling me with confidence what she wanted and where, begging me to keep going, murmuring how good it felt and how much she wanted it, soothed all my anxieties about us being together. And when her breathing caught as she tensed and shuddered and gasped underneath me, I knew this was the right place, the right time. That waiting for her was the right thing.

I hadn't realized she'd been digging her nails into my back and arms until she relaxed her grip, her whole body still trembling. Gem wrapped her arms around my back, her kiss conveying exactly how much she'd wanted what we'd just done.

"I love you," I whispered. I couldn't help myself, I had to say it, even though it felt silly and clichéd at that moment.

She blinked, her mouth twisting into a luminous smile. "I love you too. And I really, *really* loved what you just did."

"Me too."

Though I was still so aroused it almost hurt, I thought I was satisfied with what we'd already done, with how I'd made her squirm and beg me to keep going, and how that had had arousal twisting through me. I wanted her to touch me, but I would have been okay if she wasn't comfortable. I thought I was satisfied… Until Gem rolled me onto my back and without a word, began to lavish attention on my body. It seemed she knew every spot that made me tremble, and it didn't take long until the white hot sensation between my legs began to spread outward. And I couldn't do a damn thing except let myself be carried along on the waves of pleasure. Gem held on to me, kissing me deeply as I came…and came…and came.

It was unlike anything I'd ever experienced. I mean, yeah, I'd had self-induced orgasms, lots of them, but Gemma…Gemma just…*knew* how to touch me. And when I finally stopped shuddering, she didn't stop touching me. She held on to me, kept me from falling apart until I could finally speak. But then I couldn't think of what to say, because no words felt adequate. So I kissed her instead. There was still urgency in the kiss, passion, desire, but I no longer felt the need to desperately devour all of her.

Gem shifted and pulled me against her until I lay curled up against her side, my cheek resting against the smooth, soft skin of her breasts. Yes. Definitely breasts. I wasn't twelve anymore. Gemma's hand brushed up my left arm, slowly tracing the tattooed images until she paused at the red stone in the snow. My Gemstone. Her fingertip moved back and forth over the gem. "I've always wanted to ask. What is this for?" It felt like she already had an idea, and was asking me to confirm it for her.

My throat felt so tight that the words came out hoarsely. "It's *you*. You're my strength, Gem. My security."

She held me tucked against her, a hand lazily stroking my back and sides. I didn't think I'd ever felt so completely content as I did in that moment, one perfect moment in time, recalling just before as we'd…had sex? Fucked? Made love?

I exhaled an unintentionally loud sigh of contentment, and Gem leaned back to look down at me. "What?" she asked.

"It's nothing. Well it's something but it's so embarrassing and sappy that I think I want to forget I even thought it, let alone actually say it."

Gemma threatened tickles. "Come on. That's not fair."

I felt my cheeks and ears heat, and wanted to press my face against her skin to hide my flush. But at the same time, I didn't want to hide anything from her. My voice was embarrassingly squeaky when I said, "I see now why it's sometimes called making love. It just…felt like love."

Her whole body relaxed. She cupped my face to kiss me and when she pulled back, the look in her eyes told me she didn't think I was stupid or sappy. Gem lingered close. "Yes. It felt like love."

I would have been happy to stay there for a while, just absorbing everything we'd done, thinking about how incredible being with her had been, and how much I wanted to do it again. As if she knew what I was thinking, Gem climbed on top of me, our bodies touching all along their lengths. The sensation of her skin was no less exciting than it had been when I'd first felt it against mine—if anything, it was even more so—and I shuddered.

When I ran my hand down her back and cupped her ass, Gem smirked. "You know what?" she asked.

"What?"

She kissed my neck, and as her lips moved against my skin, her hand moved between us, gliding down my stomach. "I think I want to love you again…"

CHAPTER EIGHTEEN

Gemma

And that had also gone even better than I could ever have imagined. When we'd finally exhausted each other, we collapsed on the bed, trying to regain our breath. I pressed myself to Stace's side, my leg over her hip and my arm tightly around her middle, trying to get as close to her as I could. Stacey wrapped an arm around me, burying her face into my hair as her free hand stroked up and down my side. I felt so satisfied, and tired in the best way.

I'd thought sex would be good, great, maybe even amazing. But I wasn't prepared for just *how* amazing it felt to be with Stacey that way, even if I set aside the actual "having an orgasm" part of it. I kept replaying bits of our intimacy, the look on her face as she'd touched me, the sound she'd made when I'd touched her, the way we'd moved together.

And in the back of my mind was the persistent question of why did I wait so long? There were times when I was with Ashley, and to a far lesser degree, Noah, when I'd thought I might agree to sex if they asked if we wanted to go further— mostly when we were making out and things were getting hot.

But now I knew with absolute certainty that it wouldn't have been like this with anyone else. The trust and love and honesty between Stacey and me had made it so incredible, and I couldn't imagine how it could possibly be any better. I wanted to stay with her like that for the rest of the night, sleeping curled up together only to wake up and discover all the parts of her I hadn't found tonight, but I kinda needed to pee—and not just because it'd been mentioned a million times in The Maternal Note. Thinking about that made me think of what other things I usually did before bed and how it was so unsexy. I leaned up on my elbow so I could look at Stacey's face.

"What?" she asked, mouth twitching like she was trying to figure out what I was thinking.

"Movies and books and stuff don't really talk about that boring stuff around sex, do they? Like needing to pee after, and then me having to put in my retainer before bed, and putting pajamas on, or back on if you were already wearing them, or maybe not putting them on at all…" And what happened if we woke up in the middle of the night and wanted to do it all over again, but I had my retainer in? It seemed odd to pause things to take it out and have it sitting on the bedside table while we were having sex. "Just boring things."

"No, they don't," Stacey agreed with a smile. "They also don't talk about how hard it is trying to be in the right position, and not squish you or elbow you somewhere, or just trying to not act like a game of Twister."

"Yeah." I stroked up and down the naked skin of her belly, playing my fingers over the ridges of muscle, enjoying the way she tensed at my touch. "But it was fun to figure it out." And I knew there'd be more to figure out as we got more… adventurous. The thought of exactly what that adventure might be sent a thrill through me.

Her smile turned dreamy. "It sure was."

"So, um, do we put on pajamas or stay naked?" Another, super unpleasant thought came to me. "Or do you want me to go sleep in the guest room?"

She looked aghast. "Well, after we do the less romantic before-bed stuff, I want you to come back to bed with me. And you should sleep however you want to. But I won't object if you're not wearing pajamas." She kissed me, rolling so we were facing each other. "Then I won't have to take them off you again…"

* * *

I woke up with Stacey behind me, snuggling me into her with one arm under my neck and the other pulled tight around my stomach. We were both naked, and I took a moment to isolate the sensation of each of her body parts as they fit into mine and remember how amazing it had been to see and touch those body parts in a new way. We'd stayed awake past midnight—almost unheard of for her—and learned more about each other and what brought us the most pleasure. And! I'd figured out what to do with my retainer.

Despite having only slept for half the time I usually did, I felt rested and relaxed. Stacey had training, and I was surprised she was still under the covers when I came out of the bathroom. An arm snaked out from the covers. "Get back here."

"If I come back there then you're not going to get out of bed."

"I knowww." She groaned, rolling over and pushing back the covers. "Are you hungry?"

I nodded and picked up my clothing from the floor, quickly getting dressed before my willpower cracked. Stacey sat up, the covers falling away to expose so much skin that I almost caved and crawled back into bed. "I'm starving," she mumbled. "I need to refuel after last night's"—an eyebrow bounce—"workouts, or I'm not going to make it to Copper." She glanced at her watch. "Shit, I'm late." She flung herself out of bed.

"Mhmm, you are. I'll start your breakfast so you can get dressed."

"Or…" Stacey kissed me, murmuring against my mouth, "We could do more of this and I can eat in the car on the way to the mountain."

"Really? You'd change your super-strict routine for this?"

"Mhmm, I would. What is happening to me?" A lazy smile played around the edges of her mouth as she dragged light fingertips up my thigh and over my hip. "Oh...I know. You happened." After another quick kiss, she disengaged herself and I went to make her training breakfast—to-go—so she wouldn't be late, because how awkward to have Aspen know exactly why.

I didn't have insurance to cover me when the mountain was closed, so I couldn't go to watch her, or ski myself. Then she'd be napping after her morning training, and me being around would seriously endanger that. But we agreed to meet here and go to the gym together for her workout that afternoon before coming back to her place for dinner and...

Aspen was gone, and Mom was unsurprisingly still asleep when I got home just after six a.m. I took a quick shower, afraid that if I let myself stay in there, thinking about Stacey's touches, then I'd never get out. Aside from asking if I'd had a nice day yesterday, Mom was very restrained when she came down to join me for breakfast. Yeah, she knew. My stupid smile would have given me away anyways. After breakfast, I played around with my edits, got in a solid study session, exchanged some sexy texts with Stacey when she got home from Copper, did more study, and then I got ready to meet her at her place so we could go to the gym together.

If this was adulting, I was all for it.

Charlie seemed delighted to see me again, asking immediately about the film project and how he looked and if I'd edited his best side into the majority of his shots. And I swear he gave Stace an eyebrows-raised look that made me think he could somehow tell something had changed between us.

Instead of warming up on the bike in the weight room as usual, Stace joined me in the main cardio room, where we pedaled on neighboring spin bikes. She urged me on with "Faster! Faster!" while grinning the whole time like she was doing nothing more vigorous than sitting on the couch.

I pedaled as quickly as I could and was, unsurprisingly, still out-pedaled by Stace. She let out a triumphant shout, which drew the attention of the rest of the cardio crew, before dialing the bike back down and slowing her pace. I matched her slower pace gratefully, trying to take a breath that actually satisfied me.

"Are you going to stay here or come play with some weights?" she asked.

"I'll do a little more here, then I'll come in and watch you. And maybe do some weights." Or die. Either or.

She waved at Charlie, who was leaning against the door to the cardio room, then flashed me a cocky grin before slipping off her bike and cupping my face. I watched her tight butt swagger out and dropped my head to concentrate on what I was doing. I spent forty-five minutes doing half-hearted cardio before deciding it was time to do some half-hearted weights. And watch my girlfriend—girlfriend!—during her intense gym workout. There was no way I'd be able to work out for another hour and fifteen minutes, which was what Stacey had left in her session, but I could stretch and watch her once I was done pretending to make some muscles.

When I made my way into the quarter-full weight room, Stacey was finishing up a set of something she'd once told me were called core killers. Probably why she had killer abs. I tucked myself into a corner where I wouldn't be in the way, and started stretching. By the time I was done, Stacey was pushing a weighted sled across the long side of the room as Charlie, iPad under his arm, encouraged her to go harder and faster. Stacey's calves and quad muscles bunched tight as she drove the sled forward, her arms and shoulders straining. Oh yes. I could watch Stacey work out all day. And now, being free to stare as much as I wanted without worrying she might notice me, I did just that. I let my gaze linger on her strong thighs and calves. That ass. Her muscular shoulders and back. Those abs… And I thought about last night, only just suppressing my shudder of excitement.

I moved to the free-weights rack and pulled out a set for squats. All the hardcore exercises Stace did to improve her strength, coordination, reflexes, and balance were way beyond me. But Aspen had given me a weight routine to help build my skiing muscles. Not so I could race, obviously, but so I could feel stronger and more confident on the slopes.

A woman, a couple of years older than me and obviously a dedicated gym-goer, set the pair of thirty-pound weights back onto the rack. She shot me a smile. "You too, huh?"

The shock at being spoken to by a stranger made me forget my usual shyness for a second. "Pardon me?"

She gestured to Stacey, who was resting after pushing the sled the length of the gym and was, at that very moment, pulling her tank up to wipe sweat from her face. Of course, that exposed the tight definition of her six-pack and the sexy muscle over her hips. Her six-pack and hip muscle which I'd thoroughly explored with my fingertips and mouth last night. Recalling the sound she'd made and the way her muscles tightened when I'd tentatively touched her clit sent a rush through me, and I knew I was blushing.

The feeling of excitement over what Stacey and I had shared last night deflated a little when the woman gushed, "She's so hot."

"She sure is," I agreed.

"Those abs? Those tatts?" She fanned herself. "Phew. I've seen her around here a bit, she's smiled at me a few times. I think…I think I'm going to go talk to her. Shoot my shot, right?"

"Right," I said weakly. After clearing my throat, I added, "Maybe she has a girlfriend."

"If she does, I'm sure she'll tell me." She brought her hands together in front of her chest like she was praying for a good outcome. "Wish me luck."

My smile pulled my lips apart so tightly it almost hurt. I was about to tell her not to bother Stacey, because she was obviously in the middle of a serious workout, with a trainer for crying out loud, but the woman had already walked off, all swinging hips and confidence and being closer to Stacey's age than me.

Stacey looked surprised at the interruption but her surprise quickly dimmed. Even from where I was I could see her charming smile, the way she leaned slightly closer—not into the stranger's personal space, but still closer—and how her whole body language changed to cockiness. Cockiness and confidence were such ingrained aspects of Stacey's personality, but they were also tempered by her kindness and caring.

I heard Stace's laugh, not her real one but the one she kept for the public, but I couldn't hear what she was saying. I didn't need to hear to know she was flirting. They didn't touch at all, didn't get closer than three feet, but it was obvious there was a mating ritual going on that didn't include me. Charlie interjected, and the woman said something then turned away, her body language clear disappointment.

Stace caught my eye and winked. She blew me a kiss, then returned to her sled pushing. When the woman came back to stand by me, she was all but fanning herself. I felt like fanning myself to cool the heat of anger replacing the heat of desire that'd been there a minute earlier.

The stranger leaned against one of the weight machines, still looking over at Stacey even as she said to me, "Oh she is such a flirt. But you were right. She's taken. Lucky woman."

"Right," I said tightly.

I knew women found Stacey hot, because she was. And it'd always just been a thing in the background that made me feel strange because she was my best friend and I was in love with her and those women didn't really know Stace. They just saw the public persona. But now we were dating, it made me feel even stranger. Not angry. Not sad. But almost…defensive? Because Stacey was still being Stacey—gorgeous and personable and a flirt. She'd always been a flirt, and I'd always attributed it to her connecting with people. But now it made me uncomfortable. More than uncomfortable. Because if she was flirting with other people, then did that mean she still wasn't thinking of me as her girlfriend?

Obviously Stace had told this stranger *no thanks*, but seeing how she'd engaged with her made me feel sick. And all my enjoyment from watching her training had just evaporated. Thankfully flirt woman left, after wishing me a good day— ironic really. I played around one-quarter-heartedly with the weight machines while Stacey finished her workout, and once she started her cooldown and stretching routine, I did the same.

Charlie gave Stacey his usual mini-lecture about hydration and nutrition, said cheerful goodbyes, then swanned out of the gym, leaving me and Stace staring at each other.

A grin played around the corners of her mouth. "It was super hard to concentrate on this workout with you here doing all your sweaty stuff." She stepped closer, one arm slipping around my waist and pulling me to her. "So hot."

"You're telling me," I said, trying to sound cheerful, seductive. But I was pretty sure I failed. To cover my embarrassment at seeming odd, I handed her the shaker bottle to which I'd added water so it'd be ready for her when she was done.

"Thanks," she said, giving it another shake to mix her post-workout supplement. She chugged a third of it in a few gulps, then recapped the shaker. "Ready to go?"

"Yep."

She slung her duffel over her shoulder, took my hand in her free one and we walked to her car. But instead of driving away, she just sat there. *We* sat there. Silently. She swirled the bottle of protein mix around, watching me watching her. "What's up?"

My eyebrows rose. "Me? Nothing."

"You sure? Something seems to be up. You're...flat?"

"Harder workout than normal," I said lamely, and untruthfully, as if that'd explain it.

"Nice." Another third of the bottle went the way of the first, Stacey's cheeks bulging as she tried desperately to replace what she'd just burnt up. "But this doesn't seem like 'my quads and glutes are dying' flatness."

I fought with what to say, wondering if I was just being silly, and eventually decided that not saying anything would eat me up more than saying something. "That woman who came by to talk to you. You were flirting with her."

The shake paused midway to her mouth and I could see her battling with wanting to drink it and wanting to address what I'd just said. She frowned, and I could see she was genuinely confused. "I was?"

She finished the shake as I said, "Yes, you were."

Stacey carefully leaned over to place the shaker in the gym bag on the back seat. Then she just sat there, staring at her hands. "I don't really know what to say. Or even how to explain."

"Please try," I said quietly.

It took her a minute, and when she finally spoke, she seemed both edgy and contrite. "Gem, my whole identity is tied up in being a ski racer. And part of that is this." She indicated her face with a swirling finger.

"This...what?"

"This. My charm. I know it sounds stupid and egotistical but it's true. Nobody wants to watch quiet Stacey Evans who doesn't talk to fans or take selfies and sign things after races, who doesn't hype on social media. Fans don't want that, and neither do my brand partners. They signed me because they got invested in what I've done so far."

"I know that. I know you're an extrovert. I love that about you. I love how we fit together, how we balance each other out. But how do I fit into this specific image? How do I fit into your public life? Do I even fit? Because when you flirt with other women"—I lowered my voice—"just hours after you and I were in bed together, it makes me feel like I don't."

"Of course you fit," Stacey spluttered. "That's a ridiculous thing to say." She took my hands, turned them over, kissed my palms. "Why would you think that?"

"Because I'm not...glamorous. I'm not fancy. I'm just a senior in high school."

"Only for another three weeks, and then you'll be a college student on her way to being an award-winning, universally adored, in-demand documentary film maker. And then you'll be making documentaries and I'll be winning World Cup crystal globes and Olympic golds and it'll be absolutely perfect because we'll be doing those things together."

"Okay. But what about right now?"

It took an eternity before she spoke again. "Right now, it won't happen again. Gemmy, I'm so sorry. Please, forgive me. Please believe me when I tell you I didn't mean it."

"I know you didn't. You've always done it, and I think sometimes you don't even realize you are." I smiled in an attempt to soften what I'd said, but it felt shaky. "Did Bree ever say anything about it?"

She deflated. "No." Stacey glanced at me, and I could see how upset she was to have been pulled up about this. "I don't think she cared about anything except my Insta account. We were just using each other I guess. She wanted the audience she got from my social media followers, and you know that I was just shallowly attracted to how we looked in photos. She gave me nothing aside from an ego boost." Stacey grinned her slightly lopsided grin. "And we all know how much I need that."

"Ah yes. She is hot." I tried not to sound bitter, because it was an undeniable fact that Stacey's ex-girlfriend was attractive.

"On the outside, yes." She leaned over the middle console, and when I didn't pull back, she kissed me. "Unlike you who's hot inside and out." When I opened my mouth to respond to her cringeworthy line, she kissed me again, lingering long enough until I softened against her. "Apples and oranges, Gem. Both delicious, but everyone has a favorite. And you're *my* favorite. You're kind, funny, caring, and so hot that when I think about you my stomach feels all fluttery, kinda like race excitement but even more so. If I wanted to be with Bree or someone like her then that's who I'd be with. But I'm not. You're who I want."

I fought against just wanting to melt into her and let it go. "Okay, I get that. But do other people know it? Because if you keep openly inviting them in like you're single, and responding to their flirting with flirting..." I let my statement hang, knowing she'd pick up on what I was saying. "I know you can't control how people respond to you, and they do respond to you because you're so personable, but you can control how you react to that. And you *were* flirting."

Stace chewed her bottom lip, staring straight ahead through the windshield, but her eyes were unfocused. Eventually she said quietly, "I did flirt with that woman. And it's upset you."

"Yeah. It did. It just made me feel...not...unwanted, or unloved, but more like unseen, I guess."

She raised helpless hands. "You're right, I'm a flirt, and it's beyond disrespectful to you to do that."

I'd expected her to argue, and I even had a few more points lined up to give her to help my cause. But this acceptance made me swallow them. I felt sorry for her, having realized for maybe the first time that though she seemed happy enough with the short string of glamorous girlfriends she'd had, she actually hadn't been.

Stacey exhaled loudly. "I'm sorry. I'm sorry that I did it and I'm sorry that I made you feel like shit and unseen. I *always* see you, Gem. And I'll do better. I'll be better. I swear it."

"I know you will." I leaned over and cupped her face in my hands before kissing her. "Thank you. Thank you for listening to what I had to say and for understanding how I felt."

"It's just…new, right? We're just figuring out what we need from each other as girlfriends." She pulled off her ball cap, raking a hand through her hair. "Shit. Look at us talking things out and being reasonable. We are so mature and adulty."

"So mature," I echoed around my laugh.

Stace gave me a smile tinged with sadness, maybe even regret. "Gemmy, I don't want you to ever feel like that again. And if I do something else that makes you unhappy, you should tell me then too."

"And likewise." Because I was far from perfect. "I don't want us to be upset with each other over things that could be talked out."

"Deal." Stacey kissed my knuckles. "Now, I need a shower and a backrub."

"I assume you need someone to assist with that?"

This smile was more Stace, a little cocky and a lot charming. "Yes. Both things." She leaned over me and pulled my seat belt across my chest, clipping me in safely. Her gaze was earnest and unwavering. "I love you, Gem. I've never felt like this about anyone else. And I kinda feel like I don't *want* to feel it with anyone else."

I pressed my forehead against hers, wondering how she'd just articulated what I felt so perfectly. I knew she loved me—I felt it in every look and touch and word. But knowing she had realized some of my insecurity and that instead of being defensive, she'd been accepting made me feel that love even more. "I know. I love you too."

Stace kissed me, so deeply and possessively that I wanted to drag her into the back seat right there in the gym parking lot. When she pulled back, she carefully tucked a piece of my hair behind my ears. "Let's go home."

CHAPTER NINETEEN

Stacey

I felt like a complete shit. I was a complete shit.

I *knew* I was a hopeless flirt—not that I was bad at it, but that I couldn't stop myself from doing it. I'd always known it, and until now, it'd never been a problem. Women liked to talk to me, I liked to talk to them, it just turned into unconscious flirtation. No big deal, right?

But now I realized it was a big deal. I couldn't do that anymore, not when I had Gemma in my life. She deserved so much better, even if my playing with other women had just been meaningless fun. Meaningless fun that was now in the past. Time to grow up for real. And I thanked the universe that Gem was so good at articulating her feelings, and that I'd been able to kind of explain why I'd done what I'd done with that woman at the gym.

We'd talked it out more at my place, between showering together—and figuring out shower sex was slippery but super fun—making dinner, and then Gem reluctantly leaving just after eight p.m. so I could catch up on the sleep I'd missed the night before and so she could study. Because while we'd agreed that Gem staying at my place every night would be *amazing*, we quickly realized that with her school and study, and my training and love of sleep, it wasn't really going to work. But we decided we could see each other most days, and we'd figure out sex and sleeping and school as they happened. And in just a few weeks she'd have a couple of months free before starting college and we'd have as much time together as we could manage.

When I woke up—alone—on Monday morning to a mass of social media notifications, I didn't think it at all unusual. I always turned my phone to silent overnight while I slept. My parents knew to call my landline if there was an emergency, which was the only reason I'd kept one, and there was nothing else overnight that would require my attention. But texts and even a missed call—no voice mail—from Gemma was unusual. So was the text from Brick. I opened the message thread between Gem and me first, noting three messages she'd sent between ten p.m. and one a.m.

Are you awake?

Can you please call me if you get up to pee or something? Any time, please call. Nobody died but it's urgent.

I'm still up. Call please if you get this message. Bree's posted something on her socials and it's not nice.

A wave of nausea crashed over me, and Brick's message made my stomach sink even further. *Check Bree's social media as soon as you get up then CALL ME.*

What the hell was going on?

Obviously, Bree had done something. Something not nice, according to Gem. Something urgent, according to Brick. I decided to arm myself with information before I called either of them, and went straight to Bree's Instagram. Holy shit. Her most recent post had hundreds of likes and responses, a new record for her. Unfortunately, the likes were at the expense of defaming me. Or maybe not defaming, but something like it. I checked Twitter. Yep, cross-posted there too.

And she had deliberately posted it all after my bedtime—seemed she was aware of it after all—so I couldn't do anything about it and it had had hours to soak in on the Internet. I tried to make sense of what I was seeing. There were a couple of pictures, clearly taken at max zoom with a phone, of me and Gem in my car outside the gym yesterday afternoon. The first picture was of me, holding my shake in one hand and gesturing with the other. I looked frustrated, Gemma looked upset. Then a picture where I'd leaned over to kiss her. Then a selfie of Bree and me that she'd artistically Photoshopped to split in two.

Pictures could be interpreted a dozen ways, so I wasn't as concerned about them. It was the words that stung the most.

@BreeziBree

My ex, everyone's golden skiing speed girl Stacey Evans, isn't as golden as she pretends to be. She's self-centered, cruel, emotionally absent and given she's already got a new GIRL on her arm less than a week after we broke up, she probably cheated on me for our entire relationship. Looks like she's cheating again if Gemma's face is anything to go by. I totally dodged a bullet with @staceyskeez and good riddance. She may have won bronze but she's a gold medal bitch.

A gold medal bitch? That didn't even make sense.

I didn't know what made me angrier—the fact she'd implied Gemma was a kid, that she'd implied I was a cheater, that she'd said I was emotionally absent when I'd bent over backward to try to accommodate her around my hectic life, or that she'd named Gemma. I was surprised she even remembered Gem's face and name given how dismissive she'd been of her. It was lucky Bree had left Gem's username out of her vile post.

I closed my eyes, rubbing my fingertips over the eyelids. I was such a dumbass for dating her, and now I was reaping what I'd sown. It was regular time by my standards, but early for Gem. She'd been awake at one a.m. but I decided to check if she was awake now instead of just calling. *You up?*

I had a response in under a minute. *Yes.*

I don't know what's going on. I'm going to call Brick then I'll call you.

Okay.

I put my phone on speaker so I could get dressed for training while I talked with Brick. Even though my life was imploding in the virtual realm, I was still due at Copper Mountain this morning. I had no idea if Aspen had seen this or if Gemma had told her, but it didn't matter. Life didn't stop just because my ex-girlfriend had decided to rake me over the coals for something that should have been forgotten. People broke up all the time, people who actually had a connection, unlike Bree and I.

As soon as Brick said hello, I rushed in with, "Before you say anything, I know I have the worst taste in ex-girlfriends."

Brick grunted. "Yeah, you really do." I knew he wasn't mad at me. "I'll handle it. But I need you to tell me what happened."

"*Nothing* happened. Bree and I weren't compatible, we hardly ever spent any time together, had no real common interests, *and* she was mean to my best friend. So I broke up with her. I wasn't nasty about it and I *didn't* cheat on her. And it was about a week after that when Gem and I finally got brave enough to admit our feelings about being more than just friends."

"Ah shit. I assume you've seen her response?"

"What? Whose? Bree's?" His silence made something twig and I managed a hoarse, "Gemma's?" At Brick's grunted assent, my stomach dropped even further. "No? Shit. I haven't done anything except look at the post, text Gemma to try to stop her panicking, and then call you."

"Take a look. It's not catastrophic, but she needs to take it down right now and not engage any further. And speaking of not engaging, that's exactly what you're going to do. I'm meeting with the PR person at nine and we'll draft a statement refuting what Bree said and you can post that. And we'll put out spot fires as they happen. It'll die down, it always does. Put it behind you and focus on what's important."

I started pulling on thermals. "Do I get to see what I'm saying first?"

"You do. Is there anything you *wanted* to say? The PR person might not take it on board, but if it's not going to hurt you, then it might get through. You've got to look contrite over the fact you broke up, not apologetic, but not like a heartless bitch."

I bristled. I wasn't contrite, apologetic, or a heartless bitch. "I don't knowwww. Just say I could have been more mature or something, it was a short and superficial relationship, you know that. Maybe just make me seem like a young, dumb idiot who dated the wrong person. And also make it clear that I'm *not* a cheater. I never even had sex with Bree."

Brick nearly choked in his haste to smother that. "Whoa, kid. There are some things I don't need to know, and neither does the public."

"Okay, I know. I just wanted to point that out. Not that not sleeping with someone means you can't cheat. But you know what I mean." She'd done me one favor by not mentioning she'd correctly deduced that I was a virgin when we were together. She'd probably kept that in her pocket because she knew how spilling such a personal detail would look, and she was trying to maintain a wholesome image for when she became a Big Famous Movie Star.

I scrolled through the comments on Bree's post. It was so nice of them to move away from commentary on my ski performance at events. "I suppose this makes a nice change from them calling me an idiot, a choker, a shit skier, a bronze bitch."

"Ignore them." While Brick rattled off his usual "Don't let the bastards get to you" speech, I stared at the pictures Bree had taken of me and Gem.

"She took pictures of us in my car. Can we check if that's even allowed?"

"Where were you?"

"Outside the gym."

"You were in public, so there's no reasonable expectation of privacy there. Not much we can do. Sorry, kid."

"I didn't even *see* her," I said as I walked into my gear room to grab a race suit. "It's so freaking creepy. Like she was stalking me or something."

"If she starts doing that, then we can do something. But I don't think she will. I think she's just got her feelings hurt because she's an arrogant, egotistical young woman and she wanted the world to know she feels wronged."

"So basically she's still riding my coattails to get herself noticed."

He laughed. "You got it in one."

"I don't want to get all legal, but she's saying things about me in public that aren't true at all. And I hate that," I said as I jerkily pulled on my race suit.

"I know, but if you want to take legal action, we can look into our options. Being threatened with a lawsuit might make her think twice about lying in public."

"No, I don't want to do that." Not that I didn't want her to pay for what she'd done but because the thought of dealing with all that for something that should go away on its own was just too much.

"Okay. If you're sure. I think she's shot herself in the foot, because everyone who knows you on the circuit, and all the journalists who've interviewed you, think you're rainbows and sunshine. So they'll all know it's bullshit, and they'll deduce that if she's lied about that then the stuff about your personality and you cheating is suspect too. We've got the upper hand. We just need to keep it, so follow my lead and trust me."

"I will. Do you think this is going to affect my brand partnerships?"

"Not at all. I'll make sure they all know it's just a vindictive ex-girlfriend stirring up trouble and making false accusations, so don't worry about them freaking out. They also know you and your values, and we're going to get in front of this statement by a nobody who's just trying to get some attention, okay?"

"Sure," I agreed, wishing I felt at least a fraction of his confidence.

"Take care of yourself, and remember—do not contact Bree at all in any way. We don't engage with idiots."

"I won't," I promised him.

"Good, and please tell Gemma the same."

"Yeah, okay," I said glumly.

"Chin up, kid. We'll get through this just fine and you'll be unscathed. I promise."

We said our goodbyes. I finished dressing and decided it was time to see what Gemma had done. She'd responded to Bree's post which was the biggest no-go of spiteful social media interactions. As I read, I felt like I'd just had a slab of snow slip out from under my feet.

@gemstone04

Four eye-rolling emojis. *This is the biggest load of shit I've ever read. Stacey Evans is an incredible human. What's with the lies @BreeziBree? Are you so starved for likes now that you're no longer attached to Stacey's star that you have to make up lies to get people to pay attention to you?*

Oh no no no. Shit. She'd had a handful of replies, mostly unpleasant. Including Bree's. Instead of reading the vitriol, I dialed Gem, wedging the phone between my ear and shoulder so I could prepare my breakfast. Why couldn't crises happen at convenient times? Despite the fact she'd confirmed she was awake, it took a while for Gem to answer. When she finally did, it was a sleep-rough—or maybe tears-rough—quiet, "Hey."

"Hey, beautiful. Uh. So…" I actually had no idea what to say and blurted the first thing that came to mind. "Bree's a bitch, again."

Gemma coughed out a laugh, but it was so dry it sounded like she'd choked on it. "Tell me something I didn't already know."

"How'd you see it?" I asked as I broke eggs into a pan. "You weren't tagged." Thankfully.

"You were trending on Twitter when I was going to bed. I thought you'd died and had forgotten to tell me. Then I saw what she'd posted. I almost came around to your place, but Aspen wouldn't let me, said it was just an Internet thing, not a real emergency. She called Brick."

"I see." I set the phone down and put it on speaker so I could slice my avocado. "You really shouldn't have responded to it, Gem. It just pours gas on it for her to set fire to, and now they know exactly who you are. Ignore the haters, right?" We'd said it so many times, whenever there was a fresh round of trolls coming at me for something, and I almost couldn't believe she'd forgotten that rule. Though, she'd never had vitriol directed at her online and it was easy to say "just forget about it" when it wasn't aimed at you.

Her voice pitched up, cracking around her distress. "I was defending you. Defending myself! Can't I do that?"

I fought to keep my voice even and not snap at her. "Not like this, Gemmy Gem, no. You can't. Please delete it. Please. You'll only make things worse. Haven't you already seen that? They're coming at you now, including Bree."

She was silent.

I tried a different angle. "What you said about me was super sweet, thank you. But this isn't how it gets dealt with."

"How does it get dealt with, then?" she asked sarcastically.

"By the people I pay to deal with it." I was trying to flip my eggs when my toast popped and the coffee maker beeped to tell me it was done brewing. "Fucking fuck! I'm trying to do a million things right now and I can't deal with you too." Instantly realizing what I'd said sounded more than a little hurtful, I softened my tone. "I'm sorry. Please, Gem, just delete the post. Please. We can talk about it when I've finished training. I'll call you during your lunch hour or something."

There was a long, silent pause. So silent, I could hear my own breathing. Then Gem asked, with more than a little acid in her voice, "So…what then? I just have to leave this horrible thing up for everyone to see? This thing that's not only about you, but about me too?"

"She's hardly got any followers, Gem," I said weakly. "Nobody cares."

"She might have hardly any followers, but those followers have followers," she snapped back. "It's already got hundreds of interactions. That's more than *nobody*."

"Brick is dealing with it."

"I'm glad someone is."

Then she was gone. Even though I knew it was idiotic, I still asked the empty air, "Hello? Gem?"

I didn't know if I wanted to scream or throw my phone or crumple into a heap or all three. Instead, I calmly ate my breakfast, then sent Gemma a text apologizing again for Bree and my behavior and asking her to please not ignore me or shut me out.

No response. I probably would have picked one of my three losing-my-shit options, but I had work to do. As if summoned by the thought of training, a text from Aspen landed as I was pulling on my jacket. *Are you okay?*

Yes. The polite response. And I was okay, broadly speaking.

And okay to drive?

Yep.

Good. Let's skip race training and go to A-Basin for some non-regulated goodness. Just you and me, no Christina, so don't forget to bring skis or it's not going to be fun for you. Funny for me though. Take some extra time this morning and deal with what you need to. I'll see you there at 9:30. She added her usual batch of cheerful and hype-up emojis at the end.

I threw the phone onto the bed, angrily yanked off my jacket and ski pants, and ripped at the race suit zips on both sides of my chest. No need to be freezing in a race suit all morning if I wasn't doing race training. Thanks for fucking up my training, Bree. Again.

At least Aspen didn't seem angry with me for upsetting Gemma. Though this could just be the calm before the storm. Nah, Aspen wasn't the type to pretend she was feeling something she wasn't—I always knew exactly where I stood with her and she was rarely anything other than cheerful and supportive, even if she was being a hard-ass.

The hour drive to Arapahoe Basin passed in a blur. A very quiet blur. Gem hadn't responded to my texts, I'd muted all my socials so I didn't have to deal with the never-ending stream of notifications, and had been so agitated by music which just made me think of singing in the car with Gem, that I'd turned it off.

Aspen greeted me with a hug, but said nothing more about the Insta incident until we were back down by my car after a solid morning of skiing, which had made me feel about five percent better. "How're you holding up?" she asked.

I shrugged. "I'm doing okay. But I've definitely had better starts to my day."

She locked her skis in the rack on top of her car. "I can imagine. You want to talk about it?"

"Honestly? I don't even know what to say. Brick's dealing with the fallout."

"That's what he does best." She gripped my shoulder. "Come on, you don't have to hold it all in. Safe space, remember?"

Aspen was more than just my coach. She was a friend, a mentor, kind of another parent in some ways. Not long after she began coaching me, I'd had an incident at school—the usual homophobic shit—and when I'd turned up to training with a split lip from getting in between my then-girlfriend and a bitch, Aspen had been equal parts protective and caring.

I admired her so much, not just as a coach and athlete but as a person. She was everything I wanted to be as a human—an accomplished ski racer, a good and nice person, a caring and protective and loving spouse. When I eventually got to spouse stage with someone, that is. But I was screwing it all up—I was nowhere near the person she was.

I slumped back against the side of my car. "Yeah, I know. It just bugs me, that's all. Like, I know it's a lie, but everyone's seen it and most of them don't know it's a lie."

Aspen smiled knowingly. "I've never known you to care about what other people think."

"I don't, but this time I do because it's Gemma." I glanced over at Aspen. "How is she?" Hours after my last text, it was still radio silence. Sure, she was at school, but...

Aspen took a few moments before answering, and I thought she might tell me I should go find out for myself. "I only talked to her quickly last night and before she left for school this morning. She's upset, understandably." Aspen eyed me. "I overheard some of that conversation this morning. She'd probably be better if she talked to you properly, but she just needs some time. You know what she's like when she's upset."

I huffed out a laugh that felt like it was about to turn into crying. My answer felt tight. "Yeah, I do." Gem shut down and shut people out right away—her immediate instinct was to curl into an armadillo ball and protect herself. And while she was bundled up, she thought about things and then uncurled ready to talk about it. So I just had to wait until she was ready to hear my apology and explanation. I hoped I didn't have to wait too long. "I didn't mean for her to get caught up in anything like this, and I really didn't hurt her on purpose."

"Of course you didn't. We all know, Gem included, you wouldn't do that."

She was letting me off too easily. I rubbed the back of my neck, digging my fingers into muscle that felt like steel. I'd had all morning with the relaxing, rhythmical motions of skiing to shake all my thoughts loose and it had made me realize that, "I didn't handle it well, at all."

"A lot of the time, we don't." Aspen gently patted my back. "But it's how you handle it *now* that really counts."

"Right." I let out a long breath. "I'll see you tomorrow morning at Copper?"

She smiled. "You bet." As I turned to leave, Aspen asked, "Stacey? Your parents are still in Florida, right?"

I turned back, confused by the question. "Yeah, they are."

She stepped close and opened her arms to me. Without thinking, I moved into the hug. She'd hugged me plenty of times before, but right now when I was feeling so utterly crap, I fell apart. Aspen held me as I sobbed and when I could finally talk, she seemed to understand my mumbled-against-her-shoulder, "It's so fucked up. And unfair. And I know Gemma's hurt, but I don't know what to do because she won't talk to me."

Aspen hugged me tight, rubbing my back as she murmured, "I'm sorry, Stacey. It'll all blow over and things will work out. You'll see. You've just got to have patience and keep being the good person that you are. Gemma's upset, but she'll be okay. You'll be okay."

Gem might be okay. I might be okay. But would Gem and I be okay?

CHAPTER TWENTY

Gemma

It was possible that I'd had the worst day at school, ever. Worse than the time in fourth grade when I'd puked on myself in class. Worse than when in eighth grade I'd told a girl I was crushing on that I liked her, and she'd laughed and rejected me so loudly that everyone around us knew what I'd said. Worse than when my chemistry assignment, which was perfect on every test run, completely failed to work during my class presentation.

I'd known when I stopped by my locker first thing that something was up, and judging by the looks I was getting, the something was about me. It was always obvious when there was some sort of drama swirling about the halls, but I'd never been the focus of it before. And it felt horrible. Without needing, or wanting, to find out exactly what people were saying, I shrank down, wishing I could just go home and hide forever.

It was no better during my classes, and with every passing minute I felt sicker and sicker. The worst thing was I couldn't actually make out what they were saying, just snippets like my name, *Stacey*, *cheating*, *idiot*, along with the usual words to make someone feel like they were less than an inch tall. And by the time lunch rolled around, I was a big ball of anxiety and had pretty much decided I didn't want to face the cafeteria arena when Erin texted *I have something to cheer you up. See you at our usual table.*

I knew what she was doing—not only trying to make me feel better with what I suspected was my usual iced coffee, but also not letting me avoid the idiotic gossipers. So, with my best "Who cares?" expression stuck to my face trying to mask the very-much-does-care feeling in my gut, I waded through the cafeteria and slumped at our usual table with my back to the room. Hey, I'd made it, I wasn't shrinking away, but that didn't mean I had to sit there and stare at all the people who were dissecting my private life.

Private life.

I guess I'd known that dating Stacey had meant some of my private life would be public, the parts I shared with her. But I hadn't expected anything like this, and I had no idea what to do about it. Because there really wasn't anything I *could* do. I'd been told not to engage, to just sit there and let it play out. Let this vitriol—and let's be honest, it was as much a dig at me as Stacey—just float around in cyberspace.

And yeah, the post was hurtful, but it was easy to pretend I was okay with it because Bree had never liked me, and the people who'd responded didn't know me at all. Initially I was more upset that my girlfriend had to deal with something totally untrue and just plain mean. Until Stace had totally dismissed me and my feelings and steamrolled me about it, without even *trying* to talk about it, implying that I was a naïve idiot. I knew how busy she was, that she would have been trying to get ready for training and prepping breakfast as well as dealing with this. But she didn't even try to be soft. She just went straight to hard.

Erin sat down across from me, and silently slid my drink over.

"Thanks," I mumbled.

She waited until I'd taken a sip, then handed me a bag from Northside Kitchen with a donut shape inside. Her expression was soft, sympathetic. "Exciting weekend, huh?"

"You could say that." I should have been telling her about all the amazing stuff that had happened, but instead, it was all about Bree.

Erin opened her lunch bag with a dramatic huff. "I reported that post to Insta and Twitter, by the way. What a bitch."

She didn't know the half of it, but the last thing I felt like doing was dredging up all the other times Bree had made my life shitty. "Thanks." I glanced up at her. "Is it still there?" I'd been too afraid to look this morning. Too afraid to see what else people might have said. Most of it was directed at Stacey, but there were a few cruel comments about me and how young and dumb I must be. Not to mention the comments on my comment.

Erin scrolled through her phone, both her eyebrows arching in surprise as her thumb paused. "Nope. It's gone. Stacey must have some serious cyber muscle to get it poofed so quickly."

I coughed out a dry laugh. Maybe she did, but she'd sure taken her time using it. I almost didn't want to ask, but the need to know overwhelmed my dread. "Is there anything new from Stacey?" Like an apology, a rebuttal, anything. I realized immediately how dumb my question was—I had notifications turned on for her posts, but it was like that irrational paranoia that your phone wasn't working when you were expecting a call or text.

She scrolled again. "Nope, nothing. Last thing was that picture of you two at Alderfer."

I picked at my food, trying to ignore the surrounding chatter. Obviously I knew it wasn't *all* about me, but it sure felt like it. Erin seemed content to wait for me to talk, which meant we sat together quietly with our lunches. Until Aiden pushed up from his table a few down from ours, and came over. He was a friend of Noah's—an oafish jock who I doubted had two brain cells to rub together. I didn't look up, but he launched right in. "Bagged yourself a cheater, huh? You know, you had a good guy and you dumped him."

I glared, and muttered, "Fuck off." Not only did I not want to talk about it, especially not to him, but inserting himself into my ten-months-ago ex-boyfriend's bruised feelings was gross.

He leaned closer, smiling wolfishly. "What was that?"

I didn't get a chance to repeat what I'd said, or even say something more mature, because Erin stood up, her hands planted palm-down on the table. "She said fuck off. And grow up, you epic moron."

Surprisingly, he did just that. Fuck off, not grow up.

The anxiety I'd been controlling was suddenly so huge I didn't know what to do with it. I wrapped my hands around the plastic coffee cup, trying to hide my trembling. I didn't know if I wanted to run or cry or stay or puke or what. I just knew I didn't want to feel like this.

"You wanna talk about it?" Erin asked around a mouthful of kale.

I shook my head. The thought of talking, of eating, of doing anything normal, just felt overwhelming. "Know what? I'm not hungry. I'm just gonna hang out in the video lab. Thanks though. And thanks for the donut."

The lab was thankfully empty, and I hid at a workstation in the corner, balancing on the computer chair with my feet up and my knees pulled to my chest. I managed to keep my tears inside their ducts, which made it easier to go rationally through everything that'd happened.

Stacey and I had moved so quickly from best friends to girlfriends, and aside from a quick chat, hadn't really discussed our expectations. Maybe we needed to step back and look at things from every angle. Figure out how to work together as girlfriends. Because if we'd already had this happen, less than a week after we'd started dating, and a day after we'd first had sex, what did that mean? Then there was the argument we'd had about Stacey's "meaningless" flirting at the gym. Two dramas in a week. Oh, and the one about me accepting a place at CU Boulder. It almost felt like a sign that maybe we weren't meant to date, that we were just supposed to be best friends forever, best friends who were in love with each other.

Screw that.

The idea of stepping away from Stacey felt so much worse than us trying to sort this out. Because now we both knew how we felt, now that we'd had sex, how could we ever go back to being just best friends? I couldn't do it, even though it'd been in the back of my mind when I'd first started this thing—that if things didn't work out then how could we ever go back to never kissing, or touching each other that way?

I couldn't do it.

But I couldn't lose my best friend either.

So the only thing to do was work it out, find a way to deal with these issues, because now my life was tied to hers, and her life was kinda public. But she'd been so dismissive, so focused on herself, and so inconsiderate of my feelings about something that she'd dragged me into, even if it was unintentional. It felt like Stace still thought of us as best friends who now just did something more. But…she'd never been inconsiderate like that before. So who the heck knew what was going on and what I was supposed to do about it.

The rest of the day was blurry, and I rushed out to my car after the last bell, desperate to go home and burrow somewhere safe where I wouldn't have to think about this for just one damned minute. I almost skidded to a stop in the parking lot. Stacey was the last person I'd expected to see. Leaning against the hood of my car, dressed in her favorite pair of jeans, loosely laced scuffed leather boots, and one of her many Spyder down jackets, she projected the perfect image of a stylish ski punk. She tugged at her beanie, pulling it back so some of her hair puffed out around her forehead.

And I became aware of the gathering crowd, slowing to watch. They probably would have done so anyway—Stace had grown up in Edwards and was a local Olympic and World Cup hero—but now it felt like they were staring because of Bree's social media post labeling Stacey as a cheater.

I paused a few feet away. Stacey pushed away from my car, giving me a bright smile. But underneath it I could see her worry, her hurt, her distress. And the worst thing was that I still wanted to be near her, but I was so upset with her that I couldn't make myself go any closer. My resolution to work it all out had fled at the sight of her. I just couldn't find the words to tell her what I wasn't even sure I felt.

I said a wary, "Hey."

"Hey, Gemmy Gem. How are you?" She reached for me, but I kept my distance, tucking my arms around myself.

"Fine."

Her hands withdrew into her jeans pockets. "Listen, I'm sorry about today. Can we talk about it? Do you wanna come around? I was thinking about painting the Aeldari Warlocks. Then we can talk? I'll make dinner?" Her voice rose hopefully with each question.

As if Warhammer painting and dinner would make it all okay. "I have to study. And work on my film project." My heart clenched at the thought of working on the film now.

"Gem, look. I'm sorry. I'm sorry Bree is such a bitch and said what she said about you. I'm sorry she did it publicly."

I couldn't believe that she still just didn't get it. "Fuck, Stacey, it's not just about what Bree did. Well it is. Like, yeah, she's a bitch and I hate that she said those things about you, about us. But it's more about what you did, how you reacted to it." I swallowed hard. "How you reacted to *me*."

Her face almost melted, like she was just…falling apart. "I'm sorry. I panicked and I was trying to juggle everything and I just had no time to stop and think about what I was doing and saying, and I'm sorry."

"I think if you were really sorry then you wouldn't have done it. You would have thought about what you were doing, and tried harder and you would have stopped to consider how I felt before telling me to go away, like I'm just an annoying kid."

She looked like she'd been slapped. "Gem—"

"It's been *so* humiliating. Do you get that?"

"Of course I do," Stacey said, her shoulders hunching defensively.

"And not just from the people I don't know on the Internet. The whole school was talking about it today, laughing at me, making fun of me. And you didn't do anything except tell me to back off. Why didn't you do anything? It was up all night and morning. I don't care about strangers, they don't know me. But everyone at school saw it. They think I'm a total idiot."

"I *couldn't* do anything about it, Gem. I could have made the whole thing so much worse by jumping in without thinking, without getting advice from people whose job it is to deal with things like this."

"Oh sure. I forgot about your image."

"Gem—"

"You made me feel really abandoned." My breathing was shaky, and I forced myself to speak more quietly. "I've spent all day listening to them whisper and laugh and make fun of me, and now you're here and it's just making it worse because they're all staring."

Her face crumpled. "I didn't mean to make it worse."

"Look, I need to go. Like I said, I've got to study, and work on my film project, and—" My voice cracked. "I just need to go."

Stace inhaled shakily. "Are we breaking up?" It sounded like she'd barely managed to get the words out.

"No," I said hastily. "We're not. I'm not breaking up with you." I paused, and lost the hold I had on my tears. I swiped at my face with my sleeves. "Unless you want to?"

"Fuck, no! No! I do not want to break up. Gemmy, I'm sorry. I'm *so* sorry. I just want to talk to you."

"I know you do. But I can't, not yet. I'm not ready and I'm just going to get more upset."

Stacey's jaw tightened but she nodded and, without a word, walked away. And I cried the whole drive home.

Mom and Aspen pounced when I got home, but left me alone when I said I was really okay and just didn't want to talk about it right now. I wanted to talk about it, wanted to talk to Stacey, but I didn't know how. I decided to try and study, and had been at my desk for fifteen minutes, definitely not studying, when Mom knocked. She was carrying a mug, which she held up with a smile. "Brought you some tea. Can I come in?"

I nodded.

She set the mug down on my desk, hugged my shoulders, and kissed my forehead. "We're here if you want to talk."

"I know." She was almost to the door when I spun around in my desk chair. "Mom?"

"Yes?"

I hunched forward, hugging myself around the middle. "How do you and Aspen do it? Be together I mean. You guys make it look *so* easy."

She blew out a breath then came back to sit on the edge of my bed. "It's not easy, sweetie, I'm sure you know that. Being in a relationship can be hard work, but loving someone is also the easiest thing in the world."

"I'm realizing that," I said wryly. "It wasn't like this with Ashley or Noah."

She smiled. "No, I didn't think so. Maybe that's why it's harder with Stacey. Because it means something to you. Something important."

"But you and Aspen never fight, you don't even seem to disagree on anything. It's like your whole lives are just trying to make each other, and me, feel loved and happy and needed."

Her eyes widened. "Oh we argue and you know we absolutely disagree sometimes. But not about anything that's important. And we don't have our fights around you. We made that decision really early on, that you didn't need to witness that."

"Have you been reading that Good Parenting website again?"

Mom laughed. "Something like that." She paused for a few moments. "I think we had our one big fight in Australia. We got it all out of our system back then, all the hurt and anger, then we put everything out in the open and promised we'd talk frankly and honestly, and now there's nothing left to really fight hard about. Just little silly stuff."

I'd never asked Mom what that fight was about, a fight that had happened out of nowhere because from where I was watching, they'd already fallen in love during our vacation. "What *was* that fight in Australia about?"

She wrinkled her nose. "Me being an idiot. I made a decision for both Aspen and me, a decision based on my fears, and I excluded her from that decision. It was wrong and selfish, but

I thought it was the right thing for me and for you at the time. I was trying to protect you, protect myself, and I just hurt all three of us instead."

"What would you have done if she hadn't come back to Colorado and found you?" It'd been a total romance-movie-accidental-meeting thing.

Eyebrows raised, she exhaled a long, noisy breath. "I would have regretted it for the rest of my life. Making the decision to protect the family you and I had built felt like the most important thing to me, but then I realized our family is *so* much better with Aspen in it."

"Yeah," I agreed. "It really is."

Mom gave me one of her meaningful looks. "So if you make the decision about this relationship with Stacey all on your own, for whatever reason, then you need to be prepared to deal with the consequences. And the consequences aren't always nice, and they don't always work out the way it did for Aspen and me. I don't want you to regret losing your girlfriend, or your best friend, or both because you're too afraid to face up to the hard stuff."

"You think I should talk to Stacey."

"Of course I do. Avoiding a problem isn't the answer, and relationships are about sharing even when you don't feel like it. You don't have to share right away. You can take time to figure out your feelings, but if you can see yourself with her in the long term, then, Gem, you've got to talk to her. And you've also got to listen, really listen to what she has to say."

I leaned over to snag a tissue from my bedside table. "I just feel so...small. What Bree said made me feel like a kid all over again. Like I wasn't enough for Stacey, like I never would be. And then Stacey blew my feelings off, as if they didn't matter, which made it feel even worse."

"But you're not a kid," Mom argued. "You're an adult. A woman. Lord help me," she added teasingly, under her breath. "And Bree whats-her-name doesn't even know you. And I get the feeling she didn't really know Stacey either. But Stacey does know you. You have an amazing and solid and wonderful friendship. And if you love her as a friend *and* something more, then I think you've got everything you need to make this work."

"What if I've screwed it all up by shutting her out?"

"I don't think you have. I think this is less shutting her out and more just taking the time to process everything. It's a lot, especially for you. And Stacey knows you well enough to know how you deal with things."

"Yeah," I mumbled. By crawling into my little turtle shell until I felt like I could cope. "But what if it happens again?"

She pretended to look shocked. "How many stupid ex-girlfriends does Stacey have?"

I huffed out a laugh at her deliberate misinterpretation. "I mean, a few. And all of them have been Instagram addicts so who knows what they'd do." Not like me. I mean you know, socials are fine, but I didn't want my entire life to play out on social media because I'm dating Stacey. "I mean…what if we fight again and I just keep doing my hiding thing? What if I shut down again when we fight?"

Mom took a few moments to think about it. "Well, you can either try to not do that, or you and Stacey can build a toolbox so you're ready to fix it when, or if, it happens again."

CHAPTER TWENTY-ONE

Stacey

I shouldn't have pushed by going to Gem's school and waiting for her like a stalker, but she'd ignored my calls and texts all day, even those I'd timed for her lunch break when I knew she'd be free. But I was *so* desperate to talk to her. To explain. To see if she was okay. But sitting in my car in her school lot, watching her drive off, I realized she must have felt trapped by me. I'd given her no choice but to confront what'd happened, and in such a public space. I knew that when Gem was upset, she often withdrew until she'd figured things out, and if I was patient she'd come to me to talk. I *knew* that. So I'd screwed up doubly by acting before thinking.

I only knew one way to move through life—flat out, pedal to the metal, boobs to the wall...you get the idea. I charged through my days, throwing myself into everything, sometimes without thinking things through. Because if I stopped to think about the consequences of ski racing, like crashing out and breaking a limb, permanently disfiguring or paralyzing myself, or even dying, I'd never be able to do the thing I loved. Maybe the mindset of not overthinking anything had seeped into my personal life as well.

Gem was the opposite. She wasn't afraid, but she thought everything through before acting. She wasn't indecisive, the opposite really. I always knew that if she'd chosen something, she was certain. It was why I was so instantly at ease when she'd first admitted she loved me as more than just a friend—because I knew she was sure, which made my fears fall away.

Maybe that's what relationships were really all about. Balance. Things that would usually push against each other somehow finding a way to work in harmony. So I could take some of Gem's care and thoughtfulness and apply them to myself as needed. And if she wanted some of my…uh, I didn't even know what to call it. Stupid thoughtlessness? Bravery? Confidence? Whatever. If I had something she needed, then she could take that.

I replayed the conversation in my head. What she'd said about being humiliated stuck with me. My first thought had been *Geez, like it's not humiliating for me too?* Then my little head-voice reminded me that this was technically my fault, that Bree was my ex and therefore my problem, and Gem had only been pulled into it because of me. And she had every right to be humiliated, and I could totally understand why she was.

Before I left the school, I called Brick to see where we were, what he'd come up with to smooth over this whole social media shit-storm, because I really needed it smoothed. I needed it gone because it was jeopardizing the relationship with one of the most important people in my life.

As always, Brick sounded calm, and confident. "We reported the post to Instagram and Twitter and so did a bunch of other people it seems, because it's gone. So that's good—now we don't have to engage with Bree to get it taken down, which would just open up a whole new issue. One sec…I just sent you an email with a statement for you to post on your social media accounts. Sorry it's taken all day, but we wanted to be sure it hit the right notes. Let me know what you think. We took what you said, tidied it up, but it doesn't sound like it was written by a pro."

"Okay, lemme see what it says." I opened up my emails and read what his public-relations person had written to help fix one of the shittiest things that'd ever happened to me.

I'm sorry my ex-girlfriend felt the need to make our private life public. I admit I could have been more mature in how I instigated our breakup, but doing so was the best thing for both of us as we were on separate life and career paths. I want to say emphatically that none of what she said is true. I'd ask that you respect my privacy, and be happy that I'm happy in my personal life, which will allow me to get on with what I do best—winning alpine ski racing medals for my country.

It was solid, and the appeal to their sense of ownership of my victories was genius. It wouldn't sway everyone of course, but it would dampen the indignant flames of those bystanders who'd only jumped onto the #StaceyEvansCheater bandwagon because it was something new and exciting. Everyone loved someone who won medals for their country, and reminding them of that should help.

I raised the phone to my ear again. "Yep, I'm happy with that. Do you want it as text, or a video?"

"Your call," he said.

"Video's probably more intimate, shows I'm not hiding. I'll record it when I get home, then put it right up."

"Good. It'll die off in the next day or two. Something else will come up that'll take their focus away from you, especially if we don't draw any more attention to it after your statement goes live."

"Right. And I won't engage of course." And I doubted Gemma would either after the ass-chewing I'd given her. My stomach twisted as I recalled what she'd said about the kids at school. She must have had an awful day and it was all because of me. There weren't enough sorrys in the world to make up for what I'd done.

"That's the way we do it." His voice softened. "This is just a bump in the course, kid. And we made it down to the bottom just fine."

We was a loose term. My team and I, yeah, sure. But Gem and I? I still had no idea. I made a mumbly, gurgly sound in response and hoped Brick would let it pass.

He did. "Now. You need to relax. Put the statement up, then forget about it. Move on and focus on what's important. The things that make you happy, and help you do what you need to do."

"Right." Easier said than done. If it were just me, then I'd stick it in the mental trash can with all the other crap that wasn't useful, helpful, or kind. But now I had Gem to consider too.

"We'll keep an eye on the metrics, but unless it does the opposite of what we're sure it will, you won't hear about it again. And remember, if Bree contacts you, don't engage. Just tell her you don't have anything to say."

Oh I had so much to say. "Sure. I will be the very model of control."

He gave me his belly laugh. "Knew I could count on you. Now, take it easy, okay? And you know I'm here if you need me for anything."

We said our goodbyes and hung up.

My favorite part about getting home was the guy with a huge camera still camped out on the sidewalk outside my house. He'd been there when I'd come home from A-Basin, then again when I'd left for, and come back from, the gym. Each time, I'd given him stink-eye—from a distance of course, because those were not photos I wanted on the Internet—then had stuck my best game face on and driven past him without so much as a sideways glance.

I printed out and practiced the statement, tidied my appearance, sat on my back deck with the gorgeous mountain view behind me, and read from the paper stuck to a chair in my line of sight. I wasn't an actor, but the video looked pretty good. And thankfully not like I was reading from a printout.

Good fucking riddance, Bree.

I left my annoyance and anxiety outside and locked myself back inside away from the prying camera lens out front. As I was readying to turn off all notifications and hide out for the rest of the night with some binged television and some sadness ice cream, another Insta notification pinged through. I glanced half-heartedly at the screen, my half-heartedness turning full-hearted when I saw it was *@gemstone04* who'd liked my statement. My stomach both sank and soared. Okay. So obviously Gemma didn't want to cut me out of her life altogether. But she didn't want to talk to me at school just an hour ago?

No, Stacey, she *couldn't* talk to you.

This small social media interaction felt like an olive branch. And I grasped it with both hands. Gem found some conversations easier over text, where she had time to think about what she wanted to say and make sure they conveyed her meaning without her emotions skewing things. She'd explained that the lack of tone that you'd get from a face-to-face conversation was balanced by her not feeling confronted, or being slammed by feelings and trying not to fall apart in front of someone.

Heart hammering, I tapped out a text. *I'm sorry. And I'm sorry I came to school this afternoon and made you feel cornered. I just really want us to talk and work this out. And I REALLY don't want to break up.*

Typing dots appeared immediately. *Me either. That's the last thing I want. I'm sorry I couldn't talk. You know me.* Wobbly face emoji. Turtle emoji.

Yeah, I do. I love you, Gemmy Gem. Kissy-face emoji. *And when you're ready to talk, I'm here.*

I know, thanks. And I love you too. A handful of hearts appeared in another text. I fell back onto the bed, phone clutched against my chest. Relief made me feel shaky, not unlike the adrenaline comedown after a race. And I thought that yep, we'd be okay after all.

Within a few hours of my statement going live, it seemed to be having the intended effect. My periodic checks of socials—yeah, okay, I couldn't stay away—told me I was no longer trending with #StaceyEvansCheater. The team Brick had employed to scour social media for my name assured him that aside from the odd thread playing out with barely any bites, it was dying down. And those periodic socials checks also told me everyone who knew me had said something, even if just a brief message of support, on my post. So by tomorrow, I should definitely be yesterday's news.

Yay…

I did some stretchy meditation—*not* yoga which I'd never been able to get the hang of—ate dinner, tried painting the Aeldari Warlocks, then gave up because I couldn't focus on the intricacy. So I went into my home gym, hooked up my phone to the sound system and just…danced. I didn't dance well, I never had. But I needed to move, to get rid of the angst rushing around my body like a vital fluid keeping me alive.

With every jiggly, jangly, uncoordinated movement, I felt some of the horrible feeling I'd been carrying around with me fall away. Probably in horror at my dancing. So things weren't perfect, but at least Gem and I had communicated, confirmed we hadn't suddenly stopped loving each other because of this, and that there'd be further communication which would hopefully make things better.

I'd been impersonating a disjointed puppet for almost half an hour when my ringtone cut through the song. I rushed over to my phone, a little disappointed to see my mom's face instead of Gemma's. The timing of Mom's call made me suspicious. She wasn't a social media person, but I was sure my big brother, Max, had filled her in on what'd happened. She'd been over the moon when I'd texted her about Gem and me moving into a different sort of relationship—my parents adored Gemma, and vice-versa—and I was kinda scared that Mom was going to give me shit for messing things up already.

I took a deep breath and answered the call. "Hey, Mom."

"Hi, honey."

The sound of her voice made me want to crawl into her lap and cry my eyes out. I went through some basic pleasantries to give myself time to calm down. "How're you and Dad? How's Grandpa?" They'd only been on vacation for a couple of weeks, but it felt like I hadn't seen my parents in months.

"We're all fine. We've been talking, and Grandpa might come back to Colorado to stay with us for a while too."

"Oh? That'd be so cool." Since I'd started racing professionally, it'd been really hard to find time to go down and see my grandpa in Florida. Having him just ten minutes away, living with my parents, would be amazing.

"It would. But we can talk about it later. How are you, my sweetheart?" The way she asked it—soft, concerned, loving—gave me no doubt that she knew about the Bree Blowup.

I tried to sound nonchalant, but my response was shaky. "I've had better days. But I'm doing okay. Brick's on top of it."

"I'm glad to hear you're okay. And I'm glad Brick's handling it."

"It's not true, what Bree said."

"I never thought it was," Mom said instantly.

"She's just pissed at me," I said as I started up the hall, back toward the couch. "But, I mean, we weren't in love and had only been together three months, so why would she do something so vindictive?"

"Even if she didn't love you, seeing you with someone else so soon would probably still sting," Mom said matter-of-factly.

Especially when I was giving Gemma what I couldn't, or wouldn't, give Bree. My time. "You're right," I sighed. "And now the whole Internet is talking about me like I'm a gross person with no morals."

Mom laughed quietly. "I doubt the whole Internet is talking about you. I love you, and I'm proud of you and all your accomplishments, but you're not Beyoncé."

"I know," I sighed. I bypassed the couch and carefully pulled back the corner of my front window blinds. "But there's still some guy with a telephoto lens camped out on the sidewalk. I have no idea how he knows this is where I live." He hadn't budged, except to photograph me each time I came and went.

"Really? Oh those people have no shame, do they."

"Not a bit."

She paused for a moment. "And how's Gemma coping with all this nonsense?" This question was no less soft-concerned-loving, but it had a touch of caution.

That one question broke the armor I'd been trying to keep wrapped tightly around myself all day, and some tears emerged. "Not great. She's pretty upset. Mad. At me."

"Why at you?"

"Because it's my fault she got dragged into this, because I didn't handle Bree how I should have. And because she fed the trolls which you know just makes it worse, and I got…kinda mad at her for doing that."

"Oh, Stacey." The disappointment was clear, but so was her Mom-concern.

"I know, okay. I'm not proud of it. It was a super-stressful thing to wake up to, and I had Brick in my ear about it, and Gemma freaking out and I was trying to get ready for training. I'm not excusing it, but it was just a really shitty time and I didn't stop to think."

"Did you apologize to Gemma?"

"Yeah, a few times. But she wasn't ready to talk to me."

"She will be. You just have to be sensitive to her needs. Dating each other is a big change for both of you."

"I'm trying to be, but I'm also freaking out. Dating her is incredible, so much better than I ever imagined it'd be. But ever since we started, we've also been having problems we never had when we were friends." The flirting thing, my unexpected-to-her reaction about her college choice, Bree's bombshell. "Does that mean we made the wrong choice? It hasn't even been a week and it feels like we keep messing it up."

"I think it means you're learning how to be in a partnership instead of just a friendship, honey."

"But how is it different? I mean, aside from"—I cleared my throat—"the romance stuff."

"When you open yourself up, truly open yourself to another person and let them in and they you and you're honest with each other, then things happen that wouldn't otherwise. It's a new dynamic. It doesn't mean you don't love each other or that you shouldn't be together romantically. It means you're doing what you should in a relationship—being honest."

"But we've always been honest with each other."

"I know. But this is a new kind of honesty. More intimate. And it's going to take time to get used to that."

"Right. Because we all know I'm so great at being patient."

Mom laughed. "You've waited how many years for this to happen?" Her tone turned more serious. "I'm sure you can take the time to lay solid foundations to make sure it lasts."

The thought that had been brewing since I'd talked to Aspen that morning, when she'd implied that none of my other girlfriends had meant anything to me, shoved past all the other thoughts fighting for space in my brain. Because she was right. Before Gem, I'd never fully given myself to a girlfriend— physically or emotionally—because I hadn't really felt invested in any other relationships. And it wasn't that I was consciously holding myself back from her, but maybe I was still learning how to share myself that way.

The thought that I was selfish, that I didn't instinctively consider how my actions might affect Gemma—even when we were "just" best friends—was horrible. But maybe it was also true. And I really didn't want to be that person. I wasn't going to be that person. I was going to fix this. I was going to be the person who admitted her mistakes, and worked hard to never repeat them.

"Do you think I can?" I asked quietly. "I've never done this with anyone else before, never wanted it as much as I do with Gem." I'd marry her, totally, which seemed a scary thing to think at almost-twenty-one years old, and also with the shit we were wading through. But Gem made everything better, easier. And why wouldn't I want to spend the rest of my life in a partnership with my best friend?

"You can do anything you set your mind to, honey. Especially when it's something as important as this."

"Yeah," I sighed. "It's just so hard."

"It is," Mom agreed. "But sometimes the key to building good foundations is accepting where you were at fault, and working to ensure you don't make the same mistake again."

A.k.a. being an adult. Awesome.

CHAPTER TWENTY-TWO

Gemma

Mom had been right. The next day at school was almost like nothing had happened and I was back to just being part of the sea of students. The masses had moved on to the next big gossip thing, and most of my peers were too excited about graduation in two weeks. So I was all but forgotten, which made it easier to settle how I felt about it. After Stacey had reached out, another bundle of upset had packed up and left town. I really wanted to talk to her, and I knew she knew that, and thankfully she seemed to have finally remembered that sometimes I just turtled for a bit 'til I could figure out how to have a difficult conversation without melting into a puddle of tears and snot.

Stace and I had texted back and forth during the day, both our normal texts and also a few deeper ones, checking in with each other, reaffirming our love for each other, and confirming that we'd talk soon. And once I'd come home and taken a long, hot shower, I felt steady enough to talk to her face-to-face. The text I sent asking if she wanted to talk had her answering in seconds with *I'll come around, be there soon.*

And it was indeed soon when Mom called up the stairs, "Gem? Stacey's here to see you."

"Okay. Can you send her up here, please?"

A few seconds later, I heard her taking the stairs two at a time. Her smile was unusually uncertain, even shy. But when she saw me, her face softened like she'd just taken a huge relaxing breath. "Hey, Gemmy Gem."

"Hey." I stood up, walked right over to her, and dragged her into a hug. As Stace's arms wrapped tightly around me, I felt how hot and sweaty she was. I pulled back a little and looked her up and down. "Did you run here?"

"Yeah." She flashed a grin, a little more crooked than usual. "Had to work off some nervous energy."

"Ah." I didn't need to ask what the nervous energy was about. She radiated a similar tension as she did before races, but with more anxiety coming through. Carefully, I reached up and cupped her face in my hands. Stacey relaxed instantly. Then relaxed again when I pulled her down for a kiss.

The kiss was slow and soft, almost careful, like we were seeing where our boundaries had fallen after our fight. It felt like they'd fallen pretty much where they'd been before, and the feeling of our shared closeness had butterflies swirling in my belly.

"Are we done fighting?" she asked, her lips still brushing against mine.

"I hope so."

"Good." She kissed me again, then let me go. Stacey collapsed into my desk chair, her arms slung over the armrests. She took a deep, slow breath, her eyes never leaving me.

I pushed my door almost closed then dropped down onto my bed, shoving my hands between my knees. "Being angry with you is really hard work. I hate it. But I *was* angry and upset. Maybe I still am."

"What are you most angry and upset about?"

"A little by what happened, but mostly how you dismissed me."

"I didn't mean to hurt you."

"I know you didn't. But you still did." I tried to sound as neutral as possible, just telling her my truth instead of accusing her, because I really didn't want to fight again.

She sagged. "I know I did. And I'm sorry. I think I was just… trying to protect you. Trying to protect us. And when I saw you'd gotten involved, I panicked, I guess. I know I'm not a huge celebrity, but people still want to have little pieces of me, and I just wanted one part of my life that was only mine. I just wanted you to be mine. You're *my* BFF."

Frowning, I asked, "Your BFF?"

She tilted her head, her eyebrows creasing in confusion. "Well, yeah."

"Right. But I'm also your girlfriend now," I pointed out.

"Of course you are, but you're still my best friend, Gem. That hasn't changed because we're dating. I love you. As my friend, as my girlfriend. Both those things are super important to me, maybe equally important, and I'm sorry I put them in danger."

I smiled. "I think danger is a bit of a strong word."

Her cheeks puffed up. "It sure felt like that."

"We were never in danger, Stace. Just a little wobbly. And I feel a lot better now that I've had some time, and we've talked." I reached out and touched her thigh. "Sorry I turtled."

Now she smiled. "S'okay. I kind of expected it. Sorry I pushed while you were turtling."

"I know you just wanted to talk. And you were right, we needed to talk, but I—" I took a deep breath, trying to figure out how to apologize for my behavior. "I shouldn't have jumped on you the way I did, magically expecting you to fix it all right away. I knew you would be trying to deal with it on top of all your usual stuff, and I put my own feelings on you without giving you a chance to explain. I dumped on you, and then I ran away and hid. That wasn't fair, and I'm sorry, and I'm going to be more aware of it, of my insecurities, so I don't ever do it again."

"Guess we both could have done things better."

"Yeah," I agreed.

She was quiet for a while, her fingers working together nervously. "I've realized with all this that I've been really selfish in my past relationships. If you can even call them relationships," she added. "And the worst thing? I even thought about it with you, worried I might do it. And I swore I wouldn't, and then I *still* did it. With this Bree thing, I think I was more focused on myself and totally forgot someone else was being hurt. Fell right back into selfishness."

It was an interesting thing to hear her admit, especially when she'd kind of brushed me off when I'd brought up this exact thing at Beaver Creek. I thought carefully about how to word what I wanted to say. "I think we have to be a little selfish sometimes. And you've got a lot of reasons to protect parts of your personal life to protect your racing career. Keeping some things private gives you a safe space away from racing and all that attention and pressure. Maybe it was just a part of that."

She shrugged. "Maybe." She smiled, and while it was as charming as always, there was a touch of sadness in it. "It's a really hard thing to confront your own personality flaws. Especially when you really don't want to have those flaws. I don't want to be a selfish person, Gem. Not in any aspect of my life." Her forehead wrinkled. "And I don't *think* I'm a selfish friend—"

"You're not," I assured her. Our friendship had always been one of the least complicated aspects of my life, and I'd never felt she'd withheld herself from me. We understood how each other's lives worked, and we'd never pushed where we shouldn't. Stacey had skiing. And I had school. For another few years at least.

"Well that's good." She puffed out a loud breath. "So why am I a selfish girlfriend? Why did I immediately move you, and how I act around you, into that column? Nothing really changed between us, except for the…romantic stuff, right?"

"Right."

"And I still flipped the switch into selfish." She raised both hands, palms up. "So what does it mean? I don't want to be this person in a relationship, Gem, especially not with you."

"I know you don't." I debated if I should tell her or not, but decided almost right away that keeping things from her wasn't going to help us. "I've been your best friend for a while, watched you with a few girlfriends now." I smiled at her cringe, before I told her the truth again. "I think, maybe you're afraid of what it might mean to really let someone in like that, so you've kept your girlfriends at a distance. Then you can't get hurt and you don't have to manage anyone else's expectations. You can enjoy the benefits of being seen with a hot girlfriend but without having to do the hard emotional work. And now it's just a habit."

"Afraid…" she mused.

"A shocking concept for you, I know," I teased her.

Her mouth twisted, and for a moment I thought she was going to cry. "It is. And I think you're right. It's just habit." She inhaled a slow, shaky breath, and seemed to regain control of herself. "So what are we gonna do? I can't do this again. Not to me or you, or us."

"I think…we just have to be aware of how we act and react, and be honest with each other, and open to hearing that the other person is feeling a certain way. Not in a critical way, just a healthy, adult way."

"Agree."

I reached out and took her hands in mine. "Stace, I know you, and I know the parts of your life where you need to focus totally on yourself. And I'm okay with that, okay with supporting you the way I always have. It's the other parts of you I need. I just want you to keep letting me into all those other parts of your life, the way you did before we started kissing each other."

"I know. I will. I still don't even know why I did it. Like… you're my Gemmy Gem, right?"

I nodded. I loved her nickname for me. "Right, that hasn't changed at all. We're still us. Just…extra."

She groaned. "Geez, working out feelings is so freaking hard."

"Yeah, it is. But it's better than the alternative."

Stacey looked uneasy. "Which is?"

"No more of this…" Smiling, I murmured, "Come here." When I tugged her hands, Stacey melted from the chair and crawled on her knees toward me.

She pressed herself against the front of my legs, wrapped her arms around my waist and buried her face in my lap. "Gemmy, I'm sorry. I love you. And I promise I'm not going to do that to you ever again, and I'm going to try my hardest to not be selfish when it comes to us."

I leaned down, took her face in my hands, and kissed her. "I forgive you. And I'm sorry too. I was so focused on how I felt that I didn't really give much thought to how it was affecting you, how hard it was for you to be trying to deal with all that and then me too." The weight I'd been carrying around since I'd first seen the Insta post felt suddenly lighter. I was less encumbered, like I could move and breathe again.

"And I forgive you too." She kissed me quickly, then crawled up onto the bed to sit beside me. I hugged her against my side, and we sat together quietly, just reconnecting. The relief of us having worked through what'd felt a major, possibly relationship-ending issue was so enormous I couldn't even put words to it.

Stace glanced at my desk, then back to me. "Are you working on my movie?"

"*My* movie," I corrected her with a smile. The laptop was open, a frame frozen on the screen. "And yeah. I think I'm about half done."

"Can I see it?"

"Unfinished?"

"Please."

I leaned over and pulled the MacBook down, settling it on my lap. I didn't feel the need to explain nervously that it still needed this and that, and to not expect a finished product. We watched together in total silence and she was quiet for a few moments after I stopped the video. Then she slowly turned to me, a smile teasing her mouth. "You know what I think?"

"Aside from it being a masterpiece?"

"Aside from that." She took my hand, turning it over to study my palm. "I think it feels like a love letter. I see it now when I didn't during filming."

Smiling, I agreed, "I guess it is."

"Good. I love it. And you. It's perfect. You're perfect." She kissed me, another gentle, lingering kiss. When she pulled away, Stacey covered a yawn with her hand. "I am so tired."

"Then stay here for a while. You can nap while I study." I climbed off the bed and put the laptop back on my desk.

Stace didn't argue, just shuffled herself across the bed toward the wall. "You coming back?" she asked quietly.

"Course I am. Just grabbing my stuff."

I stacked up all my pillows so I could lean against the bedhead, and once I was comfortable, Stacey moved closer. She lay snuggled up to me, arm over my waist and her head against my boobs. Breasts. Whatever. I leaned down and kissed her temple, smoothed her hair back from her forehead. She was a master napper, and it took barely five minutes until I felt her relax, her breathing getting deeper and slower. And then she was out.

We stayed that way for almost an hour and a half, me studying, and Stacey sleeping away her troubles. I'd forgotten to pull my phone from my back pocket, and had felt the vibration of a couple of text messages, but I didn't want to risk disturbing Stacey, who looked so adorable sleeping against me. Given the time, it was probably Mom or Aspen telling me it was time for dinner. Usually they'd just come up and knock, or call from the bottom of the stairs, but they probably thought we were making up from our fight in the naked way.

At the quiet knock on the partially closed door, I said, "Come in." I wondered who'd drawn the short straw of coming up to check on us to potentially discover something parents should not have to discover.

Mom's head peeked through a small gap in the door. I had to give her credit for not looking at all alarmed about the fact Stacey and I were in bed together, even though we were both fully clothed and on top of the covers. And one of us was asleep and the other reading. Not exactly having sex. I wasn't even sure where Mom and Aspen stood on that matter. Given we hadn't had A Discussion about sex in my parents' house, probably where they stood on most things—as long as I'm happy with what I'm doing, not breaking any laws, or hurting anyone, they'd be okay with it. But sex when my parents were in the house felt way too disturbing.

Mom smiled apologetically, and spoke just above a whisper. Being quiet when Stace was sleeping was unnecessary—she could, and did, sleep anywhere, including an almost-packed cinema during a movie one time. "Dinner's ready. We assumed Stacey would stay."

I glanced down at Stace. "Good assumption." She never turned down food, and it was past her fairly rigid dinner time. She'd be starving when she woke.

As if her name and the mention of food had somehow permeated her unconsciousness while she slept, Stacey stirred against me. She propped herself up, then quickly sat up, running a hand through her sleep-mussed hair. Her voice was rough with sleep when she said, "Hello, Mrs. Archer."

Mom smiled fondly. "Hi, Stacey. Dinner's ready when you two want to come down."

"That sounds amazing. Thank you very much." On cue, her stomach growled its protests.

"We'll be right there," I told Mom.

When we were alone again, Stacey rolled over and onto me. She lingered on top of me for longer than someone just getting up and out of bed, kissing me deeply. "Shame about dinner…" she murmured, before climbing off me and walking to the doorway.

* * *

After dinner, I insisted on driving Stace home. When I suggested it, she made a half-hearted protest but I didn't want to worry about her walking or running home in the dark.

"You wanna come in for some tea?" she asked once I'd pulled up.

"Sure." I wanted more than tea, and judging by the way she'd been stroking her hand up and down my thigh as I drove, so did she. The fact that we both still obviously wanted each other after our fight was such a relief, I could have cried. Except crying wasn't very sexy.

Stacey locked the door behind us and held out her hand to me, and when I took it, she pulled gently. But I didn't move. Instead, I pulled back, and she closed the small space between us. The moment she was in kissing range, I did just that. There was urgency in this kiss, more than our first time, more than the other times we'd had sex. I needed to touch her, and I slid my hands under her sweatshirt to stroke her skin.

Stacey inhaled sharply, then, still kissing me, she hooked her hands under my butt and lifted me up. Stacey playfully picked me up, or piggy-backed me all the time. But never like this. I wrapped my legs around her waist, sucking her neck as she carried me toward her bedroom. But she'd barely carried me ten steps before she stopped, right by her kitchen table. And when I pulled back, the *why* already forming in my mouth, she said hoarsely, "I want to fuck you right here."

I inhaled sharply, both at the rawness of the words and the mental image it'd elicited. The mental image that had excitement racing through me. I gripped her hair roughly, tilting her head back so I could kiss under her jaw. "You do?"

Stacey bit her lower lip. "Sorry, was that too much? It sounded hotter and more confident in my head."

"It's not too much," I assured her. "And it *was* hot." Then, with a sexiness I hadn't known I possessed, I told her to, "Put me down."

She lowered me to the table, her body not breaking contact with mine. She pressed herself between my legs as we both peeled away our sweatshirts and tops. I could taste the sweat as I kissed her neck and shoulder, sucked on the delicious tantalizing skin of her breasts. I helped her yank her jeans down, and she helped me wriggle out of mine.

This *was* amazingly sexy. But I wanted to touch all of her. To feel that full skin-on-skin contact as she lay on top of me. "I want to touch you properly," I croaked out.

And just as she had before, she lifted me, carrying me to the couch and laying me down so my head rested against the arm. I'd said nothing more than that, but it was like she knew what I wanted. And maybe she wanted it too. I opened my legs so she could fit between them as she had before, loving the feel of her, the weight of her. And though we were still a little clumsy at times, it was so utterly perfect that I could have stayed like this with her forever.

The sensations were absolute, all-consuming, utterly electrifying. I couldn't narrow it down. But I had to or I was going to come completely apart. The feeling of her fingers on my nipples. Her lips making a wet path over my belly. The quiver of her stomach muscles when I touched her. The sounds she made. The sounds she made me make. The sensation of her fingers inside me. Her tongue against me. I had no idea her tongue could do that and now that I'd felt it, I wanted more. This time was rough and fast, and every bit as incredible as before when we'd been slow and sweet.

I'd barely finished shuddering and gasping when Stacey pushed herself up, bracing a hand on either side of my shoulders. The look she gave me was almost desperate and I pushed my hand between her legs. I could feel how aroused she was, and with each of my thrusts, she panted, her hips moving in time with me. *This* was what I loved the most about being intimate with her, aside from coming of course, this feeling of being *with* her, of being completely in sync with her. Stacey dipped her head to kiss me, her tongue playing against mine before she pulled back. But she stayed close, keeping eye contact as I stroked her, and I could feel her breath against my cheek.

Her breathing caught and she made the sound that made my pulse race as she shuddered hard against me. I pulled her down, held her close, and kissed her long and deep. And when we parted, I saw everything I needed in her eyes. All of her love, her trust, her desires. And I hoped it reflected back at her from me. I looped my arms around her neck, and my voice was tight with emotion when I said, "Stace, I *really* hated fighting. But, yeah…now I can kinda see why they say making up is so fun."

CHAPTER TWENTY-THREE

Stacey

The snow gods were granting me favors. We'd had excellent spring snow to not only keep my training momentum going—into June by the feel of it—but to ensure Arapahoe Basin was still open at the end of May. And I'd woken up on Sunday morning so excited that I was almost doing backflips. I could think of no better way to spend a day off training than spending a morning skiing with Gem, coming home to take a long, hot shower together before settling in for a relaxed afternoon and evening.

We could have gone out for some backcountry fun, but I knew the idea of being dragged somewhere without a lift or snowmobile just to ski was right at the limits of Gem's love for me. Only I thought a day of hike to the top of a mountain, ski down, repeat all day was one of the best things ever.

It was still early, and I decided that lying in bed with Gem for another fifteen or thirty or sixty minutes was better than spending those minutes on the mountain. I snuggled into the warm, naked body beside me. Gem inhaled deeply, and let it out slowly. It was a long contented sigh, and I hugged her tighter, pressing my face into her blond curls. "You know the three words every woman wants to hear?" I murmured.

"Fresh pow day?" she joked, her voice rough with sleep.

"Close. I was thinking more along the lines of…I love you. But we can just say 'fresh pow day' instead. You'd love that, wouldn't you?"

"Mmm." She wriggled back against me, pulling my arm tighter around her. She mimicked me. "Fresh pow day. Fresh pow day too."

Laughing, I tugged her waist until she turned over. Framing her face with my hands, I kissed her. I hadn't thought it possible, but two weeks after our fight, it felt like things were better than ever. The fight, as horrible and upsetting as it'd been, had made us realize the importance of what we had, made us realize how we could work together, made us look at the things we needed to work on in ourselves. And that feeling of understanding, of love, of trust, made me feel like I could do anything.

Gem kissed my nose. "I can hear you thinking."

"I'm not really. Well I kinda am. But not about anything bad."

"What about then?"

"This. Us. How I never want it to end."

"It doesn't have to." She reached down and took my hand, pulling it up and holding it between us. "I think we've shown we can weather some storms."

"Mmm." I played with her fingers. "How're you feeling?"

Gem's eyebrows rose. "About what?"

"Graduation, moving on to college, that adulty stuff." She'd completed her senior finals—acing them of course—and would graduate on Wednesday. Three days, and then she was officially finished with high school.

Her forehead wrinkled. "Not sure yet. It's been such a weird blur that I don't think it's actually sunk in yet. All that time thinking about these last few months and what they meant and now I realize I don't really remember any of the school stuff. Seems kinda silly when I think about it, about how much brainpower I spent worrying about it."

"I get it. I feel like that about the Olympics. I hardly remember any of it, except for missing you and our FaceTimes. Oh, and then the medal ceremony. The rest? Blurry noise."

Her teeth brushed her lower lip. "You're still coming to my grad ceremony, right?"

"Wouldn't miss it, even for the best pow day in the world." I patted the top of her head. "I can't wait to see you in your cute little cap thing."

She reached around and slapped my butt. "Well that's a level of certainty I'm happy with."

We lingered in bed for another ten minutes, snuggling, and maybe making out a little, before Gem declared she could *feel* my desperation to get onto the mountain. She packed snacks and water while I sorted through the gear I wanted and loaded the car with our skis, poles, and gear bags. And as if knowing I wouldn't want to linger over breakfast when there were fresh tracks to make, she'd also made coffee and some grilled cheese sandwiches to eat in the car.

I leaned over to kiss her. "How is it you always know exactly what I need? Even when I haven't said anything."

"Because nobody knows you the way I do." There was a double entendre there, but I ignored it in favor of the truth of her statement.

"Nobody knows me the way you do," I echoed. And that was exactly how I liked it.

A-Basin was fairly busy, no doubt due to the weekend, fresh dumps and the imminent threat of the mountain closing for the season. But we managed to find a secluded spot to prep, and once we'd sunscreened-up, Gem smiled at me, her cute little secretive smile that made me suspicious she was about to snowball me or something.

"What?" I asked as I applied a generous layer of Chapstick.

"Nothing. Just a bet with myself."

Oh I knew the bet—that someone would approach me for a photo or an autograph. Today I was sure it'd be before we'd even clipped in to our skis, given the Instagram thing, and the fact Beijing was still fresh in people's minds because they were still skiing or boarding.

"Yeah yeah," I drawled.

"Whaaaat? It's funny. Because you still get so weird and shy about people recognizing you."

I raised my eyebrows. "You still think that after Bree-gate? That being recognized is fun?"

Gem shuddered. "Oh, yeah. Maybe not."

"Know what? I'm going to bet you one massage that someone recognizes *you* first today."

"I'll take that bet. Kiss on it?"

We sealed the deal with a kiss, then double-checked our packs, clipped in to our skis, and made our way to the lift line. I lost the bet in under two minutes, when a young snowboarder in camo snow pants—because green camo worked so well in white snow?—waved at me and called out, "Yo! Stacey Evans! Sick runs in China, dude!"

"Thanks," I said, as everyone in the lift line turned around to look at me. Determined to prove Gemma wrong—I so was not weird and shy about fans—I reached over for a fist-bump.

He side-hopped his snowboard over and obliged me, then left like he hadn't said anything. Thankfully, after a few seconds, everyone turned back to waiting to board the lift.

Gemma leaned into me as we shuffled forward in line. "I win," she murmured. "I win, so hard."

"Dammit. But you don't even enjoy massages."

"Oh no, I'm going to give you a *massage*." The undercurrent in that one word made my legs feel wobbly. Thankfully the chair came to scoop us up.

The snow provided prime spring skiing, and we spent a chill few hours cruising around until it was time for snack and selfie breaks. We stopped off the side of the trail and moved down out of everyone's way. Gemma looked around. "I know it's dumb, but I still feel odd skiing here. After the avalanche adventure," she clarified as she shrugged out of her backpack and set it down.

Four-ish years ago, Aspen and I had encountered an avalanche here at Arapahoe Basin when we'd come for some off-piste reaction training. She'd done the Aspen thing and shoved me down the hill to safety and been caught in the avalanche herself. Obviously, she'd survived, but not without a handful of bumps and bruises, and a broken wrist.

"It was an adventure indeed." I bent at the waist and leaned on my poles, taking a slow look around, absorbing the calmness that always came with being on a snowy mountain. Twisting, I looked up at Gem. "But remember, it was a week after that when you and me first skied together. You were so cute and sweet and adorable."

"Any more synonyms?" she asked dryly.

"I'm sure I'll think of some."

"I had a few synonyms of my own for you too."

I clipped out and dumped my pack on the snow. "Care to share?"

Smiling angelically, she shook her head, and passed me a sandwich. So I created my own synonyms for myself. Charming, hot, funny, not good at finding synonyms.

We ate as we usually did, sharing things back and forth until my hunger had been satisfied, and Gem's hanger had been staved off. She stuffed the empty trail mix bag into her pack, dusting her hands off on her ski pants. "I was thinking, if I can make it line up with my classes, that I could maybe come to some of your races overseas. I'll be there for every single one I can in the States, of course, but it'd be awesome to travel *and* see you race at the same time."

"I think that would be amazing. And I'd love to have you there." I snugged an arm around her waist. "May as well practice for the future, right?"

She went very still and quiet. "What do you think our future is?"

Her reaction made me panic, but instead of brushing it off, I said, "Oh, y'know, marriage, a kid or two, your film premieres and awards, my World Cup globe wins and Olympic glories." It'd just been a joke but once I'd said it, I could totally picture the whole scene. What a great life.

"Oh cool. That's exactly what I was thinking," she said, totally deadpan. Or at least her voice was deadpan, but her face wasn't. Her face said she'd thought the exact same thing I had—that I wanted a wife and kids, success in my racing career, and to support my partner's successes. And I could see it so clearly with Gem, even though it felt ridiculous to think it *now*. But I couldn't help myself.

Gem broke the tension, and the fact I now couldn't stop thinking about wife, kids, success, with a quiet, "Selfie before we move on?"

"Sounds good," I managed to say around the *wife, kids, success* merry-go-rounding in my head.

We both pulled up our goggles, rotated around to find the best background for the picture, and took a mountain selfie. Or more accurately—a few selfies, because Gem was addicted to burst-mode photos. I kissed her cheek, staying there until the phone camera went quiet. Then I kissed her mouth. When she handed my phone back to me, I swiped through the pictures. Damn, we were cute together. I'd already had a couple of my sponsors tell me, through Brick, that they really liked the "wholesome" dynamic Gemma and I projected. The unspoken implication was that my other girlfriends had not projected a particularly wholesome image. A fair assessment.

Gem had thought the "wholesome" thing hilarious, but I'd also caught the undercurrent of worry that she thought we'd have a repeat of the last time people became aware of her on the Internet. Everyone from Brick to brand partners had promised they'd be monitoring it, and we'd only put up as much as she was comfortable with. And I'd promised myself that I'd okay every picture with her.

I held up my phone. "Can I put this on Insta?"

"Sure," she said easily.

But I still felt squirmy about it, even though she didn't seem bothered, and rambled, "You know, just gotta keep the ol' brand partners happy and my followers interested into the off-season. But I can just put one of me up if you wanna take it."

"It's fine, Stace. Really. It's not the first time I've been on your Insta. And I have to say, I look really good."

I stole a kiss. "You look gorgeous."

Her cheeks pinked. "Thank you."

"Geez, no reciprocal 'You're smoking hot, Stacey'?"

"You're smoking hot, Stacey," she said around a grin.

Tapping the screen, I said, "I might do a video too." I liked to put up short boomerang videos, just because I found them hilarious.

Gem nodded and I passed her my phone, then started side-stepping up the mountain until I was about twenty feet above her.

"Ready when you are," she said.

"Aren't you supposed to say 'Action!'?" I called down.

"You're such a pain. And, action," she called back.

I pushed off, skated to gain some speed, then came to a sharp hockey-stop almost on top of her, spraying up a good arc of snow.

"So mature," she deadpanned.

I brushed down her pants, apologized with a kiss, then edited the video so it was just boomeranging me stopping with the snow spray back and forth, then put both it and the great selfie up on socials. *Spring fun with my favorite skiing partner @Arapahoe_Basin #weareskiing #BeWhoYouAre*

I tucked my phone back into my pocket. "I love this."

"I know you do."

Laughing, I said, "No, *this*. Us. Being here with you. Being anywhere with you."

It'd been far more than I'd ever expected. I'd imagined the intimacy, the fun, the trust. But I'd never expected to become *more* because of her. To be pushed to face up to my personal failings and to do something about it because there was something more important to me than my own egotistical feelings about being called out. Maybe this was what being an adult was about.

"I love it too," she said seriously. "I'd follow you anywhere, Stace. I mean it. Even down a double black. Very slowly." After a wink and a quick kiss, she asked, "Ready to go?"

"Of course." I helped her into her CamelBak and after I'd made sure she was set, we moved off to pack in as much skiing as we could.

By early afternoon, I could tell she was getting tired, and we agreed to make this our last run. I glanced over my shoulder, then cut quickly across the mountain and came to an abrupt stop, sliding off to the side of the trail. Gem carefully turned to stop beside me. "You okay?" she asked.

"Of course. Just gotta do this." I stepped out of my skis and pulled my glove off. Bending down, I carefully drew a huge heart in the snow banked by the trees, using my fingers to scoop it deeply so it would be really obvious to anyone who'd ski by it exactly what it was. "I love you, Gem," I said seriously. Pointing at the snow heart, I added, "I wrote it in snow, so you know it's true."

She placed both hands to her chest and sighed heavily. "It's beautiful. I'll cherish it forever."

I shrugged. "Or until it melts."

Gem gave me a withering look. "My love for you will never melt. It'll be like glacial ice, here forever. Or at least for a few hundred years until climate change ruins everything."

"Oh are we doing love puns? Even morbid ones about melting glaciers?" I pulled my glove back on. "I've been dying to pull some out." Not morbid puns. Great puns.

"Should I be afraid?"

"Oh yeah, very afraid." I drew myself up and cleared my throat. I'd been desperate to find an opening for this one for a while. "Gemmy…You're my Super G."

She groaned, apparently unimpressed with my perfect merging of her name and skiing. Tough crowd.

Undeterred, I tried again. "Okay okay. How about…my love for you is like a rolling snowball? It just keeps getting bigger and bigger."

"That's no better."

"My love is an avalanche? Kinda out of control and wants to swallow you up."

"That's even worse. You are *so* corny."

I leaned in and booped her nose with mine. "But you love it."

"I do. I love everything about you, Stacey." She wrapped her arms around my waist, and I shuffled my boots until I was standing in between her skis. "I have from the moment I met you. I really did schuss down that love hill, and boy did I go hard and fast."

I rolled my eyes. Her lame snow-love joke was no better than mine, and it wasn't even hers! It was Aspen's. But I let it go. "Usually I'd say that's bad, but in this case…" I pulled her goggles up onto the top of her helmet, then did the same for mine. "I say race all the way to the bottom."

"No slowing down?"

"Nope. Schuss!" I dipped my head and kissed her. Our kiss was soft and unhurried and when I pulled back, Gem's eyes were soft with emotion. I gently cupped her face. "I'm the safety netting. And I'll always catch you."

"I lov—" She grinned, her eyes sparkling. "I mean…Fresh pow day."

I kissed her again. "Fresh pow day too."

Bella Books, Inc.

Women. Books. Even Better Together.

P.O. Box 10543
Tallahassee, FL 32302

Phone: 800-729-4992
www.bellabooks.com